SAL.....

DREW GUMMERSON

HAYWOOD BOOKS

HAYWOOD BOOKS

an imprint of Renard Press Ltd
124 City Road, London EC1V 2NX
United Kingdom

info@renardpress.com
020 8050 2928
www.haywoodbooks.com

These stories, in different versions, first published on ABCtales in 2020
Saltburn first published by Renard Press Ltd in 2025

Cover design by Will Dady

Printed and bound in the UK on carbon-balanced papers by CMP Books

ISBN: 978-1-80447-154-8

9 8 7 6 5 4 3 2 1

EU Authorised Representative: Easy Access System Europe – Mustamäe tee 50, 10621 Tallinn, Estonia, gpsr.requests@easproject.com.

CONTENTS

Saltburn

My father grew up around Saltburn-by-the-Sea, Marske, Redcar, Boosbeck. My intention with these stories was to write something of a memoir, but they became something completely different. May the residents of the real Saltburn-by-the-Sea and neighbouring towns forgive my mermaids, my nuclear-power stations, my foetus museums and so on and so on. They were written with love.

The author would also like to take this precursive opportunity to forewarn the perhaps unwary reader of both the spicy nature of some of these stories and for the views expressed by certain of the characters within them – these views, again, in no way reflecting upon the real people of Saltburn, etc., and so on ad infinitum.

MELTDOWN

A Falling Mother Falls

One night, while his mother was out cleaning at the university, Arthur watched a flickery black-and-white documentary, mostly in Russian, on their six-inch Binatone TV set. The long and short of it was that during a late-night safety test at a nuclear-power station an explosion had taken place, releasing highly radioactive material into the air, which was then carried across Russia and western Europe.

'Wow-weee,' Arthur said out loud.

The next day, still thinking about the show, he stole the tomato-sauce dispenser from the condiment table of Mavis' Roadside Café and called up Albert and Reggie and invited them over for a game he had named Meltdown.

Albert and Reggie resembled each other exactly, like the identical twins at school everyone had christened Bumface One and Two on account of their moonlike faces. But in fact Albert and Reggie were hardly even related, sharing only an elderly great-aunt in Bridlington who owned eight miniature sausage dogs and a collection of antique teapots. Disguising herself in one of the many second-hand wigs she was famous for around Bridlington's cafés, she had managed to get the teapots, or a selection of them, on *Antiques Roadshow* eight programmes in a row, convinced that somewhere in that collection her fortune lay. It would just take the right eyes to see it.

Albert was living with this aunt now, expelled from school for wiping his English teacher's spam and onion sandwiches on Balder's – the blind boy's – bum. Claymore, the English teacher, was not a popular figure. It was thanks to his campaigns that sausages had been banned from the school menu, due to their resemblance to willies. He was a stickler. On his jacket he wore a selection of badges handed out at New Puritanism rallies – *Ban the Bum, No More Nudity, Keep Your Private Parts Private!*

Reggie, something of a rebel too, dressed in the kind of clothes public-service announcements on the radio warned the general public about: military-style coats, big boots, very skinny trousers with an accentuated crotch. On Tuesday nights men sporting this kind of clobber would descend on Park Pond and place illicit spectacular bets on clandestine mock maritime battles or flock to Proctor's Peep Show, bags of change bulging in their pockets, exhorting the elderly women dressed in tight blond wigs and pink leotards into making ever more lascivious poses.

'And good luck to them,' Reggie would say. 'Who are we to police people's innermost desires?'

Scandalous words.

After Arthur explained the game to his two pals, the winner of Meltdown being the one who best faked their own death from acute radiation sickness, the three boys stripped down to their birthday suits and, while Yves Montand's 'Les Canuts' played at full volume on the old phonograph, took turns under Arthur's mother's sunlamp, having rubbed the stolen tomato sauce into their bodies to simulate maximum burn effect, extremities and private parts not excluded.

Then it was just a question of striking spectacular death poses and marking each other out of ten, the numbers crayoned on cards attached to the ends of wooden kitchen utensils.

When Arthur's mother came home several hours later she found the three boys, completely exhausted from their death throes, naked, the dried tomato sauce on their bodies flaking and stinking, lying on top of Arthur's single bed together.

Pulling at her hair and ears like she had once seen Jane Fonda do in *Barefoot in the Park*, and subsequently taken on as a tic of her own, she feared the worst.

It was happening again.

Seven years before, jobless for eighteen months and at the end of all their tethers, Arthur's father, Langston, had been recruited by two men to work on a men-only cruise liner, *The Pride of the Sea*, plying its trade on the rough stretch of water between Stornaway and Kirkwall. Although he regularly sent home tiny bundles of pound notes packed, for safety, into Swan Vesta matchboxes, and told her the work in the kitchens was both 'hard and hot', she knew the truth: he dressed in tight pants and let the elderly male guests fondle him on the poop deck, and down below, for tips.

Having turfed the visiting boys one by one from the house, not even allowing them time to dress, Arthur's mother sat him down and told him Reggie and Albert were banned from ever coming to the house again. 'No arguments.'

The following day she was up before daybreak. Soon after she found herself standing outside the window of George's Tea Shop, still in her dressing gown.

There it was: below a notice for a litter of terrapins that would be available at the end of Tuesday week and above an advert for Rangar's Recalcitrant Dog School was the flyer for Male Aversion Therapy, run by Rector Barnabas. A man of the church! Surely someone who could knock some sense into her son. She made a note of the number.

Arthur lay in bed and worried over what exactly he had done wrong. It was just a game! And anyway, he thought, slapping the covers, his mother was a *flamin' hypocrite*! Some of the pale, skinny philosophy students she brought home from the university where she worked as a cleaner got him to do things, and he knew that she knew because he had told her.

One had bought him a wooden sailboat filled with home-made Napoleonic soldiers and, telling him it would be a 'learning experience', took him down to Park Pond for a lame reconstruction of the Battle of Waterloo, making him remove his trousers and underpants to stop them getting wet as he was cajoled to enter the water to launch the boat. Another had made him sit dressed only in a pair of skimpy swimming trunks astride one of the tired, flea-bitten donkeys that plied their trade up and down the seafront. That had been almost OK until the man had mounted the donkey behind him and whispered lascivious tales in his ear concerning 1930s Hollywood movie stars – Claudette Colbert, Carole Lombard, Greta Garbo, Joan Crawford and others of their ilk.

These philosophy men didn't work so much, and often his mother would leave them naked in her bed, their pudenda still moist, *Thus Spoke Zarathustra* open at a pertinent page, while she was out at her day job selling wallpaper from a wooden cart. She was hopeful the philosophers would still be there on her return and, maybe, marry her, or take her to one of the southern resorts where the penny arcades had been specially adapted to accept fifty-pence coins, or other similarly shaped coins from the continent: octagons, polygons, impossible dodecahedrons.

But the bed was always empty on her return, the sheets stripped by Arthur himself, then washed and hung out on the municipal line.

It had to be this way.

Her bed, by day, was their dining table, and the place where they did jigsaws – their favourite one made of only four pieces and displaying Mount Sinai in complete darkness (it wasn't as easy as it sounded).

But sometimes when his mother came home she was too tired for jigsaws, her limbs sore from pushing the wallpaper cart around, and then Arthur would rub hazelnut and tamarind paste into her weary arms and feet.

'You're OK, though, aren't you, Mum?' he would ask. 'You're OK?'

Rector Sebastopol Barnabas, organiser and chief factotum of the Male Aversion Therapy course, wore a top hat, fingerless gloves and a bright green Adidas tracksuit that might have fitted a smaller man well.

Knocking on the door Arthur found the house full of the Rector's famous suitcases. Made by Barnabas himself, bulk-bought Naugahyde stretched over a balsa-wood rigid frame, the suitcases would be sold to parishioners at church fêtes, whist drives, harvest festivals, the money raised used to fund an annual retreat for poor penitents in Poulton-le-Fylde. If they could be sin-free in that north-western hotspot, then they could be sin-free anywhere!

For his first lesson the Rector read aloud a long Bible story that Arthur was unable to follow – Abraham begetting Elijah begetting Ishmael and so on. The drone of his voice had been largely drowned out by the drumming of harsh February rain on the window until, drawing closer, with breath redolent of harsh prairie oysters and mildewed After Eight mints, the Rector had recounted something of his own early life: an alcoholic father, beatings in the woodshed, the son of a dairy farmer he had become *over-fond* of, mistaking the stink of soured milk on his fingers for a kind of aphrodisiac. Then, tears in his rheumy old eyes, the Rector donned a steepled canonical hat and put Beethoven's Symphony 10 in E Flat Major on the mighty Columbia Grafonola phonograph while he held up a series of grainy flash cards of Marlon Brando in the nude while he ordered Arthur to rub himself roughly between the legs with a stiff hairbrush.

That night Arthur cried like he had never cried before.

The next day he told his mother he was cured, and that if the sessions with Rector Barnabas were to finish, come to an absolute full stop, he would promise never to see Reggie or Albert again.

That was the deal.

The following summer, despite protestations from his mother that they would *manage* and that *ends would meet, maybe not in the middle, but near the middle,* Arthur got a job helping out George in his tea shop. Everyone in the know – and that was almost everyone, it being a small gossipy town – knew that George's Tea Shop wasn't only a tea shop, the cakes in the window being a front – no, George made the bulk of his income from the making and selling of alchemical potions, age-old recipes he had learnt in his youth in the souks of Cairo and the bazaars of Constantinople.

Traditional alchemy, he explained to Arthur on his first day, was concerned with the transformation of base metals into precious ones, the creation of an elixir that brought about immortality and certain panaceas that could cure any illness. He, however, and he said this with his eyelids drooping, a sign that Arthur was later able to understand indicated a heavy heart full to the brim with disappointment, specialised in cures for erectile disfunction, love potions, remedies for period pains and hair loss.

George lived in the storeroom at the back of the tea shop, its walls filled with shelves, the shelves filled with boxes of flavoured crisps, huge tubs of whale oil, tins of sardines, rolls of old promotional posters for corned beef hash, pemmican, ox tongue and bottle after bottle after bottle filled with the liquids he used to make his potions.

Serving old ladies with blue rinses, swarthy labourers with fingers as thick as the rungs of ladders, nurses with musical instruments attached to their tabards, Arthur worked in the tearoom every night after school.

Except on a Wednesday. On a Wednesday George closed early and disappeared. This might have become something of a mystery, except on the third Wednesday Arthur found

George waiting for him outside the school gates with a ham sandwich wrapped in yesterday's front page of *The Courier* and an exhortation to, *Come with me boy – it's time.*

As they walked along George explained that on a Wednesday he attended a 'whist event' – and here his alchemy-stained fingers formed inverted commas in the air – with other local small-business owners at Benny's Bingo and Karaoke Centre.

Arthur had never played whist before, and for the whole journey fretted over what 'whist' might be, but he needn't have worried. Whist, like the cakes in George's Tea Shop window, was simply a front.

The meeting was opened by the clashing of a pair of symbols by Trev, owner of Trev's Fabulous Keyboards and Stands, and one by one each of the local businessmen or women was given a chance to make a short statement before the meeting proper started.

It was a heated, raucous affair. In short, they were all concerned by big business steadily encroaching upon the town – huge bowling complexes, gleaming fish-and-chip emporiums with buxom serving girls on roller skates, shoe shops larger than the Titanic...

The chief instigator behind the majority of these businesses, his name repeated again and again, was that of Evans, an industrialist from the north-west, who, through a series of aggressive underhand moves, was buying up huge swathes of land in the area and was reputed to be planning an enormous retail park filled with his own franchises that, it was commonly agreed, would be the death of the town.

There was beer at the meeting, served in tiny cups by a ginger-haired lady wearing a shark's-tooth necklace. Slightly drunk on the way home, Arthur, feeling a new intimacy with George thanks to the trust shown in inviting him to the meeting, told George about his mother's men, the philosophers, and the strange things they did to him. The latest, a follower of Zeno of Elea, for a *thought experiment* had filled Arthur's mouth with Ritz crackers and made him stand naked on a street corner wearing nothing but a gold ankle sock over his willy – which, of course, was completely illegal, the New Puritanism Party having banned the public display of bums in one of their first edicts.

George didn't say anything then, but the next day, as Arthur was finishing up, he was presented with a small plastic package containing a red paste. Arthur was used now to the harsh smells of George's potions, Aqua Fortis, spirit of turpentine, caustic potash, ordered sotto voce by women in colourful hairnets with their pot of teas, Chelsea buns – *a little something* to put a lift in their husband's drooping dick, maybe, or *a little something* to take them out of themselves – but this one was different.

'So what does this do?' Arthur asked.

George smiled and tapped his nose. 'The paste of a Carolina Reaper chilli, liable to burn. Handle with caution.'

That winter there was an election during which milk bottles filled with petrol got thrown. One protestor was killed outright; another lost his legs under a tram. But once all the votes were counted the New Puritanism Party were returned with an increased majority, and one of the first new laws they passed banned the selling of anything from handcarts, even shellfish of any kind.

This came as a blow to the many winkle and cockle sellers whose gaudy carts lined the seafront in the summer months. A petition of appeal was started, only to be pooh-poohed by the emboldened Prime Minister. *Health and safety* for the general population was tantamount, he claimed – *better to be able to monitor cleanliness*.

But a week later the Prime Minister was photographed in one of Evans' amusement arcades being passed a bag of loose change behind the Nebuchadnezzar the Great slot machine. A bribe, it was said, on the quiet – which held out when another week later the footings for Evans' new shopping mall were dug. Advertising banners appeared by the side of the motorway:

Evans – from cockles to winkles and everything in between.

For a time Arthur's mother took her wallpaper cart out by night. While previously she had wheeled it around the town, ringing a bell to announce her arrival, now she would position herself beneath a low-hanging tree, whistling stealthily at any passing trade – drunk sailors from the port, moon worshippers in their long white robes, the gangs of men who prowled the streets at night, wearing only nappies, crying for their past sins and misdeeds. But then a car-park attendant, who had a long-held aversion to wallpaper – anything pasted to a wall, in fact, ever since a Howard Jones poster had unpeeled itself and smothered him as a boy – reported her, and under a glaring, unforgiving sun government agents arrived at their home, cast out the cart and smashed it to smithereens right outside in the street for everyone to see.

For two weeks Arthur and his mother lived on tins of sardines and cans of Spaghetti 'n' Sausages, bought with the money Arthur earned from the tea shop and his mother's paltry cleaning wages – but all too soon the rent was due and Arthur needed new trousers for school, ones that didn't ride up his bum crack, dividing his cheeks so decisively that when he needed to perform his ablutions they came together like friends at a party who hadn't seen each other for years.

That was when his mother took out one of the long black cigars she made from pampas grass and leftover hair dye and declared she was going to move into the black economy. What she had been giving away to those no-good philosophers for free she would now charge for. Prostitutes, she had heard, were needed at the port.

The sailors carried flip-up photo albums with grainy photographs of all the ships they had sailed on and, before getting down to the deed, they related many a rum-soaked tale. At night, though, after his mother had gone out for snacks – for if she fed them, she thought, they might take her away to Martinique, or French New Guinea, or Vanuatu – they were even worse than the Philosophers.

After being surprised by the first one, a huge barrel-chested man with enormous earrings he had made himself from spent matches and toenails dried to brittleness in the Caribbean sun, Arthur remembered the paste George had given him. He found it worked best if he put it up their bums – easier to accomplish than he supposed. Not one of them said no when he offered them a finger. By the time the third sailor got taken to the emergency room, word got around, and the sailors avoided his mother like the plague.

Night after night she stood on the docks, lifting her skirt jauntily above her knee and calling up to the railings of the ships in the manner of a mermaid. She even tried the tug hands – in the pecking order of sailors, the lowest of the low.

'I'll pay you,' she said one night, taking out the last pound note from her cleaning-job pay packet, and thrusting it towards Archibald. He was the captain of *Little Dolly*, a two-man crabber that plied the waters around the Faroe Islands and was often gone for weeks on end.

But even Archibald had heard the tales. 'Look, love,' he said, 'keep your pound.' But then he had a change of heart and sold her one of his deep-sea red crabs for 97 ½ p, and it didn't even have much meat on it.

Arthur believed he had done the right thing. He had saved his mother's shame. But he was a boy, and he didn't understand shame.

Three weeks after Archibald's rebuff, and unable to take any more – the loss of her wallpaper business, the ignominy of selling herself and of not being able to sell herself, of not being able to support the son she loved – Arthur's mother wrote a short farewell note and then walked two hours out of town to the Humber Bridge. She didn't even flinch as she flung herself from it and down into the water below.

Falling Upwards

On the day the social worker came for *The Intervention* Arthur stole a Stylophone from Trev's Fabulous Keyboards and Stands and played 'Land of Hope and Glory' with all the gust and zest he could muster.

'Land of Hope and Glory' was the only song he knew all the way through, although he made up his own version of the words: '…Mother's in the sea.'

After he finished he explained he was going to get a monkey 'from somewhere' and go busking down at the station, where he was sure to make a killing.

The social worker was as thin as a long slender branch, and Arthur imagined her on a tree with other social workers, rustling in the wind, scaring children with their antics.

He was terrified she was going to take him away and put him in the children's home. The boys there were made to work in the municipal gardens and hand out inspirational tracts around the shopping centre on weekday afternoons, the electronic tags fitted to their ankles quietly beeping.

Despite Arthur's protestations that he could care for himself the social worker said it wasn't typical for fifteen-year-old boys to be left *to their own devices*. This was often repeated by the hypocritical establishment, because it was common knowledge that many parent-less boys would gather behind the old theatre on a nightly basis.

The most daring would wear backless underpants and a luminous lipstick that would shine brightly under the halogen street lights – all the better to entice the rich men from the southern resorts, driving their flash cars with plastic toys on the dashboard, with wives who thought they were both more controlling and loved than they were.

The social worker was all ready to sign him up when George, having seen the distinct official car outside and sensing something was up, appeared and said quite simply that he would take *the boy* in. Arthur, he said, would be able to carry on working in the tea shop after school, and they would fix up a bedroom for him in one of upstairs rooms.

George had used to rent out these rooms for £2 a week to the cockle and winkle sellers, but since the banning of the carts the sale of cockles and winkles had gone underground and the sellers were keeping less high-profile accommodation, moving, so it was said, with the wind.

It was a fait accompli.

The social worker was sent packing, folding her long skinny body into her vehicle in the manner of a bereft praying mantis, and Arthur had only to collect his scant belongings before making the move.

A new life awaited.

Although the old one, as lives are wont to do, did still linger.

Despite her best efforts, Arthur's mother hadn't died when she jumped from the Humber Bridge, and every Sunday Arthur would take the special 'madhouse express', as it came to be known by its regular users, from Central Bus Station out to the sombre establishment where his mother was housed, and it was these trips which beat like a metronome, marking the time of his teenage years.

The long dark corridors of the institution, from which water always seemed to drip, and which were adorned with signed black-and-white photographs of directors past, present and future, filled him with a kind of dread – as did the blank faces of the hospital patients and staff. But he maintained the habit of going and, although there was never any perceptible response, he would recount the recent facts of his life to his mother: certain mishaps in the tearoom, a dropped tray, an old man's miniature schnauzer pissing against one of the table legs, gossip he had learnt from the regulars, usually petty infractions against New Puritanism edicts, Agnés, the lighthouse keeper's wife, going to Abdul's Mini-Mart in a lime-green boob tube and sorting through the display of courgettes in a manner that suggested an ulterior motive, a certain group of teenagers staging a same-sex kiss-in at the black-light theatre performance of *Annie Get Your Gun*... He told her how George was teaching him the basics of the alchemical craft, adding powder to powder to liquid in the back storeroom and creating the most marvellous concoctions, how they had both got themselves passports and gone on long bus journeys together, first to Prague, then to Antwerp and Flanders; how the weather was cold and wet; or how, in Prague, it had snowed, piles and piles of it stacking up against their hotel window, covering the whole city, giving it a uniformity and blandness he would later find tough to shake from his mind – especially when, before the snow, the vistas had been most spectacular, gargoyles and saints twisting their bodies to the full moon from elaborate gothic towers.

Once, remembering his mother's obsession with hamsters – she had owned a dozen as a little girl, ten in a row all named Charlie Bucket after Charlie in *Charlie and the Chocolate Factory*, her favourite Roald Dahl book – he had obtained a baby one from Libby's Pet and Fish Shop and placed it quite carefully on his mother's bed.

He thought it might jolt something from her, from her past, from the recesses of her dead mind, but she and the tiny beast had merely stared at each other, one set of black eyes boring into the other, and then somehow he had lost it on the bus ride home – or perhaps it had escaped, sensing the chance for freedom and a better, more fulfilling life.

Despite feeling as though his heart was continually breaking, he persisted.

One weekend he brought pictures of his room above the tea shop, converted into a den just for him, with its posters of Kraftwerk and Yazoo on the wall, his set of British Manly Exercises barbells, his collection of Hammond Innes books – *The Lonely Skier*, *The Blue Ice*, *Wreckers Must Breathe* and, his favourite,

The Angry Mountain – the racks of test tubes, bottles of powders and crystals that towered above his narrow bed, the bed itself with his soft Hong Kong Phooey plush toy his mother had given him years ago, and which he still slept with even now.

When he was of an age he told her of his affairs. It was Albert, his old school friend and long-term survivor of the Meltdown game, who became his first amour. They made a kind of love in one of the cramped units of Mario's Self-Storage while Mario was otherwise engaged, twisting themselves around old bicycles, stacks of slow cookers still in their boxes, an upright piano with a long associated seat, the lid of which Albert liked to bang to hide the sound of his accumulating passion; and then it was Juliette, the daughter of a road sweeper, whose face was always dusty and whose clothes smelt of the detritus her father trudged through on a daily basis – which bore not only odour but also a heft and a weight.

And at the end of each visit to his mother Arthur always said the same thing. 'You're all right, aren't you, Mum? You'd tell me if there was something on your mind, wouldn't you? You know you can trust me. I'm your son.'

But then one day when he turned up at the institution, instead of being directed to make his own way to her room – *You know the drill* – he was taken to a side office by a doctor with an unhealthy squint and rolled-up shirtsleeves, a set of coloured Biros in his top left pocket, and was told that his mother had died suddenly.

'She wasn't alone when it happened,' said the doctor, pinching the end of his nose as if to stifle a sneeze, or as though he was about to dive into the deep end of a pool. 'There was a nurse in there with her – one of our newer members of staff, who had taken a great interest in your mother, and was often to be found brushing her hair. And this is the thing: before your mother passed, she opened her eyes and said a single word: Mermaid. Does that mean anything to you?'

'She tried to drown herself,' said Arthur. 'In the water. Where mermaids live. That's the reason she was in here.'

'In that you are mistaken,' said the doctor swiftly. 'She was in here because she *didn't* drown herself. That is quite a significant difference.'

And then the doctor had sighed, apologised for Arthur's loss, and moved on to the funeral arrangements.

George was big on learning, and when Arthur passed his school exams, achieving a range of straight As, the letters standing like the first line in a children's primer, it was George who sent off for the university prospectus, coached Arthur in his responses, and stood next to him mouthing encouraging words as Arthur underwent the gruelling two-hour telephone interview.

'You'll be grand,' he said at the train station on the day Arthur was finally to leave. 'Just as good as anyone. You'll see.'

The university was in Capital City, a metropolis the likes of which Arthur had never seen before. With its seething streets, huge concrete monolithic tower blocks and pulsing neon signs Arthur felt he had stepped on to the *Bladerunner* set. *Bladerunner* was George's favourite film, and he held a special screening in the tearoom on each of their birthdays; sitting on one of the hard-backed chairs, devouring a Chelsea bun, Arthur had never imagined he would find himself in such a place. But here he was.

Scouring the accommodation ads in a butcher's shop window, Arthur found himself a single room in the attic of a Northern Quarter fish market. Thanks to the thin-tiled roof and the huge blocks of ice stored in the room below, to chill the freshly caught fish, the room was so freezing that during that first winter Arthur had to sleep in two pairs of long johns and an aardvark-skin hat. But as the spring and then summer came around, the sun beat down on that same thin-tiled roof, heating the room to a super-high temperature, and Arthur found he had no choice but to climb out on to the flat roof and sleep there, quite in the nude.

The men who worked in the fish market were mostly Nigerian, and the first time a group of them – tall, slender, handsome men with fish knives secured in their narrow belts – came up on to the roof for their regulation early-morning cigarette break and found Arthur lying there in the buff they had let out a communal whoop and holler. Startled from his reverie Arthur had leapt up, whooped and hollered back, and then, a certain amount of proverbial ice being broken, shared a cigarette with them – an act which soon became a daily occurrence.

It was the first time since his early teenage years with Albert and Reggie that Arthur had felt a sense of belonging to the world – of being part of a like-minded community.

Arthur mixed rarely with the other students at his university. The fish market was some distance from the campus, but living any closer, in one of the luxury chrome tower blocks where the other students lived with their up-to-date sound systems, smartphones, third-world cleaners and baggies of experimental drugs hidden in sock drawers, was beyond his means.

In order even to make ends meet, for five nights a week Arthur worked in Tom's Bowling Alley and Fun Factory. The Fun Factory part was a range of rusty climbing frames covered with a tarpaulin: it had been closed down early that summer after a five-year-old child had fallen on to the mouth of a rough sleeper. The bite marks had appeared on the front cover of the *Daily News*, and a national campaign, backed by the Prime Minister, had been started to have the teeth removed from all homeless people. Several high-profile private dentists had come on board, and a crowd-funding site had been set up. Donators could go for a single incisor, a molar, a wisdom tooth or – the pièce de résistance – a whole mouth. A well-known reality TV star had sponsored the first whole mouth, and had appeared on the front page of several national newspapers with his arm around the homeless man whose teeth he had paid to have removed. Rumour had it that the homeless man had been snapped up by a literary agent and a cookbook was in the works, *Eating Without Teeth*, with a potential follow-up already on the cards, *The Art of Sucking and Seeing.*

Arthur's job at the bowling alley was to hand out the special lime-green rubber bowling shoes and to scrub them clean on their return. It was difficult to get the smell of feet out of his nose, and at night he dreamt of big toes, verrucas, athlete's foot. Naked, disembodied lower limbs would surround him, before slowly closing in, suffocating him as they filled his every hole, squirming and squeezing inside him.

He told all this to his tutor, Professor Bermann, a frighteningly tall Calvinist whose great uncle, a German Jew living in Prague some time before the Second World War, had been the basis for a minor character jeered at and then knocked from his horse in an unpublished story by Franz Kafka.

'And these toes enter you from behind?' asked Professor Bermann. Arthur blushed, remembering his brief affair with Albert. Albert had liked to do things with his feet – and cheap dog food, with jelly around the sides. He would make Arthur bark like a dog and lick himself, getting angry when Arthur couldn't lick his own butt. Arthur wasn't sure if this shame was a new one or an old one; like many things in his life it was about balance, and he was unsure where, or when, to put the weights on the scale.

Arthur was studying the sciences, and at the end of the first year the university held an Innovation Fair in the hired-out neo-Gothic waiting room of the Central Railway Terminus. The other young men, whose parents were wealthy, had elaborate stalls to show off their creations, fancy installations to represent breakthroughs in scientific fact, each adorned with hand-stitched flags displaying ferocious-looking griffins or dragons or representations of the family dog scampering gaily around their holiday home in the Lower Algarve. These other young men stood proudly behind their stalls, dressed in top hats shiny enough to reflect light and skinny black trousers that showed off their perfectly toned calves.

Before Arthur set up his own stall, a tea-stained tray he had stolen from the canteen and to which he had attached thin bamboo legs, he walked around the hall, and felt more and more sickened.

There was a working volcano, Krakatoa or Etna, tiny mountaineers scaling its sides, a walk-in wind tunnel, boys visible through its glass sides, their long hair streaming behind them like banners, a diorama of the town of Pripyat held in time shortly after the Chernobyl meltdown and, most striking, three competing life-scale models of Nikola Tesla, Guglielmo Marconi and Edwin R. Scott inventing the Death Ray. Arthur had only some tiny bags of powder, George's erection giver, improved by himself and tested late at night in his rooms above the fish market. Standing naked and proud, he had been able to hang all manner of things from his upright member, consoling himself with the thought that if all else failed he could always become a coat rack or be incorporated into a car as a living gearstick.

But as it turned out, his bags were a roaring success, the queue at his stall long and sinuous. Erections in the lower region being a thing young men covet, word soon got around. The price was 25p, and by the end of the day Arthur had sold out.

Two days later Arthur was called to the principal's office. The principal's secretary wore a pince-nez and had large gold rings on each of his fingers.

The principal himself didn't stand up from his desk upon Arthur's entry. The curtains were drawn, and the only light came from an illuminated globe with pins in to indicate the towns in which the affiliated colleges of the university existed – Obal, Hrodna, Navahrudak, Pinsk and Minsk.

As the principal talked on, Arthur was taken back to that time years ago when he had been scolded by his mother over the incident with the tomato sauce and his and Albert and Reggie's naked bodies – he felt the same sense of ambition and endeavour being turned into shame and humiliation.

The long and short of it was that there had been a scandal, and he was to blame.

On the night after the Innovation Fair police and various other emergency services personnel had been called to the chrome tower block where the other students lived. An orgy or something of the kind was going on, young men naked and running along the corridor or engaged in heinous acts in their rooms, and even, it was said, *six going at it on and under the reception desk* – much to the shock of Harold, the elderly concierge.

An investigation had traced the cause back to Arthur and his powder. Taken on its own it had the effect as advertised. Mix it with alcohol and the effect was something else. 'Bacchanalian' was the word the principal used. Lustful. Horny as all unholy hell.

Several boys were in hospital, bleeding from orifices not usually discussed in public, and for decorum's sake extra male nurses had had to be brought in from the suburbs.

Arthur was now publicly – as well as privately – ostracised. News of his powder had been printed in *The Bottom Line*, the university paper.

To take his mind away from his troubles, to exhaust his body so he could sleep, Arthur took on more hours at Tom's Bowling Alley and Fun Factory, but even events there conspired to antagonise him.

Eric, Arthur's friend and coworker, left abruptly after a hold-up at the club. Eric had been on duty, cashing up for the night, when masked men in tight, dark-coloured turtlenecks had broken in. Not only had they taken the money, but they also made off with half a dozen bowling balls and a good deal of shoes. Eric couldn't take the pressure any more. He was seventy, and had long craved a quiet life by the sea, growing tomatoes and reading the works of Agatha Christie and Marcel Proust in their entirety. Now he would.

Then, to add insult to injury, George died suddenly in a boating accident. Or it had happened on a boat. The details were sketchy. All Arthur was left were George's last letters, stories of problems at the tea shop, declining trade, Evans' new *spectacular* tea shop opening further down the High Street, offering two-for-one on all drinks twenty-four hours a day and waiters who had been cosmetically enhanced to be the spit of George Clooney. The final straw, it seemed, was the *anonymous* report to the Health and Safety Department: inspectors had swooped in one Tuesday morning, put 'condemned' stickers on all of George's test tubes, stipulated *no more potions.*

Arthur invited Albert and Reggie to the funeral. The pair were lovers now and, as a symbol of their love, had run lengths of string between their bodies, connecting them together in the fashion of Lord Ashberry of Sutton and his favourite slave girl, Mercy.

At the wake there was dancing, and Arthur, quite drunk from the many tiny glasses of port upended into his mouth, trying to get between Reggie and Albert, had become entangled in their strings and an argument had ensued.

Didn't Arthur know where some of these bloody strings were attached? He did not.

All he had felt, for a moment, was comforted, supported, as it were, in a cat's cradle of his friends' design. That it proved to be false severed his own heart's strings.

Another year passed and then another, a lonely time spent either at his lectures or the bowling alley, and at the end of these years Arthur attended a ceremony in which he was handed a rolled-up piece of paper indicating he had been awarded his degree and was ready for the world of work.

A man at last. Except sometimes he still felt like a little boy.

He missed George. And he missed his mum. He had photographs of them both, which he kept in a leather pouch, secured by strings, over his heart.

Sometimes in his sleep he would put his hand over them, and he would dream – or he believed he would – because the only thing in his mind when he awoke was a single image: that of a mermaid, deep underwater, her hair floating above her in the manner of a halo.

The Spectacular Death of a Bearded Socialist

The money George had left Arthur was beginning to dwindle when the envelope arrived.

The power station was on the outskirts of Saltburn-by-the-Sea, a north-eastern coastal town not so far from where Arthur had grown up. Although he was a recent graduate they were offering him the post of Assistant Chief Nuclear Engineer. It was certainly a step up from handing out shoes in the bowling alley.

For the majority of the train journey Arthur sat between two square-jawed soldiers who were tightly packed into musty-smelling khaki uniforms. The soldiers ate a whole plastic Evans bread-bag full of sandwiches, from which a fish head and tail stuck out from each end, as if the fish still believed, given half a chance, they could make a break for it upstream to pools where dolphins and sharks cavorted in idle company.

The soldiers talked of life in a war zone, the fear of being shot at, the regularity with which their colleagues had lost body parts, legs, arms, dicks to IEDs, the sound of shells detonating in the dead of night. They silently mouthed 'kabooms' to each other like they were blowing soft kisses. When one came back from the stinking end-of-carriage toilet – they were interchangeable, these soldiers, as alike as Mattel die-cast models produced on a production line – the talk turned to desert sand, and for quite some time it was mostly this: how the desert sand got between their bum cracks, deep down and in, around their balls, under their foreskin, so they would scratch at themselves long into the night, but not in an act of masturbation – oh, what it would have been like to have an easy grit-free wank, and then, perhaps, they could have withstood the eternal horror of war.

As the train was leaving Doncaster – a godforsaken place, it seemed, tired old donkeys on the platform accompanied by women in hairnets carrying skinny chickens in home-made wicker baskets – one of the soldiers leant over to the other and breathed the name Lanky Jones, recalled how Lanky Jones was shot because he had his fingers up his arse – that was the whole story – how Lanky Jones was trying to scoop out the bloody desert sand rather than having his finger on his trigger, eyes on the horizon, and he died like that, face forward, fingers still inserted, arse in the air, and it wasn't funny, no it wasn't funny, but they pulled their lips back from their gleaming army teeth and wheezed with laughter like happy old smokers.

Arthur was sad when the soldiers got off the train, because he had fallen a little in love with them. Since George had gone he was always forming random out-of-the-blue attachments to men he hardly knew. For two weeks he had worn a shabby donkey jacket and hung around the canteen of the local refuse depot after a kind word from his binman. He had even tried to emulate the toffs in his study group, feigning an interest in exclusive skiing holidays, kumquat salads, liver-spotted dogs who only walked to heel, but then he overheard them talking about him, mimicking his accent and calling him *cheese-eyes*.

At the next stop the soldiers were replaced by a family of four: a mother, a father and two small boys. The father had an eyepatch and was dressed in a woollen overcoat much too big for his pipe-cleaner arms and pigeon chest, and the mother had a chemical perm that had gone wrong, but she was clearly trying to make the most of it by placing seven or eight chopsticks through the tight curls. Upon closer inspection Arthur noticed each of the chopsticks had 'The Efficient Panda Chinese Restaurant With Free Parking' stamped on them.

Both of boys had blond unkempt hair, bitten-back fingernails and trouser legs thick with wiped bogies and damp sand from a seaside somewhere. As soon as the train left the station they took a battered board game box from a lime-green Mace plastic carrier bag, the Mace logo faded from spending too long in the sun, and proceeded to set the game up on the shiny Naugahyde table.

A small lump formed in Arthur's throat when he saw the title on the front of the box – he had used to play The Spectacular Death of a Bearded Socialist™ with Arthur and Reggie in Reggie's garage. The idea was each player took a token representing a company paying less than 0.001% tax. The winner was the one who acquired the most public services for the lowest price. There were bonus points for disposing of homeless people or setting fire to food banks. The game had 125 plastic interlocking parts. At the end of each round a marble went down a runway, knocked a domino which hit a lever which started a merry-go-round which sent another marble rolling which landed on a see-saw which fired a non-elected-governmental-advisor at a target, the hitting of which released a cage which descended and trapped a bearded socialist who then spontaneously ignited, burning fiercely until he was nothing more than a pile of ashes.

The game came with six bearded socialists. Replacement packs were available to be bought in Evans' Pharmacies and Evans' Toys. As the game was so popular these had flown off the shelves, and the money raised had been used to fund various New Puritanism causes: leafleting warning against the dangers of exposing your bum in public – *You don't know who's watching!*, a multiple-choice quiz designed to weed out sexual deviants and male hair stylists, posters advising of the dangers of Eastern European women (the women appeared on the posters in traditional dress, snapping up all the fruit-picking and toilet-attendant jobs, or queuing up to buy pickles outside ethnic stores, severe-looking gun belts strapped tightly, and with menace, around their waists; this one read 'SUSPICIOUS PICKLE EATING? PHONE OUR HOTLINE: 0800-333-PICKLE').

As Arthur watched the family opposite him one of the young boys held his arms up in silent triumph as he reached the last square that meant he had won the round and he could set the marble rolling to bring about the death of the bearded socialist. But unfortunately, as many of the plastic parts had either been lost or stolen, the marble rolled off the first runway, bounced across the table and fell down into the aisle of the train, where it was lost under the chair of an extremely fat man who was silently pressing the keys of a broken Hammond organ.

Arthur's stop was the last. Stepping out on to the platform with its broken chocolate vending machine and empty newspaper kiosk, there was the smell of the sea in the air, overcooked hot dogs, tanning lotion, the blue rinse of a distant hair salon.

He was supposed to be being met, so the letter of appointment had said, by Arkwright, the nuclear superintendent.

Arthur found the rendezvous point, a crumbling statue of a seal, easily enough. The creature sat staring mournfully over the chopping waters just opposite the train station entrance, decades of guano encrusted on its once proud head. Arthur sat on its pedestal and joined the creature in its gaze, although his was not out to sea, but up and down the road.

After an hour of fruitless waiting, jumping at the sight of any likely Arkwrights – *What would an Arkwright look like?* – Arthur gave up and set off along the front, his suitcase banging painfully against his ankles.

Despite the decrepitude of the environment, faded shop fronts, peeling paint, abandoned shopping trolleys on the sand, there was a certain quality to the air, lucid, that he had never encountered before. And he could taste it.

I'm going to like it here, he thought. Here I have no past, only a future. And, like the air, this future would be lucid, steadfast.

He set his suitcase down, climbed up on to it, pumped both fists wildly above his head.

There would be no more darkness, dank corners. Misery. Shame. This was his new life.

There were any number of B&Bs along the front, tall imposing buildings with flaking window frames, dead pines in potted plants outside their closed doors, rotting signs that said *Vacancies* – or not.

Taking trust in his new steadfastness Arthur knocked boldly at the door of one. Waiting a time, he knocked again. It was some minutes later – long minutes, in which Arthur felt his boldness fading – that the door was opened by a huge woman sporting a curled mass of blue hair, the set of which Arthur believed he had smelt on the station platform earlier.

'I was wondering,' he said, then stopped. What was he wondering? The situation had quite overcome him. 'A room?'

This was enough. She was, as George would have said, a talker.

She said she didn't usually *take in* guests at this time of night, but since Cyril had died she had a spare room. It was in the attic. The bathroom was on the floor below. He would have to share that with Mr Rogers and Mr Stanley. They were actors, and two of her long-timers. They had come to the town fifteen years before for a production of Harold Pinter's *The Birthday Party*, and never left. It was a shame, but the old theatre had closed now. For a while it had been turned into a gentleman's public convenience, then a haberdasher, but apparently there was no money in that. She didn't stand for funny business, or put on trips, but if he liked she was friendly with one of the local fishermen, who could take him out across the mudflats to see the seals – only he had to be careful they didn't bite his hand. The seals, not the fishermen! He could lose one of his beautiful fingers. Not many out-of-town folk knew that seals were biters. And she had noticed his fingers, and his brown corduroy suit. So rare to see a well-dressed young man these days! And then, of course, there was the Foetus Museum and the Aquarium just along the front. He could visit them under his own steam, although the aquarium didn't have any *actual* fish any more – not since *the incident*. But still, it was worth a visit. It was amazing what you could do without fish these days.

'Like what?' Arthur had asked, genuinely intrigued – but just at that point a bell had rung somewhere, and she had unlocked the door to the attic room – they had arrived right outside it – pressed the key on its huge wooden fob into his hand and left him, apologising that she couldn't offer him sandwiches, because she had no bread, not until the bakery opened, and that would be some time away. But if he was desperate she could open him a tin of beans and sausages. Or SpaghettiOs. Her son brought her a suitcase full of those when he visited from the States once a year. He was on the vaudeville circuit in Florida.

'I'm OK actually,' said Arthur. 'Not hungry.'

For most of that first night Arthur stood in his new suit at the window. There was a bottle of hair tonic on the bedside table and the yellowing pillow on the bed had a shiny spot in its centre where a head may have lain. Cyril's, he supposed. He could imagine him, Cyril, a small man who walked with a frame and who still had a collection of VHS tapes – *Carry On* films, *Cagney and Lacey*'s best episodes, all of Benny Hill's Christmas specials and a Swedish fondue set he had purchased from British Home Stores in 1977.

Arthur thought the sound he could hear, intermittent, cascading, was the distant sea, or the gulls, maybe, but then he noticed the glow of neon lights along the curve of the front, spelling out words: 'Ginny's Palace, Amusements'.

A penny arcade.

George had taken him to one once. They had had a budget of 40p, and had been down to their last 5p, two 2ps and a 1p when they had hit the jackpot.

George was made up, gambolling along the promenade like a kid, insisting they spend the winnings on a battered sausage and chips, which they shared in an abandoned bus shelter, the timetables water damaged and yellowing, advertising buses that would never come now.

At three or four in the morning, still awake, Arthur saw the neon tubes on Ginny's Palace were finally extinguished. Minutes later, the door opened and out of it came a woman. She had silver hair and a tight dress that gleamed like scales. Arthur let out a small gasp and cowered back. She was the most beautiful creature he had ever seen.

This wasn't entirely true. He had seen her in his dreams, deep underwater, her long hair rising above her like a halo. His mother's final word haunted him: Mermaid.

After a succession of phone calls, a wrong number, a receptionist and then Arkwright himself, Arthur met his new boss the following day. There was no mention of the missed appointment by the seal statue at the train station either on the phone call or at that first meeting.

'It's easy work,' said Arkwright, lifting his coffee cup, holding it poised in the air like a magician with a wand at the end of a pier.

They were sat in a tea shop. The decor reminded Arthur of where he had grown up, although instead of Arthur ferrying cups of tea, bacon sandwiches, eggs done in many ways, there was a young red-faced waitress with a pad and jaunty Deely boppers on her head, large angry-looking live prawns attached to each of the springs. They stabbed at the air as he placed his order.

'The power station practically runs itself,' Arkwright said, and winked mischievously. 'It's running itself right now while we're sat here carousing. That's the beauty of nuclear. Put atoms together in the right way and they just get on with it.'

'But what about meltdowns?' Arthur pushed a button mushroom across his plate. It was shaped exactly like a cloud he vividly remembered from a documentary he had watched as a boy.

'Couldn't happen,' said Arkwright. 'Not unless you wanted it to. Now let me show you the ropes.'

And they had set off across the mudflats towards the concrete silos that dominated the horizon, Arkwright in front, Arthur behind, both leaving their footprints in the sand, Arkwright's larger, Arthur's smaller, and both impermanent, at the mercy of the waves.

And that was it. It was as simple as that. This was Arthur's new life.

For between eight and ten hours a day Arthur sat in a white room in front of a series of screens, lights flashing, green lines pulsing like those of a heart monitor, the whoosh and swoosh of airtight doors opening and closing before returning at night alone to the B&B.

Sometimes he would watch TV with the other guests, Mr Rogers and Mr Stanley – repeats of *The Onedin Line*, *Howard's Way*, *George and Mildred*, *On the Buses*, *Only When I Laugh* – or he would sit in his room and read. Remembering Eric, his friend from the bowling alley, he tried Proust, but he didn't get on with him. It was too much about the past, remembering, going over and over. Agatha Christie was no better. Too many people crowded into a varying small space, all with the same but different devious motives. So instead he immersed himself in stories of the future – *Brave New World*, *1984*, *Fahrenheit 451*, *A Clockwork Orange*, *The Day of the Triffids* – and the days moved forward.

On his days off he visited the Aquarium, learnt of its strange history, spent one Saturday morning in the Foetus Museum, although the tiny deformed babies gave him nightmares and put him off the pickled eggs and gherkins at Chippie Chips. He got to know the nuns from the lunatic asylum up on the hill – not biblically, but by sight – and the dog walkers on the beach, and their dogs, the tradespeople and the local characters, the postman with one leg and extremely long eyelashes, the fishermen, who were always with different women, and one night he found them cavorting naked on the beach around a tall, burning bonfire.

The owners of the shops, who relied on the influx of tourists in the summer months to bolster their living, knew his name now, and they would greet him with a smile and a good morning. And of course there was the lady he had seen that first night through his window – the one who worked at Ginny's Arcade, and who he was still plucking up the courage to speak to.

With no reason to return *home*, both his mother and George dead, his father never heard from, Arthur felt no guilt in referring to Saltburn-by-the-Sea as home, talking to himself on his nights alone in his room, after he finished masturbating into his special sock and before he picked up one of his books. *Here I am, at home, in Saltburn-by-the-Sea, and I am happy here.*

Arthur's trial period at the nuclear-power facility lasted three months, and after that, his continued employment assured, he decided it was time to put down some proper roots.

He gave the obligatory week's notice at the B&B, had an emotional final supper, Mr Rogers and Mr Stanley acting out selected highlights from *The Birthday Party*, and moved into his own apartment. For the house warming, Mr Rogers and Mr Stanley being otherwise engaged, he invited the only other person he knew well: Arkwright, his boss and mentor at the nuclear-power facility.

On the night in question Arkwright was early by more than two hours. Arthur was surprised when he opened the door and found him standing there, a rare look of botheration upon his face. Arthur asked if everything was OK and Arkwright said Yes and then No and then, when he had got his breath back a little, asked if he could come in.

The apartment had once been the old train station toilets, and there was still a stained urinal down one wall, the flushing of which, every five minutes, had initially kept Arthur awake through the night, but now he was used to it. On the wall opposite the urinal were eight wooden cubicles. His landlord told him the graffiti was an original feature; Arthur could still remember, his face flushing again at the memory, how, almost without thinking, he had read out, 'Juliette sucks cock. Please call,' and then the number that followed.

'Disconnected,' said the landlord, winking. 'To save you the bother I've tried. And who says landlords are exploiters? Look, that's one less job for you already.'

One of the conditions of the lease agreement was that during the football season, when the town's team, Saltburn Uninvited (there had been a cock-up with the shirts, and no money to change them), played at home, the apartment would be opened up for its former use.

Arthur didn't mind the queues of raucous supporters trailing out of his front door, as it gave him both an excuse and the impetus to get out, and on those days he would go to Ginny's Palace and try and engage the young woman he had seen that first night from his window in conversation.

He knew her name now, Peggy, and that she was attracted to sailors – or tried to be. Several mornings on his way to work he had seen her half-submerged on the rocks, singing out to the fishermen, swishing her hair, attempting to catch their attention as the sun glinted on her scales.

Arthur had told Arkwright all about Peggy, and he was hoping that, at his house-warming party, he and Arkwright could get a little tipsy and go down to the arcade before it closed – and maybe, with Arkwright there, he would finally pluck up the courage to say something. But Arkwright was behaving oddly, dancing, although there was no music playing, and refusing all of the food Arthur had prepared – tiny sardines on slivers of bread, pickled onions and chunks of pineapple skewered on toothpicks, prawn roe set in spheres of aspic.

So while Arkwright did his strange dance, politely apologising before locking himself in one of the wooden toilet cubicles, Arthur played the role of host, walking around with the tray of food he had prepared held at shoulder height until finally, when Arkwright had gone into the furthest of the cubicles, locked the door and stayed there for a good fifteen minutes, Arthur went into the next cubicle, got down to his knees, put his mouth against the glory hole cut into the wall, and asked if everything was OK.

'Well,' said Arkwright, getting down on his knees too, putting his mouth to the other side of the glory hole, 'the truth of the matter is I owe you a profound apology.'

'For what?' asked Arthur. Outside he could hear a group of night crawlers going past – men who, from the shame of the damage they had inflicted on the planet, had taken to crawling on their hands and knees at night. Arthur noted that some of them had also taken to wearing terrycloth nappies, and it brought back a sharp memory of his mother. She had told him of such men as this, right at the end, when she could only try and sell her wallpaper rolls at night.

'I got you here under false pretences,' said Arkwright. 'To Saltburn-by-the-Sea, I mean. I never needed an assistant chief nuclear engineer. I can run that place myself. As can you.' Arkwright paused before the next words came out, all at once. 'I want you to take over my job.'

'Me!' Into Arthur's head came a vision of all the levers, flashing lights, buttons. He had a recurring nightmare in which an old lady in a wheelchair wheeled herself up to the perimeter fence of the nuclear facility, hit a rock and fell – and then, as Arthur went out to help her, she jumped up, ripped off her disguise and revealed herself to be a Russian terrorist with a large moustache, and she took Arthur hostage, stripped him naked and attached a twelve-volt leisure battery to his scrotal sac, running powerful current through him until he gave up the codes for the reactor.

'Yes, you,' said Arkwright, and he put his mouth right up to the glory hole, pushing his lips through. 'Truth is I'm not long for this world. The Big C. Cancer. In my liver, my kidneys, every bloody where. And it's a shame, because in some ways I feel I have only just made my first footprint. Do you feel that? That your real life is out there somewhere, just waiting for you to catch up with it before it can begin? And now it never will. But before I go, there is something I must show you. Come, come now!'

They exited the cubicles then, and Arkwright led Arthur outside, down to the seafront and under the full moon they tramped across the mudflats to the nuclear plant.

In the distance, out at sea, the seals churned, joyous for the spring tide, tossing their heads both in and out of the waves. And it was beautiful, but sad, because, as with all beautiful things, they hold within their hearts a notion of their own transience.

Radiation

They were in the control room. Monitors lit the room – an incessant light that meant all was well in the world. In this particular world.

'First a toast,' said Arkwright with some jollity – a jollity that was shown to be false, as his hands shook while he mixed them both a martini. Then, as they clinked glasses instead of the usual *bottoms up*, he said, 'Inside,' quietly and without any of the usual bonhomie of a toast.

'Inside?' said Arthur, puzzled.

'Yes, my son, we are going inside the reactor.'

Arthur remembered the training from his first week at the facility. It was all about putting on your anti-rad suit when nearing the reactor, checking daily for leakage, monitoring the equipment. Arkwright had told him, very clearly, that entering the reactor itself was strictly out of bounds, meant certain death, even with a suit on; so Arthur wasn't sure if he had heard right, but then Arkwright was taking down the emergency reactor key from its peg and putting it in his pocket, not a sliver of protective suit in sight.

'Don't worry, son. You'll see!'

As Arthur followed Arkwright down the tunnel, radiation warning signs affixed to the wall every few metres, in his mind he rattled through the symptoms he had memorised: nausea and vomiting, diarrhoea, severe headache, fever, ditziness and disintegration, weakness and fatigue, total body hair loss, internal bleeding leading to blood vomit and blood shits, massive infections, low blood pressure, death.

But if he did get sick, then maybe Peggy would come to the hospital to visit him. It might be just the kind of icebreaker he needed.

They could fall in love, in spite of his failing organs, the blood pouring from his bumhole, the persistent beeping of the machine indicating his heart was still beating.

Or maybe he could wrestle Arkwright to the ground, stop this madness.

The concrete reactors loomed out of the darkness like giant Martello towers with cherries on the top – red flashing lights warning away the lobster and crabbing fleets, anyone who might decide to visit in a helicopter. There had been a Harrier jump jet land once, so Arkwright had said, on the mudflats, the pilot, a prize nincompoop, having mistaken the lights for that of his airbase.

As Arkwright fumbled with the keys Arthur squinted out to the horizon, where the little fishing boats bobbed, pulling on their night anchors. That was heroism, going out there every night. What he did, was doing, was nothing. But.

'You're going to die,' said Arthur. 'I don't want to. I don't know why. Except life – it beckons you on.'

'Don't be a bloody fool,' said Arkwright. 'What do you take me for? I'm not going to kill you. Come on inside. You'll see. I promise you. No danger. The truth is I've come to love you as a son. Both a son and my protégé.'

Having unlocked the heavy iron door Arkwright paused while Arthur stepped in after him and then he slammed it shut again with an ominous clang.

'The beating heart of the baby. Very hush hush.' If Arthur wasn't mistaken Arkwright was actually giggling. 'The truth is there was never any need for the anti-rad suits. They were just in case anyone was watching.'

'Watching?' Arthur was becoming more and more puzzled, not less.

'From the mudflats, I mean. We get them sometimes – nosey buggers with binoculars, wondering what all this nuclear malarkey is about.'

It took some time for Arthur's eyes to adjust to the light – or rather, the lack of it. He had a sense of space, of walls being far away. He might have been in a church, or a planetarium, or one of those long low buildings on the edges of new towns where they grow climate-inappropriate fruits, massive super-red strawberries, tomatoes as big as footballs.

He had visited one of these buildings once, on a university trip, and he kissed a girl behind a banana tree and then told her bananas didn't always use to be round, like clock faces, or motorbike wheels. In the past, he had told her, they had used to be shaped like *men's parts*, and he had pointed down at himself. *Sort of curved. With a bit of give in them.*

'You're a brute,' the girl had said. Her family were from one of the southern resorts, her father big in artisanal sandwich development and crockpots, and for the whole journey back he had had to listen to her being comforted by her enclave of girls. The final snub was that, when the complimentary biscuits came round, his were broken into crumbs, and Wally Withers, who was rumoured to have three balls, stared at him hard and told him he should do something about his cheese-eyes and wandering fingers or he *would be crumbs too.*

'Behold,' said Arkwright, and with quite a show he pulled a lever and the room was bathed in brightness. 'Prometheus' Cave! A miracle of wonders and northern grit.'

With the pulling of the lever Arthur had expected heat, a kind of X-ray effect – that, holding up his hand, he would see the precise delineation of his bones beneath his flesh, like in the movie *X: The Man With X-ray Eyes*. Instead there was a musty smell, a low but gentle moaning and a sense of beasts. And then, as his eyes grew accustomed to this new bright light, he saw the movement – a pack of them, heads and hooves, matted grey and brown sides.

'Pit ponies,' said Arkwright, confirming. 'After the closing of the pits there were hundreds of them, and those hundreds bred. We could never have afforded proper nuclear, although it sounded pretty great. A few of us got together and...'

He gave a dull hacking cough, put a hand out to steady himself.

'...So instead we've got this. Heavenly beasts of burden. They walk around. They turn the turbines. The turbines produce electricity. It's a win-win for everyone. Because the turbines are much lighter than a wagon full of coal the ponies think they're in Elysium. And their breathing – they breathe like angels these days. They're better off here than on a mountain in Norway. Or down a pit. Or being slaughtered. The truth is, I love them, and I'm trusting you to take care of them when I'm gone. That's my legacy. Yours too, if you want it. What do you say, Arthur?'

Two weeks later Arthur was with Arkwright when he died. The nurse closed his eyes and said she always admired those who died peacefully. Last week they had had a diver who the seals had gone at. 'More cunts than I have ever heard in a row.' She shook her head as if to shake out the memory, and then she had asked Arthur if he had visited the hospital gift shop, and handed him a brochure with jaunty images of key rings, pencil cases, handheld fans and miniature plastic farm animals on the front.

'And we've still got some sea monkeys left. In our special Sea Monkeys Hospital Edition you can watch them swim in and out of A&E, undergo open heart surgery and even have their little limbs removed. But if you want one you better hurry – they're selling like hot cakes!'

Arkwright's last words to Arthur had been that he should get a bit of gumption, stop worrying about the whole bloody world and to go and speak to that lass you fancy.

'You're a bloody loss unto yourself. That's what you are. If I could I'd grab you by the balls myself. You only get one go in this life. I'm proof of that, aren't I, lad?'

He was right, and that very night, striking while the iron was hot, Arthur put on his Bjorn Borg headband, matching pair of John McEnroe wristbands and Vitas Gerulaitis jocks he had picked up at Delicious Gifts' Tennis Legends Accessory Sale and walked along the front to Ginny's Palace.

Peggy was there, sitting majestically behind her Perspex screen adorned with peeling adverts for battered sausages, long-dead end-of-pier comics, old black-and-white movies staring Carole Lombard and Charles 'Buddy' Rogers.

In response to her 'Hello, Krakatoa's not paid out in three days – you might want to give her a go,' (she had hardly even looked at him) Arthur had blushed and said, trying to impress, how he was now in charge of the nuclear-power plant out across the flats. Then he pulled at the keys hanging from his belt in a proprietary manner – this had been a tip from Mr Rogers and Mr Stanley, whose advice he had sought beforehand – and asked Peggy if she had change for a fifty.

There was some confusion as hands went back and forth to the till drawer, to the neatly organised stacks of ready prepared coins, and Peggy admitted that she would struggle to break a whole fifty pounds.

Arthur blushed again, said he meant fifty pence and not fifty pounds. He had never had a fifty-pound note, never in his life, and you had to be careful because a lot of them were forgeries.

But that was it. The ice was broken.

From fake notes they moved to crime, to train robberies, to train holidays, to holidays in general and where in the world they would most like to visit. For Arthur this was Pripyat, scene of the Chernobyl nuclear disaster. In fact, he wanted to open a B&B there – show visitors around the site. 'If we can't learn from our mistakes, what can we learn from?'

Peggy wanted to go Poulton-le-Fylde. It was where she had been conceived. 'My mam's a regular person; my father's a merman. Came up out of the sea, so my mam said, and then buggered off back again.'

The conversation flowed. Arthur might have stayed there all day if it hadn't been for the queue of fragrant fisherman forming behind him, wanting their 2p and 1p pieces for The Perils of the Deep, Ginny's Palace's latest slot machine, with a top prize of £3 and a 50p-off coupon for Chippie Chips.

But before Arthur moved off he did what he had wanted to do for so long: he asked Peggy if she wanted to go on a date.

'A bag of cockles and a walk along the front. If you fancy?'

She, apparently, did. She said yes.

Meltdown Countdown

10

Eighteen months later Arthur was with Peggy when their baby was born. The nurse who was assisting wore a pair of perfectly fitting kid gloves. Pinned to her uniform were other gloves: cotton, wool, silk, some with shining malachite buttons. Each pair had a price tag dangling from them on a short piece of string and a sticker with the words: *Available in our gift shop. Please visit on your way out.*

'It's a boy,' said the nurse, smiling, and then, going pale, she told them to wait. She didn't even hand them a brochure of newborn accessories to browse through, although there was a stack of them by the door.

The doctor arrived, playing the overture from *Die Fledermaus* on a harmonica. Hanging from his shoulders on straps were a guitar, a banjo, a violin and a tiny ukulele.

'We've got a special on tambourines,' he said, 'in the gift shop,' and then, apologising for the stringent advertising quota all staff were required to meet, he took the baby from Peggy and went into a side room, calling over his shoulder that Casio made the best portable organs. 'And for a reasonable price. Finance options available!'

'Do you think it'll be OK?' asked Peggy.

Arthur took her hand. 'It? He's a boy. And he's ours now. Don't worry. He'll be perfect, whatever is currently the matter is with him.'

9

Arthur and Peggy had converted one of the toilet cubicles in their apartment into a nursery. In another of the cubicles Arthur sat flushing the cistern over and over to hide the sound of his sobs.

'Oh, Atlas,' he said. 'Oh, my little Atlas.'

They had called the boy Atlas after the son of Poseidon and the first king of Atlantis – except like a king their son did not look.

Only work provided a distraction.

Arthur, now in sole charge of the nuclear facility, instead of sitting in the control room smoking Egyptian cigarettes and drinking martinis while keeping watch over the useless buttons and displays, let himself into the reactor chamber and tended the ponies.

He found comfort in their beastliness, their persistence, the way they turned their big eyes up at him when he treated them to cubes of sugar.

For a moment he could forget that he had a son who would never walk. Never crawl. Never, in all likelihood, speak.

Everyone he had ever loved had died or been damaged in some way.

'Better that I myself were never born!' he cried, and he imagined lying down on the dung-strewn ground, letting the ponies trample over him with their non-cloven feet.

But he didn't, because he had promised Peggy that their baby would be perfect whatever he was.

Just that morning, standing over the crib he had made from a lobster pot, watching Atlas' little arms and legs flailing, his heart had filled with love – both love and despair. That's how it would be.

8

It was the day after the annual Saltburn-by-the-Sea Prawn Festival, when dusty plaster busts of prawns would be burnt ceremoniously all along the beachfront and prawn-inspired songs sung, that Arthur, at work and half-asleep, was alerted by the klaxon of the perimeter alarm.

The night before he and Peggy had drunk too much prawn wine at the festival, and then they had danced almost naked on the beach, little Atlas in his basket by their feet, so it took some time for his eyes to focus on the security camera screen. But there, in grainy black and white, was the image of a person on the mudflats walking slowly backward and forward around the nuclear facility's fence, blatantly ignoring the RESTRICTED AREA, DANGER OF RADIATION signposts.

It was the perambulator he recognised first. He had made it himself, attaching the big wheels of two penny farthings to a scampi basket.

It was Peggy. And little baby Atlas.

The next day she was there again, and then the next.

7

Plucking up the courage, fearful, almost, of the answer, on the fourth night while they were lying in bed, he challenged Peggy about her perambulations, running his hand through her hair, salt-encrusted from the many hours she still spent half-submerged in the sea each morning.

'I've seen it in the comics,' she said, choking back tears, and she listed them off, pulling the comic books from where she had hidden them under the mattress. 'All these heroes given special powers by radiation.'

There was Cromoman, whose eyes could pierce through solid metal; Firestorm, who could perform nuclear pyrokinesis; Atom, who was able to shrink to subatomic level; and Flash, with his superhuman speed.

'The townsfolk have always complained that having a nuclear-power station so close is dangerous, but maybe radiation will give our baby special abilities. Just imagine – like one of these characters in the comics.'

6

It came to Arthur the next day, as he watched the ponies going around and around, turning the turbine that generated the electricity that powered the town, that allowed people to work, to pay for their electricity, that allowed him, as nuclear superintendent, to buy food for the ponies, that life was a circle.

First his mother had gone, then George. In their place had appeared first Peggy, then Atlas.

'Oh Peggy,' he said. 'Oh Atlas.'

One of the ponies from the feeding zone came up to him, nudged him in the side, lifted its mouth for a sugar cube.

Not an atom colliding with a neutron as everyone in the town believed, but a living, breathing animal. And all the better for it. Arthur patted the pony on its head, rummaged in a pocket.

He smiled, reality dawning on him. One thing could appear to be another – the ponies were testament to that. A lesson in life.

He had an idea.

5

Waiting until Peggy appeared on the security camera, pushing her perambulator, Arthur smiled at the sight of her and his son.

'If they want radiation,' he said, 'then radiation they shall get!' And with a roar of laughter he fetched the key from its peg, unlocked the huge loading doors and, putting his back into it, pushing first one and then the other, he opened them wide, letting light flood in.

It was the ponies from the feeding zone who came over first, noses lifted to the fresh air.

'Fly!' Arthur screamed. 'Fly!'

He prodded at one and tentatively it stepped out on to the sand, soon followed by the others.

Next Arthur went to the ponies connected to the turbines, released them one by one, unbuckling their heavy leather harnesses.

At first reluctant, soon they too were streaming outside.

4

'What's going on?' asked Peggy as he joined her out on the mudflats. He had mounted one of the ponies, and was sitting proudly on its back.

'We're having a meltdown,' he said. 'Right now!' And he waved his arms around his head in the manner of a TV naturalist he had once seen describing a stampede of brontosauruses. 'Radiation is flooding out from the reactors. The whole town will be radiated, of course, but those who are closest to the epicentre will be radiated the most. And this,' he said, 'this is the epicentre. Me, you and little Atlas are slap-bang in the middle of it all.'

3

Right on cue another of the ponies sidled up, its blinkers like window shutters, its little hooves sinking down into the sand. It let out a low moan, as though it might have been a wolf in another life, and then there was another and another, until Arthur and his family were completely surrounded.

'We are all made of atoms,' explained Arthur, 'billions of atoms, and each atom in turn is made of protons, neutrons and electrons. The protons and the neutrons make up the nucleus, and around the nucleus fly the electrons. And that is something that all matter is made up of. We are all the same. Whatever we are.'

2

Arthur reached down for Atlas, lifting him gently from the perambulator, and placed him in front of him on the pony's back. Then he reached for Peggy, holding her hand as she hauled herself up, snug behind him.

And like that, still surrounded, moving as one, they set off down the beach, a mushroom cloud of heavenly creatures.

They were an allegory, a special moment, a tipping point.

1

Their child didn't need a special power – that was the thing. He already had one. He was part of the world.

Or, at least, their world, their life, lives, the three of them, in the converted public toilets just off the seafront.

They would be OK. They loved each other. That was enough. It was enough.

Enough.

THE AQUARIUM

If the Glove Fits

On a cold spring morning in 1931 Francis Sheldon Sr. stood erect on the Saltburn station platform in an extraordinarily tall top hat and a pair of squeaky shoes, polished to a high shine by his servant Wilson. He was a proud man.

Already a success, he had envisaged this moment, *this launch*, as the beginning of a new age – a new age filled with gloves. His gloves.

They would adorn the hands of royalty, of the Hollywood starlets filling the screens of Saltburn-by-the-Sea's Electric Palace Cinema, of all the ladies who would woo and then marry his offspring. He was creating a dynasty.

'Be safe, my son,' he said, 'and remember, *Sheldon, Sheldon and Sheldon*.'

'*Sheldon, Sheldon and Sheldon* my arse,' mouthed back Francis Sheldon Jr., loose lips largely obscured by the grimy windows of the stopping train that was to take him south to London. He said it again for good measure. '*Sheldon, Sheldon and Sheldon*, my arse. My father, you are a prime buffoon. I have bigger fish to fry.'

Francis Sheldon Jr. – or Ferdi, as he liked to be known, citing an imagined striking resemblance to Ferdinand Magellan, that famed first circumnavigator of the planet, a statue of whom stood proudly at the entrance to Ferdi's summertime sex haunt, the Poulton-le-Fylde Lido – saw himself as something of an innovator.

The previous spring, eschewing the loose-fitting knee-length drawers favoured by other boys of his class, Ferdi had purchased, via mail-order – *direct from the United States of America!* – seven pairs of Everlast trunks – the tight-fitting silky shorts worn by those pugilists he so admired and listened to on his wireless late into the night: Jack Dempsey, Gene Tunney, Luis Firpo, Tom Gibbons, Tom Heeney, Jack Sharkey, Max Schmeling.

He loved boxers. The men. Their pants. Their sweaty cracks.

He hated gloves. Ladies. High society. Bosoms.

The train having safely left the station, Ferdi picked up the embossed suitcase his father had lovingly packed and presented to him – the handling of the sample gloves not to be trusted to the servant Wilson – and carried it along the swaying carriage until, reaching the end, he knocked and then locked himself in the stinking WC, and placed the suitcase on the tiny stained sink and opened it up.

'Hell's bells,' he uttered. 'Even worse than I thought.'

All the gloves of his youth materialised before his eyes: long chamois ones, gloves made of kid, sealskin, lambskin, elbow-length Berlin lisle gloves, Nemoskin gauntlets, double-silk mittens, white opera muffs as delicate as petals, and as pointless, even the ones usually reserved for Delicious Gifts, to be sold to tourists, Saltburn-by-the-Sea stitched into them by fishermen's wives paid a pittance to toil in badly lit rooms while Johnson, the overseer, growled as ferociously as his famous dog Bones.

On and on they went, truly making him sick. It was time to take a stand.

Choosing the star of the line, an Italian silk lady-in-waiting's glove with exquisite malachite buttons, Ferdi dropped his trousers, yanked down his Everlast pants and, placing the glove over his appendage, he pissed through it down into the pan.

Then, for *good sodding measure*, he wiped the pernicious thing on his behind before placing it, sodden and soiled, back in the case.

He heard his father's imperious words as he took his seat once more in the carriage: 'Make us proud son. Spread the word of Sheldon, Sheldon and Sheldon. We will take the world of hands by storm.'

'Fuck that.' He allowed himself this expletive, not caring for the stern look he got from the tight-lipped prelate sitting opposite him on the face-to face seats.

He was on his way now. Alone. A man. For the time being at least, in charge of his own destiny.

Ferdi was amazed by the bustle of London, its sights, its smells, its promiscuity.

He spent his first night away from the family pile in a palatial hotel in Victoria. The barman had a walrus moustache, a bow-tie with stiff horizontal ends. On the stage a jazz quartet played: a trombone, a trumpet, a double-bass and a surly singing man with a saxophone hanging by a cord from his shoulder, louche, dangling, as all-out erotic as a bared John Thomas.

After a number of potent beers Ferdi found himself dancing. Secretly he had always danced to his mother's treasured records – W.C. Handy's *Tin Pan Alley*, James Reece Europe's *Castle House Rag*, Louis Armstrong's *Big Butter and Egg Man* – but he had never done it in public before. Or with such abandon.

He threw himself into his moves, performing dives and pirouettes, two-steps and ankle-twists, until, finally exhausted, his shirt sticking with sweat to his body, and finding his former seat taken by a rather prim-looking lady smoking a cigarette in a long ivory holder, he took a seat at a table almost filled to its brim by two extremely large men.

These men, he saw, on closer inspection, sported enormous gold rings with serpent's heads on each of their fingers, had wide mouths distorted by several (at least) missing teeth and, most strangely of all, bodies packed precariously into lime-green leotards serving to show off splendidly the immense rolls of fat around their bellies.

What a brave new world he had entered! Confidence spiked by all the alcohol he had imbibed he gave them a *What ho!* and inquired what was with all the fancy clobber.

The men, it transpired, were German wrestlers, fresh from an exhibition of Bavarian brawn – two thousand working-class cockneys squeezed into a heaving Alexandra Palace, braying and whistling, while the guys worked each other over.

'Like zees,' said one of them, and, as if it were a piece of doll's furniture, he plucked up the very table they were seated at and cleared a space.

So began the demonstration: chin-lock, claw-hold, camel-clutch, an impressive performance only curtailed when the walrus-moustached barman pranced over and said in a blistering tone of high dudgeon that, 'This 'ere is an 'ighfalutin hotel, and ladies are present, thank you very much.'

Apologies given, table returned to its correct spot, Ferdi found himself displaced; squeezed now between the two Bavarians and stuck, so to speak, he stayed there drinking with them until the early hours of the morning when, finally getting up to go, the two bruisers, sharing the words between them like an infant-school round robin, quite casually invited him up to their room, one eye on each of their faces lasciviously winking.

It wouldn't be his first time.

Back home in Saltburn-by-the-Sea he had lost his virginity numerous times to the fishermen, his virginity being the catch of the day for those men of the sea and its tempests, who liked to think they were the first to screw the posh-boy glove-master's son – a thought not unpleasant to the posh boy himself, his father's shocked, disappointed, *Not what is expected of a Sheldon* face coming to him as he licked stinking sardine skin off salt-encrusted bodies, kissed trout lips, played with ecstatic electric fizzing eels between wide legs, swallowed spawn more tasty than fish roe.

Seamen.

Semen.

He was killing two birds with one stone – both pleasuring himself and pissing on his father's chips.

It was the sun that woke him. He was naked between the Germans, a chipolata between two thick Bratwursts. Feeling beady eyes upon him, he sat up to find a small dog with a black patch around its left eye silently watching him from the corner of the room. It was also – its image, at least – on one of the fliers scattered around the floor.

Helmut und Helmut
Und kleiner Peer
die Wrestler

Peer was the dog.

That made him laugh – Peer: one who pees – for he recalled, in that moment, the wrestlers expelling their beer over him in the hotel's grand pissoir, heads back, laughing. And he had laughed too. Anything to do with water pleased him. As a child, he had been told, he could swim before he could walk. Then, when he could walk, he was always running off to the sea.

One of his earliest memories was forging out as far as he could go, *to be with the fishes*, legs kicking, arms twirling, his mother standing at the water's edge screaming while his father stood, ridiculous, further back, fully suited, as upright as his ivory cane with its silly glove-shaped end planted in the sand.

Climbing carefully from between the two Germans, Ferdi caught himself in the room's full-length mirror. He had bite marks on his buttocks. From the dog? Surely not.

He could remember first being held aloft, firm hands on his back and thighs, his nose and winky almost touching the ceiling. Then they had showed him some moves, tossing him between them as though he was a rag doll or one of those medicine balls the oiks back home liked to show off with down on the pier, stripped to the waist, chests rippling. But oh how these wrestler men were gentle, their bellies as soft as beds filled with goose feathers.

Although loath to leave this newly found sanctuary – *Come with us, next we perform in Bristol, then Bath* – Ferdi made his final goodbyes, and only just made it to the station on time, ignoring the shouts of the station attendant to slow down as he ran for his train.

The Pullman carriage was luxurious, gilt like one of Faberge's precious eggs. Once he had caught his breath and managed to place an order with the waiter, who was sporting a Hungarian moustache and tight trousers that showed off splendid buttocks – *like eggs tied in a handkerchief*, he thought – he was brought a cup of beef broth, a ham-and-egg sandwich and a complimentary copy of *London Illustrated News*. The front page was filled with garish advertisements – *Dinneford's Solution of Magnesia, Seccotine Fish Glue, Yorkshire Relish* – and there at the bottom, which made him feel queasy: *Sheldon, Sheldon and Sheldon. Gloves: a perfect fit for any hand. Why not try yours today?*

Could he never escape?

Signalling to the waiter that he would just be a moment, he took his suitcase to the toilet. *It is a small act, my father, but one of prodigious intent.* He selected this time a lace glove with pearl buttons – *Why have a pearl necklace when you can wear gloves as beautiful as these?* – and urinated through it, before wiping it on his behind, as before, for good measure. Putting it away, he was a little shocked to notice it was spotted with blood.

Retaking his seat, carefully, aware now of the dull pain, he closed his eyes and relived his night, playing it backward, then forward, until he drifted into a kind of happy stupor that lasted until Dover, where, under heavy rain and a glowering sky, spectacular backlit thunderheads, he descended from the train.

Here, under the direction of numerous sopping guards, tall lanky men with the same uniform lampshade moustaches, he ascended the dock stairs and boarded his first sea-ferry, Southern Railways' *TSS Canterbury* – which, so the glossy brochure declaimed (he had read it numerous times), had a capacity for *seventeen hundred first-class passengers*.

Seventeen hundred! Even discounting the ladies, he figured there would be more than enough men for him to choose from.

His dander was up. Or his pecker. What was wrong with him?

Having left the port, Ferdi made his way directly to the bar, its location indicated by one of the many sets of plans affixed adjacent to every doorway, and was on the point of ordering his usual beer from the *TSS Canterbury*'s barman – a man giant in stature but sporting the tiniest of pencil moustaches, so that it seemed almost to exist like an optical illusion both there and *not there* – when he changed his mind and instead asked for a glass of *the best red* and a packet of Gitanes to go with it.

Catching himself in the mirror behind the bar – it had been a day already of reflection – he wondered if he could pass for a Frenchman. Thanks to Madam Giroux at school, his French was passable. Frenchmen he had heard were supposed to be great lovers. And *liberté, égalité, fraternité* meant more to him than God Save the King. In fact, fuck the King, and all he stood for. Or rather not – Georgie, *bless him*, was not much of a looker.

When the glass of red was gone he ordered another and, slightly tipsy and desiring company, he sat himself down, all of a moment, at the only other table that contained a single person: a pale, nervous-looking man with round spectacles and eyebrows like toppled exclamation marks.

'I'm Ferdi,' he said, reaching out a hand. 'After the explorer, Ferdinand Magellan, you know?'

The man, it turned out, did know – Portuguese by birth, discoverer of the Strait of Magellan, although, like all discoveries, no doubt, it was there before him – and, this riposte being made, perhaps worrying that he had sounded a little tart, the man said he was just plain Raymond, named after his father, also a Raymond, and like him a Protestant minister.

'The only thing I can call my own is this,' he said, and held up a case, which he placed on his knees, and took out a small stringed instrument. 'This ukulele. Would you like a tune?'

'What I require, my man,' said Ferdi, 'is a drink. Another one. What do you say? On me.'

Raymond, so he was told over first one bottle of red, and then another, was on his way to the Congo, via Paris, where he would teach, in his own pious words, 'soulless black folk about God and hard work'.

'In the beginning was God and God was at the beginning,' said Ferdi, and then, to change the subject – religion only gave him wind – he asked Raymond to show him his hands.

He had been planning, drunkenly, on doing a palm reading (something his mother had been keen on – as a child she had always been telling him his fortune – 'You will be rich, have four children, be happy'), but, reaching out for the hand, he had found himself simply holding it – an act quite intimate amidst the masculine bustle of the bar.

'You have rough fingertips,' he said, his words coming out in something of a nervous stammer; and Raymond, reading rightly, perhaps, the situation, echoed this stammer in his answer back – something absurd about playing the ukulele quite vigorously.

'That indicates to me submerged passions,' said Ferdi, and to his surprise, their hands still entwined over the tabletop, neither having the gumption to let go, Raymond had blushed and said a man's passions were his own business.

'We shall see about that,' said Ferdi. Confidence returned, he pulled Raymond towards him, sending several glasses flying, and whispered intimately in his ear, 'What with you off to the Congo and all that God stuff it might be your last toss of the dice.'

Raymond had a single cabin on the lowest deck. It contained a creased cassock discarded on the back of a folding chair, a metal bed affixed to the wall, a grimy porthole that looked out over a churning sea. The only nod to jollity was a gaudy red rug, half rucked, sneaking out across the dull floor from under the bed.

'Would you like a slice of bread or something?' Raymond asked, starting to fumble at a paper bag that, no doubt, contained provisions – packed by his mother, probably, tearful that her only son was leaving but proud that he was to do God's work.

On their journey down to the cabin Ferdi had felt Raymond press against him more often than could just be blamed on the swell of the sea or the drink, and he found this whole preamble irksome; so, without further ado – 'To blazes with your slice of bread!' – he slipped out of his clothes and, quite in the buff, searched around the room until he found something they might use for lubricant, landing on a bottle of Chesebrough Manufacturing Company's Vaseline Hair Oil: *a liquid preparation for preserving and restoring the strength and beauty of the hair.*

Dipping a finger in, he spread a generous dollop between his bum cheeks – a not unpleasant tingling sensation – before positioning himself doglike on the narrow iron bed.

He didn't watch, or care to watch, Raymond getting undressed, imagining his undercarriage small, his body like a pear boiled and stuck with four forks, two for arms and two for legs, so he was surprised with the assuredness and muscularity with which he was entered, and the depth then rhythm achieved. All that praying, he supposed, translated itself into a certain fervour of endeavour, and as the stovepipe came out for a final time, the prelate having lowed in the manner of a cow as he came, the release was rather like giving birth; the emptiness he immediately felt postpartum.

Turning around, Ferdi was surprised to find the prelate already dressed – if ever he had undressed – for the unbuttoned fly, drawers half-mast around pale thighs, shoes still on feet, indicated perhaps he had not.

That was an insult. As was the look of horror upon the priest's face as he found himself face to face again with his lover.

'Oh God, what have I done?'

Ferdi hated a sniveller. He'd had a few of those – married men who rushed back to their wives before their semen had even had chance to dry on him, or, if in him, finish its pointless swim in search of a waiting egg.

'My man,' he said sharply, 'what you have done is you have fucked my arse most royally. You don't need your blasted God to tell you that. It is those young men and women of Africa I am worried about – I don't go in for all that colonial nonsense. Those darker-skinned people are just as good as us, and more numerous. Let them inherit the world. Or better still, let us join together and smash down the Old World together.'

Speech made, Ferdi had bowed, gathered up his discarded clothing and made his way, still in the nude, to his own room, where, before tossing himself on to his bed, he threw up quite violently in the water closet, his vomit red like the blood of Christ, but, in fact, only red wine.

L'Amour Doux

Ferdi's mother was dead.

Her body had been found on the family tennis court, brimming with enough opium to fell an elephant – if one had been stupid or sad enough to imbibe the noxious liquid. Ever since her death Ferdi had been trying to envisage a different life for her – one away from his father.

The week before his trip he had come across an article in the *Saltburn Flier*. The local postman, Fletch, had been stealing postal orders in order to pay for his monthly trips to a place called the Moulin Rouge. 'Behind these wholesome-looking windmill sails,' it read, 'lies a cave of debauchery, scantily clad women performing a dance so outrageous it has been banned in thirteen European countries!'

His mother had been a keen dancer herself – ballroom for show and respectability, but Ferdi had disturbed her on more than one occasion twisting alone to her jazz collection, eyes closed, a look of concentration on her face and, behind that concentration, joy, happiness, freedom.

Descending from the Flèche d'Or, the impossibly glamorous French train that had brought him to his final destination, the cavernous Gare du Nord, Ferdi approached one of the attendants and, having asked for directions, made his way towards le Pigalle, home of that famous red mill, sure that that is what his mother would've wanted.

There was a church on a hill, made, so it seemed, of inverted alabaster beehives, streets cobbled enough to break even the sturdiest of ankles and bar after bar packed to the brim with moustachioed raffish men, cigarette butts dangling from the side of pert mouths as seductive as anuses.

The hotel he finally chose was named L'Amour Doux. There were red curtains in all the windows, a man with no legs outside on a wooden trolley, and a landlady named Giselle whose hair was stacked to resemble that most famous colossal iron building dominating the skyline, drawing your gaze always towards it.

After he had spoken to Giselle in what he believed was his best French – he would like la chambre for une semaine – she had laughed, and told him, in perfect English, that the hotel was the kind of place where *ladies of the street* brought their amours for one hour at a time, not the sort of place for a young English *boy* on vacances. *Boy* – the word bristled; hadn't he had a prelate's cock all the way up his butt only a short while hence? He wanted to say, without causing offence, that he wished to make his arsehole a fuckery of riches, when the landlady's face softened.

'After all, you have come in our quiet season, so why not?'

And reaching behind her she plucked a key off a board and said there was *one* room in the attic that might suit, but he shouldn't say she hadn't warned him. She indicated he should follow her up a narrow staircase, the walls of which were adorned with soft-focus photos of ladies in various states of undress.

It was a whole new world.

Ferdi was woken on that first night by a rhythmic banging and a need to urinate. The bathroom, he recalled from the landlady's introduction, was one floor down. Still half-asleep he opened the door to find a French policeman, identifiable by the dark-blue kepi perched lopsidedly on the back of a tousled head, trousers halfway down his legs, arse as hairy as a bear's, pissing into a heavily stained pan.

At first, as he was manhandled down the flight of stairs, the seat of his Everlasts twisted tightly around the French policeman's meaty paw, Ferdi thought he was being arrested *– you are hereby charged with one count of voyeurism, a second count of inappropriate undergarments –* but then he found himself in one of Madam Giselle's boudoirs, all crushed crêpe and brocaded plump cushions, a lady déshabillé on the divan. After much gesticulating, and a request from Ferdi to the policemen that he slow down *– moins vite s'il vous plaît, je suis anglais –* he realised that he was merely being required to photograph le spectacle, and for this he would be given a quantity of francs.

So, Kodak box camera thrust his way, Ferdi perched himself on the narrow window ledge and, only half-watching the policeman and his whore go at it, snapping only when and where he pleased, he found himself more enamoured with what was going on outside the open window, the carts below, the shouts in a foreign language where every word sounded like love, the gentle breeze on his back, and in the distance, rising up over the rooftops, the splendid sails of a windmill, an indicator of a life more bizarre and exotic.

He took his breakfast at a café with small bronze replica cannons on the tables and pictures of Napoleon on the walls.

From Saltburn-by-the-Sea Public Library he had borrowed a copy of *The Pocket Guide to Paris* (published by the DAILY MAIL TRAVEL & INFORMATION BUREAU 5, Rue Scribe, Paris).

There was a map that folded out from the inside cover; moving his coffee cup, he spread it wide across his table and traced a finger along the narrow representation of streets and highways – République, le Marais, Place de la Bastille, Nation, all the way to the Bois de Vincennes.

This was where the Exposition Coloniale Internationale was taking place – his reason for being here in the first place – or at least his father's reason.

The article had appeared in the morning edition of the *Alnwick Mercury*, passed to Francis Sheldon Sr. by his servant Wilson, along with his habitual boiled egg – four minutes, no more, no less, and six rigid soldiers. It was there in bold letters on the third page. Nine million people were expected to come from all over the world to bask in the magnificence of France's colonies. Native arts, crafts and sundry goods would be displayed in glorious reproductions of huts, temples, cabins, chalets, shacks, pagodas, tabernacles, shrines. And, although Saltburn-by-the-Sea was not a colony of France *per se*, Paris *was* the spiritual home of fashion, and so the exposition would be the perfect place to drum up trade for Sheldon, Sheldon and Sheldon and their *top-of-the-line* gloves.

'I am sending you as an emissary, my boy,' his father had said. 'Don't let me down. Don't let our family down.'

The closer Ferdi got to the Bois de Vincennes the more people there were, ladies with umbrellas, men in top hats, and those less obviously sophisticated, sporting clothes of every hue and garb, babbling in more tongues than Ferdi could ever hope to recognise.

It was overwhelming.

Finally, being so jostled by the throng that he could hardly move forward without his cumbersome case colliding with someone, Ferdi stopped to take stock, and it was then through the trees, like whales hiding in the blue of the water, he spied vast pagodas, colonnades, African huts pumped up and amplified, alabaster mansions with decking and pitch-perfect lawns transferred to a Parisian field.

Putting a hand up to his forehead in a salute, serving to shield his eyes from the beating sun, rising above it all a huge wheel came into focus, tiny waving figures just visible in its cars, a feat of enormous engineering as miraculous as Eiffel's tower itself.

Suddenly, and for once, Ferdi was overawed. What did he have to offer? One single suitcase containing his product – or his bastard father's product.

Sod it.

He would set up where he was, under this tree that a mountain of a Great Dane and its barrel of an owner were both pissing up.

The suitcase, designed and developed in his father's own infernal factory, had legs that retracted outwards, so that once they were extended the case itself formed a kind of small rigid stall. Open the lid and, hey presto, there stitched on the inside were the words Sheldon, Sheldon and Sheldon.

'Roll up, roll up,' he shouted half-heartedly, mimicking the tradesmen he had seen on Saltburn's pier end, grimy-eyed men selling rollmops, poorly carved shark-tooth earrings, cloth hats embroidered with *I Love Saltburn*.

Although Ferdi had no desire to secure glove contracts for his father, in the short term, the advances on any glove contracts he might secure would give him the money he needed to stay in Paris – until he came up with his own moneymaking plan; for he had decided Paris would be his future, and short of selling his arse he wasn't sure how he was going to bring that about.

So he called out. 'Gloves! Gloves! Gloves for sale!'

There was most interest in the two gloves he had soiled. First a tall black man with a trolley full of elaborate rugs asked if it was a tribal pattern. Ferdi said that it was and, playing the fool, he acted out a small skit in which he and his tribe made gloves under a full moon and used them to strangle the first born of every family in the kingdom. And then he had blushed bright red at his own racial stereotyping, cursing himself that he was no better than that sodding prelate.

Then a white lady with a disinterested pale entourage of white men in colourful jodhpurs lifted up one after the other.

'Pas mal,' she said, but could the design could be changed? And could there be quatre? They would be perfect for le cheval.'

'A horse?'

'Mais oui!'

What strange new world was he in?

After eating his lunch – a baguette and a hunk of cheese provided by Giselle – Ferdi found his interest in selling his wares had waned, even past the poor show he had put up that morning. What was he going to do?

It was then a notion came over him – so crazy and so wanton that he threw his head back and laughed. It would be a statement of freedom, at least.

And so, shutting up the glove case, leaving it right there on the grass for any lucky finder, he strode purposefully through the massive entrance gates into the park proper. There was a certain exhilaration in movement, a concomitant freedom.

Picking up speed, lifting his knees higher and higher, pumping out his elbows, he ran past a bountiful zoological garden, startling the real-life gazelles grazing there, circled swiftly around a grand lake containing two bijou islands to which sweating paying guests were rowing in a procession of small bobbing boats, zoomed through an Italian basilica dedicated to the former Roman Emperor Septimus Severus, fated founder of the last dynasty of the Roman Empire.

This was it!

Even the groaning men and women in the working replica of a Belgian hospital lying prostrate on iron gurneys while ersatz doctors applied greasy sucking leeches to their buttocks and other intimate regions didn't cause him to pause. He was on a roll. Nothing could hold his attention.

Not the stall selling rubber goods, sheets, shoes, gaskets, tubes, thick submarine battery cases resembling grotesque sinister eyeless diving helmets, nor the crenellated kiosk vending many kinds of pungent coffee bean, graham crackers, tea biscuits, tiny tins of rabbit meat, large rotting pineapples. Not even the splendid intricate diorama of hooded muffled Eskimo and their panting packs of pulling dogs stopped him in his tracks. No, he went past all of these wonders until he came to the huge slowly rotating wheel the top of which he had spied earlier.

La Grande Roue de Paris
Un Merveilleux Voyage!

Up close it was even more spectacular – a mass of interlocking iron tubing, cars big enough for a family of four to move into, beds, baggage, the lot.

Ignoring the cries of the heavily bearded operator, done up like a prancing and preening Napoleonic soldier, Ferdi leapt over the protective barriers and, hand over hand, he climbed the iron structure, up and up, passing one by one the swinging cars, the shocked faces within them, until he was perched right at the top, wind whipping his hair.

'Bonjour Paris!' he screamed, and then, because he wasn't sure of the French for it, it not being part of one of Madam Giroux's lessons, 'Kiss my skinny white arse! I am me. I am not my father's son. I am here and here I am staying! Fuck gloves!'

So this was his statement of freedom.

Although now he was up here he wasn't exactly sure what next. The problem was taken out of his hands almost immediately by the appearance of a gendarme ascending the structure, cursing, probably, although Ferdi couldn't catch any words, his kepi growing steadily larger and larger.

Ferdi could easily imagine his father's face when the news came back – his son arrested and in a French prison.

The former gave him joy; the latter made him think perhaps he had been a bit hasty – that perhaps he should have thought about his statement for freedom a little more carefully. But when he came face to face with the policeman, and when the policeman had removed his cap, revealing the hairy-arsed flic from the night before – the very same one who had manhandled his Everlasts and put on the show with Madam Giselle's whore – they both smiled in recognition.

'Prends plus de photos ce soir,' said the policeman. 'Et je ne t'arrête pas. Oui?'

That was a deal. If Ferdi became the policeman's official *sex* photographer he wouldn't be banged up.

Why not? 'Oui,' said Ferdi and they shook hands.

Back on the ground Ferdi contemplated his new life. Around him were faces of all ages and colour, children bearing clouds of candy floss or blown-up bright bobbing balloons, grandmothers and sailors and gaudy women in bright dresses. From a nearby tent came the scratchy sounds of an audiophone, feet tentatively tapping a makeshift dance floor in a toneless accompaniment, a percussion of glasses clinking. It would do splendidly.

Tucking his shirt into his pants – it had come loose amidst all the fuss – Ferdi set off back through the park with no real plan of action. It felt akin to that prelate's cock coming out of his arse – a pain, an emptiness, a void. What *exactly* would he do next?

And that was when fate presented him with a sign. Literally.

Aquarium tropicale de la Porte Dorée

Returning from a trip to London several years earlier – sent there by their father to sell a new exquisite range of sealskin gloves to the up-and-coming politician Oswald Mosley and his growing pack of devoted followers – his older brother Wallace had told him of just such a building in Regent's Park.

'A dolphin,' he had said. 'They had a fucking dolphin in a tank of water, kiss my arse.'

The first thing that struck Ferdi was the smell. It took him back to his morning walks along the beach; the wind, the air, the salty tang of the flotsam and jetsam.

Breathing deeply, he walked with awe amongst the exhibits. In room after room there were many dozens of glass cases, some filled and vibrant with fast-moving colours, while others were pond-like and murky, hiding the mournful eyes of bottom-dwellers.

Stopping at one of the tanks, Ferdi pressed his hands and face up against it. A school of blue gourami swarmed towards him, beating their little bodies against their side of the glass. Invigorated, he greeted next the clownfish, then the butterfly fish, the angelfish, groupers and monos. When he entered the room containing the squids, cuttlefish and octopuses he let out a squeal of joy.

One time, six years old, he had found a baby octopus while scouring the beach and placed it on his head as a kind of hat, its tentacles hanging down across his face. Later the same day he had screamed the house down when his mother said he *could not* go to the church like that; and he only reluctantly removed it when she promised that it would be waiting for him on his return home.

That his father had had it disposed of in his absence was yet another reason he hated the old shit.

Ferdi was still in the aquarium when its doors finally closed for the night. It took an elderly attendant, the stub of a cigarette hanging languidly from the corner of his mouth, brandishing a stiffly bristled broom, to shoo him out of a side entrance.

But he was there the next morning at opening time.

And the morning after that. He felt at home.

And so it was that on his seventh morning in Paris, when he should have been repacking his case and making his way back to the Gare du Nord, glove contracts having been secured, that he went instead to the bureau de poste of the quartier and sent off a curt telegram.

Not coming home. STOP Stopping in Paris. STOP I will be swimming with the fishes. STOP

Aquarium

It had been on his fourth day at the Aquarium tropicale de la Porte Dorée that Ferdi had been approached by the young man who was to change his life.

Of course he had seen the man several times before. How could he not have noticed the outlandish clothes, the green jumpsuit with tasselled gold epaulets, the moleskin ankle-length loafers matching those eyes, as dark and staring as a Black Moor goldfish?

But it was more than that. He had not only noticed but *admired*, arranged himself so he could collect glances as the man negotiated the glass cases, stored those glances to include them in the slideshow fantasies of his morning masturbation. The way, for example, the thin material of the man's jumpsuit clung to his long muscular thighs. How might he negotiate the toilet? Did the whole thing come off in one piece, or was there a discreet zip?

He was momentarily speechless. Could the man sense what he was thinking as he marched up to him and said 'I've seen you looking at the fish'?

The man's lips pulled back in a smile. 'Every day. Zut alors!' He spoke with a strong French accent, and held a thick book with a fish's skeleton on its spine under his arm. He held his hand out suddenly and the book went tumbling to the floor. 'They call me Nemo.'

Up close now, from his skin emanated the stink of brackish water, like that which might come from a fish fattened up and kept in the bath.

'Captain Nemo to my friends. Would you like a drink with me some time?'

'I like your earring,' said Ferdi, and he lifted a single outstretched finger to push at the golden miniature sub dangling from his new friend's left ear. 'Do you know anywhere good? For the drink, I mean.' He found himself hot under the collar, blushing. 'Now?'

They went, Nemo leading the way, to a bar on the Rue Edmund Nocard. Its name – Le Petit Homme, 'small man' – Nemo explained, had come about because the owner had intended to employ only midgets, but then had struggled both with the applications (not enough) and the practicalities (how could these small men reach the optics or even the high tables that were common in establishments of this type), and so the idea had been ditched and now the bar only employed regular-sized people.

'He'd have been better off calling it something more generic,' said Nemo. 'Like The Ten-Toed Man, or The Man Who Breaks Wind.' He laughed in a way that Ferdi grew to love.

The bar had a live singer, but she sang so quietly and at such a distance from the tables that it was necessary to stand right next to her to hear. Customers on their way to and from the single toilet would pause for a moment, struck by the voice, and then would come away, tears in their eyes, shaking their heads, saying it was the most beautiful thing they had ever heard.

The two young men talked, words tumbling out of them, and Nemo revealed, over one pastis and then another, that he was studying oceanography at the Sorbonne, that quite unusually he had received a full grant, that his parents could never have afforded to send him there as they both worked as lowly road sweepers in Nancy. Nemo had smiled then, leant across the table, said in a whisper, although why it should be a secret was not clear, that both his parents were huge fans of Jules Verne, which went some way to explain his name, Nemo – only some way because he had added 'Captain' himself since coming to Paris.

It was also then that he had started dressing so outlandishly. 'In this city you have to stand out to get noticed – and that is what I want: I want everyone to know my name.'

Ferdi giggled. 'But everyone already does know your name. Everyone knows Captain Nemo!'

If his new friend heard this quip he didn't show it. For now he was frantically leafing through the book he had been carrying under his arm earlier. He was clearly searching for something, because with a relieved look on his face he retrieved from within the tome a thick square of yellowed paper, which he proceeded to unfold.

'You see,' he said, tapping the paper enthusiastically. 'Still over eighty-five per cent unknown. I'm going to be a deep-sea explorer.'

On the paper was drawn a map of all the oceans of the world, one of them circled again and again in pen. It was here Nemo was tapping.

'My first planned exploration! You are looking at the first discoverer of the mighty kraken!'

After drinks Nemo invited Ferdi back to his apartment, which transpired to be an old storage room above the Gare du Nord, sublet from a shady Moroccan businessman. There was a family of bats that lived in the high ceiling, many boxes of knock-off designer dresses – Christian Dior, Cristóbal Balenciaga, Coco Chanel, Pierre Balmain – overspill stock from the chain of backstreet boutiques owned by the shady businessman, and, scattered across the bare floorboards, dozens of copies of *20,000 Leagues Under the Sea*.

'These are all mine,' declared Nemo, holding up one of the copies between a thumb and forefinger. 'Special delivery. Parent express.'

On the first of every month a new copy would arrive, its pages interspersed with francs his parents had raised from selling the items they had found on the road.

'Look,' he said, passing Ferdi a note filled with tight neat handwriting. 'They also send me this. It's good, apparently, for us paupers to know where money comes from. Behold! An itemised list of every single sale.'

Taking in Ferdi's puzzled face, Nemo snatched the list back and translated it into English in a declamatory voice:

1. Brooch with broken pin on the corner of Rue Gabriel Mouilleron and Rue Saint-Léon. 5 francs.
2. Amber hair comb in the shape of fiddler crab. Parc Sainte-Marie. 3 francs.
3. Art-deco terracotta bookend with Chinese man. Rue Sainte Barbe. Not one of a pair. 35 francs.
4. Papier-mâché bust of Napoleon (hat broken off). Rue de Hollande. 125 francs.
5. Red pillbox with bird motif (bird missing). Rue du 8ème Régiment d'Artillerie. 54 francs.
6. Bronze gazelle mirror (broken). Av. des Jonquilles. 250 francs.

The majority of this money was going to pay off a debt Nemo owed. Training to be a deep-sea diver, apparently, was not a cheap endeavour, and with a bow and a single push of his foot Nemo sent a screen on wheels shooting off across the room to reveal an enormous tin bath with an aqualung propped up against its side.

These, Nemo explained, he had obtained on exorbitant credit from a shady one-legged man in the Bois de Boulogne.

'You can watch me train if you want,' he said. And before Ferdi could reply Nemo had stripped down to a pair of streamlined briefs, climbed up a short step ladder and dived with a splash into the bath.

'I do one hour with the aqualung,' he said, face reappearing over the side, 'and one hour without. I need to be prepared.'

'Prepared for what?' Ferdi asked.

Nemo put his head back out and laughed. 'Haven't you read your Verne? In case the aqualung is ripped off one day by the kraken. They don't want to be captured, you know?'

Later that day Ferdi returned to the L'Amour Doux and collected his belongings. He had been meaning to look for new lodgings anyway, so how could he have ignored Nemo's throwaway comment about the relative size of his lodgings, how he had room for two in the storage room – possibly even three or four? And besides, already he was more than a little smitten.

Ferdi stopped at the landlady's door to settle his bill.

'You are returning to England, my handsome boy?' she said, leaning towards him so that her hair became the Leaning Tower rather than La Tour Eiffel.

'Not just yet,' he replied. 'I rather think I am going to make Paris my home.'

She lifted a hand and chucked him under the chin. 'So you have fallen in love,' she said.

He was still blushing as he came out of the hotel. Was he so transparent? But this was Paris. He had heard of such things happening.

It was as he was arranging his belongings in the room above the station that Ferdi saw the shoe box stuffed full of letters. Did he already have a rival for Nemo's love?

He was picking up one of these letters – he would just have a little look – when Nemo came clattering in. Guiltily Ferdi pushed the letter back – but not quick enough, it seemed, for Nemo had spied him, and on doing so he let out a laugh.

'Ah, you have discovered my secret. Come, choose a letter, any letter, and I shall read it out to you.'

There was some backward and forward then, a stammered apology – *you really don't need to* – but a few moments later Nemo was sitting cross-legged, a letter open before him.

Chère Mademoiselle Solitaire,
I am in such emotional pain that I can't sleep at night and, exhausted each day, I fail spectacularly in my job. I am a hairdresser by trade.

Last week I destroyed a poor woman's hair with a surfeit of chemicals, and then today I severed a poor sailor's earlobe.

My problem is this. My husband tells me that he loves me, but he will not touch me as a man should touch a woman. I have tried everything: foods that are said to be aphrodisiac; scandalous clothes bought in the backstreets of La Marais. I have even gone so far as to whisper to him that I would do anything. Anything! But he merely pushes me away, falls into a slumber, snores, having declared he is a working man, tired from his daily chores, unable to contemplate such a thing. What can I do?

'But what is it?' Ferdi asked.

'It is a job,' said Nemo, and he explained that, in order to pay for his food and the rent on this space above the Gare du Nord, he worked for *Le Courrier de l'intérieur*, one of France's top newspapers.

'Ah,' said Ferdi, as Nemo translated another of the carefully handwritten letters. 'Agony Aunt. We have the same thing in the

Saltburn Messenger. I know how they work. And I am good with words. Perhaps I can help? I need to do something to earn my keep.'

And as easily as that a new life began: a home, a job, of sorts, a partner in crime.

While Nemo studied at the Sorbonne Ferdi explored Paris, his daily perambulations somehow always taking him back to aquarium. Gradually his French improved, and week by week, when Nemo returned from the offices of the newspaper with a new batch of letters, Ferdi was able to deal with them more and more often by himself, merely passing them to Nemo for corrections.

'As long as I speak to people only about their misfortunes I shall be fine,' he said, only half-joking.

'This is Paris,' replied Nemo. 'People speak of nothing else. You *will* be fine.'

The day eventually came when the Exposition Coloniale Internationale closed its doors for the last time, and all the pagodas, temples, ersatz huts and other sundry buildings were dismantled, packed up and transported back to whence they came, convoys of laden vans blocking the Parisian streets for days on end, a smog of exhaust fumes permeating the air.

It being a Saturday, Ferdi and Nemo found themselves standing together outside the entrance to the aquarium. It was a great relief to Ferdi that the Aquarium tropicale de la Porte Dorée remained, the building now appearing lonesome in the once heaving and bustling park.

'But with plenty of space to expand,' commented Nemo, throwing his arms out to indicate the large grassy area where children were playing with a ball and a tall angry-looking man was restraining a black dog on a stout lead.

'Eh?' said Ferdi, puzzled.

'When I return with my kraken,' said Nemo, placing his hands now on his hips, 'where else do you think I want to show it? Here!'

That week Ferdi had been down to the Seine with Nemo five pre-dawn mornings in a row, Ferdi helping to lug the equipment, an aqualung and various rubber suit parts, and then standing on the bank with the timer while Nemo submerged himself in the murky water.

'Come back up,' he would murmur. 'Come back up.'

And it was always a relief when he spied the tarnished gold of his lover's helmet coming back out of the water like a ginormous gilt crustacean, the visor of the helmet being pushed up.

'How long was I under this time? Tell me.'

If Nemo was obsessed Ferdi was yet to truly acknowledge it, for we do not see in our lovers what we would perhaps recognise in a stranger. Choppy waters turning to churning ones turning to ginormous waves in which it would be all too easy to drown.

Ferdi's French now being sufficiently good that the writing of the Agony Aunt letters took only a fraction of the time it had previously taken, he was looking around for something more rewarding to do, and he arrived at the aquarium one day to find Augustine, the head attendant, putting up a sign:

OPPORTUNITÉ PROFESSIONNELLE
Doit être bon avec le poisson

Ferdi, who was quite comfortable with all the staff by now, calling them by their first names and sharing coffees with them in nearby cafés, ripped the sign down immediately with an exaggerated gesture of disgust and stormed directly to Fabienne, the manager's, office.

'What kind of connerie is this?' he demanded, slapping down the ripped notice in front of her. Why place this putain advertisement when the answer to their staffing shortfall was staring them right in the face? Wasn't he the man for the job? Who knew the place better than him? Didn't the fish rush to the glass as soon as he arrived? Sometimes a passion for poisson can go a long way.

Fabienne, as pretty as a cuttlefish, with high dark eyes and long protruding lips, laughed gaily. 'You an English *gentleman*,' she said. 'I never would have…' She tapped the desk thoughtfully. 'The money is very small. You must be good with a broom.'

'I'm fucking amazing with a broom,' said Ferdi, laughing, and mimed sweeping around the office, throwing his arms and legs into it with gusto.

He started the next day.

Between 9 a.m. and 5 p.m. he collected admissions, handed out ticket stubs, sold programmes that he had designed and made himself, pointed customers in the direction of the WCs, snack bar, gift shop, and then, after hours – and this was the greatest part of the job – he was responsible for the upkeep of the molluscs, the squid, the cuttlefish and, best of all, his beloved octopuses.

In the quiet of the after-hours he would sing to them, or recite long heroic poems in which he changed the names and made the octopuses the heroes.

Odysseus as an octopus. Perseus as an octopus. Achilles as an octopus. Aeneas as an octopus. Best of all, Icarus as an octopus – and when he flew too near the sun and his wax wings melted, he tumbled into the water and formed a new watery kingdom, and this is how octopuses came to live in the sea.

In this way, and others – for there were spats, makings-up, wild times and duller ones – four whole years or more passed by.

In general Ferdi was happy. There was no ache to have a prelate's thick cock up his arse or a wrestler's sweaty balls in his mouth. He had nothing to prove any more. He had a job he loved, a man he loved, and he was no longer his father's son.

But trouble, as they say, is always on the horizon.

Trouble

After Nemo finished his degree he attempted without success to gain himself a place on a deep-sea expedition. He would talk of this and nothing else and there was one particular *fact* which ailed him.

'Because Paris has no coastline, and therefore no ocean-going boats,' he mused, over and over, while they ate their dinner, whispering the words into Ferdi's ear while he was *trying* to sleep, even shouting them down the corridor while Ferdi sat on the toilet, 'we must cast our nets further. Ferdi, I *must* put myself in the way of large vessels.'

And so it became their habit, four times a year, exactly three months apart, to take the train down to Marseille and hang out around the port, mingling with the gangsters, sailors and scoundrels who congregated there, in search of a likely boat.

'A squat, snub-nosed doughty craft with a hardy wind-worn captain and an eccentric backer – someone who had made his money in tins. Or pineapples.'

'Or pineapples in tins,' said Ferdi, joking, and Nemo, who had taken up smoking and seemed to have a preternatural control over the smoke, making any shape he desired, blew a kind of exclamation mark that hovered over Ferdi's head to show his disapprobation.

They were in L'ancre d'or, a favourite café of theirs in one of the side streets radiating from the port. The café had dusty crab pots fixed to its walls and a machine by the door that sold cigars, stamps and soda in paper cups.

'Or Brazilian rubber,' said Nemo seriously. 'I heard there's pots of money in that.' He paused to scratch his arm, then his leg. Their hotel seemed to let bedbugs stay for free. 'Did I ever tell you what a kraken actually looks like?'

'You did,' said Ferdi, but Nemo was already up and out of the door.

Cupping his hands over his mouth, he shouted back towards where his lover still sat in the café from where he now stood, some way down the street, 'ONE OF ITS TENTACLES WOULD REACH AS FAR AS THIS. WHERE I AM STANDING RIGHT NOW. FURTHER, PROBABLY.'

That same season Nemo made up some leaflets:

> Disponible à la location.
> Spécialiste de la marine.

There was a grainy photo of himself, details of his degree from the Sorbonne, some Latin words in a fancy script he assured Ferdi would *mean something to the right person*, and the phone number of the fleapit hotel they were staying in.

Each morning they would hand out these leaflets until they had none left, and then they retreated to their hotel room waiting for contact, for the concierge to come clomping reluctantly up the stairs, to rap on their door and tell them there was a strange man, or woman, enquiring for them at reception – one who smelt of briny water and who had harpoon nicks all across their hands.

'One day I will be famous the world over,' Nemo said.

It was not yet dawn, but already Nemo was poking Ferdi roughly in the side. 'Are you awake?'

'I am now,' said Ferdi, rubbing at his eyes. 'What hellish time is this?'

Going over to the shuttered window, Nemo stood before it naked. He punched his right hand against his chest, over the place where his heart would be.

'Right before you here you see the man who will one day be known the world over for capturing the kraken. A beast more mighty than King Kong himself – that so-called king of the jungle and ravager of New York.'

Ferdi had lost count of the times Nemo had dragged him to see *King Kong* at their local cinema, L'Atalante. In the end they came to know the box office girl, Bébé, and usherette, Claudine, by name.

'Carl Denham is me! Don't you see? Except, unlike that poor fool I won't let my monster escape. We will be the talk of the town. Captain Nemo and his kraken – the world of fantastic fiction come alive!'

It happened that, one season in Marseille, some years into their sojourns there, Nemo aligned himself with a brilliant young explorer he had met in a seedy bar down at the port, and all Ferdi heard for days on end was Jacques Cousteau this and Jacques Cousteau that.

'He's a man after my own skin,' said Nemo. There were in the same fleapit hotel again, the same room, Gaston, the concierge presenting it to them with a toothless smile as if there was joy to be found in the threadbare mat, the bed that bred more bugs each passing year, the pisspot hanging on the back of the door. 'At last, someone who understands me.'

And this hurt Ferdi, because did he not understand Nemo? For years now he had been accompanying him down to the Seine each morning before his shift at the aquarium. He had stood there in all weathers, stopwatch clutched in his hand, timing each of the underwater practice sessions.

As he sat and watched Nemo and this Cousteau smoking pipes together, discussing crustaceans, ocean currents, tides, the shortest cuts to undiscovered regions, he could see only one thing: that Cousteau, like all brilliant men, was both selfish and driven. He was only out for himself.

So when, one day, Cousteau was suddenly gone – to Shanghai and Japan, apparently, funded by a Greek millionaire who had made his money in Scandinavian pine – Ferdi was not surprised. It was Cousteau this year, but it had been someone else the year before that, and the year before that. There was always someone ready to take advantage – that was the way of the world.

'Your time will come,' he said to Nemo as this man he loved more than any other wept over the front-page photo of Cousteau standing proudly on the deck of the doughty ship they had always imagined for themselves, wearing his own patented underwater goggles that would soon make him famous around the world.

And then their trips to Marseille were curtailed by the coming of war and the invasion of Paris by the Germans in 1940. Life, for the time being, was concerned only with the getting along of it.

Some nights, in the early days, they would watch the German soldiers on the station concourse through a hole in their floorboards. Big strong boys, the most of them, who looked lost and sad.

'They are just like us,' said Ferdi. 'The only difference is an arbitrary border.'

The aquarium remained open, but the customers, slowly, like the turning off of a tap, dried up. When life became about finding food – sometimes he and Nemo had to walk many miles just to obtain a stale half-baguette or stub of cheese – looking at fish was a luxury.

The agony letters sent to *Le Courrier de l'intérieur* were now mostly too angry or too sad to print – people wrote of the smells coming from their Jewish neighbours, who were hoarding bags of rice, sides of beef, while true Parisians starved; and there were letters from Jews, speaking of relatives who had disappeared suddenly from their apartment overnight, and now there was a new *French* family living there who claimed to know nothing – the letter writer had been to the authorities but had been met with a wall of silence. Where could they go next? What could they do? Can you help?

And then one week there was a large number of letters from the Jewish letter writers repeating the same troubling message: they had been told to pack a single case. Come to the Gare du Nord. Do not worry. It is a simple act of relocation.

'We have to do something,' said Nemo.

His obsession with the kraken, for the time being, had been replaced by an obsession with the Nazis – not the poor boys they saw loitering around Paris, but the high command sequestered in their fancy buildings in Berlin. They would be the beast he would destroy – or do something to maim, at least.

On the day identified in the letters, the one when the *relocation* was to take place, Ferdi went out for croissants and coffee first thing in the morning. Neither he nor Nemo had slept that night, or the night before, a sense of despair overcoming them both.

When he got back he found Nemo wearing a French station porter's uniform. There was another one, apparently, for him.

'Put it on,' said Nemo. 'We find ourselves with a unique opportunity. History and our position in it have dovetailed right in our laps.'

The plan was a simple one.

'With such a big crowd, who would notice if there was a slightly smaller crowd?'

So for the next eight hours, sometimes singly, sometimes together, they went down the stairs, out of their unobtrusive door and on to the platform, and selected their next candidate.

Why wouldn't they accompany a station porter? What did they now have to lose, all their portable possessions packed in a single case?

By the end of the day, Ferdi doing the head count, they found they had spirited one hundred and seventy-nine men, women and children away from the platforms and up into their room. One hundred and sixty-nine of them were wearing the yellow star, ten a pink triangle.

'This means that I am a homosexual,' said an elderly man, flicking off his triangle. He was sitting on a case of ersatz Christian Dior bodices, a small dog resting its snout on his shoes. 'What a nonsense. Who should care who anybody loves? Pah!' Then his face had changed, transformed into a smile. 'But thank you. I rather think you have saved me. Us.'

When the war ended Ferdi and Nemo took a trip to Marseille once more, Nemo's obsession having become even more pronounced, his break from it only increasing rather than diminishing its power. Ferdi had been promoted to assistant manager of the aquarium, and this time they could afford a hotel with a balcony overlooking the port.

It was in the bar, done up to resemble the state room of an ocean liner, that they made the acquaintance of Omar and Omar, Egyptian scientists who dressed like the Thompson Twins from the *Tintin* books that Ferdi and Nemo loved.

'It is auspicious, this chance rendezvous,' said the first Omar.

'What did our mother say of the fates?' said the second.

The Omars had a penthouse suite, pictures of French Emperors on the walls, an elephant's foot they used as an umbrella stand, row upon row of china tea sets.

It was in this suite that a map was unrolled and an expedition planned. They would go to the Gulf of Oman, the Bay of Biscay, the Red Sea and beyond!

Nemo, sitting on their balcony later that evening, could hardly contain himself, but Ferdi had a feeling in his water – it was Jacques Cousteau all over again. These men were all the same. They fed on Nemo's expertise, pumped him for information, and then used it for their own ends.

So Ferdi was not surprised when, the night before they were due to embark, there was a knock at the hotel door and two policemen compelled them to accompany them to the station.

Over the course of the following week it came out that Omar and Omar were a pair of fraudsters, the expedition a front for drug running.

'Why me?' cried Nemo, beating his chest in that manner he had. 'Why can't something wonderful happen to me?'

The following month Ferdi used all his savings to take Nemo to Coney Island in the United States of America.

Week by week Nemo had become more and more depressed, staying in bed all day, not even going to the Seine in the morning with his aqualung.

Having got Nemo to Le Havre under a pretext, Ferdi thought his lover's eyes would light up at the sight of the magnificent art-deco liner, but Nemo had only stalked off to their designated cabin, asked the steward if he would put on room service and then got royally drunk.

On the second morning on the ship Ferdi said to Nemo, 'I want you to be my husband – that's what all this is about.'

Although they could not officially marry, Ferdi had arranged for one of the sailors – the brother of Fabienne from the aquarium – to perform the ceremony. He had bought them second-hand white suits and cheap, slender rings.

Nemo consented to go ahead with the ceremony – *You have arranged it, so why not?* – but when the sailor, Henri, said, 'I now pronounce you husband and husband,' and Ferdi slipped the ring on to Nemo's correct finger, Ferdi noticed Nemo's eyes weren't on him but were gazing out to sea, ranging across the waves, hoping, no doubt, for a glimpse of a kraken. Even spotting one of its tentacles would have made him happy – but not Henri's words. That's what hurt Ferdi's feelings the most.

After this inauspicious ceremony it was a given that the honeymoon would be a maudlin affair. Nemo was melancholy amidst the glamour of the boardwalks of Coney Island, between the strings of gaudy lights and muscular boys and pretty girls. They ended up in an argument.

'If only that Omar and Omar had been genuine. They could've been the making of me.'

Behind Nemo an oiled bodybuilder flexed his muscles on the beach, and a group of young studs gave a round of applause.

'At some point this has got to stop,' said Ferdi angrily. 'An obsession is OK as far as it goes, but even the sea has a horizon.'

'I saved nearly two hundred Jews,' said Nemo. 'You think God owed me one.'

'Their god belongs to the Old Testament,' said Ferdi. 'King Herod was eaten from the inside out by worms, Nadab and Abihu burnt alive. And to say you saved *them* in order to gain something for yourself is beneath even you – you who would do anything, it seems, to get what you want.'

On the liner on their return home, a majestic beast with parquet dance floors and a rambunctious live band bursting with jazz standards sung by a throaty singer, Nemo wouldn't come out of their cabin. He even went so far as to pull the curtain across their porthole so he wouldn't have to see the sea. He was done with it all.

It was springtime in Paris when they returned. Ferdi decorated their apartment with daffodils and, in an attempt to amuse Nemo, walked around naked except for the aqualung.

'I'm underwater,' he said. 'I'm a fish, a crustacean, a deadly orca.'

'I should put you in one of your blasted tanks, then,' said Nemo, and took himself off to bed.

He had been there for two weeks, stinking and unshaven, and Ferdi was at the end of his tether, when the telegram arrived from his brother, Wallace, whom he hadn't seen since the time he left England. The message was both simple and clear:

Father dead. STOP Return to England. STOP Don't stop.
STOP

The Aquarium Again

Their father's funeral might have been a sorry affair if Wallace and Ferdi had gone, but they did not. The two brothers were pleased only to attend to each other, and they drank long into the night at the Jolly Fisherman, swapping histories.

Wallace had been in prison for outraging public decency. Caught masturbating against a ginkgo tree in Saltburn's Botanical Gardens, high at the time, he had no memory of it – a defence which hadn't cut the mustard with the elderly judge, who had put him away for six long weeks. It was his probationer who had got him his job as a night porter on the Scottish sleeper service. He had a tin whistle, wore narrow trousers and kept the key to the linen cupboard around his neck on a chain even when he wasn't on duty, paranoid that he would lose it and someone would use it to steal the sheets.

'With my history they'd blame me, and then I'd be banged up again. I wouldn't want to go back to prison. Full of crooks, it was.'

Drunk, Ferdi admitted his own unhappiness. He had met the man of his dreams, but that man was sinking, his failure to fulfil *his* dream causing him deep mental anguish.

Looking out of the pub's window he could see the fishermen's boats huddled together in the harbour.

'And you know I think these days Nemo'd even settle for a skinny sloop, a lobster pot and one of that blasted Cousteau's self-contained underwater breathing apparatus.'

'I'll drink to that,' said Wallace. 'Sounds like freedom to me!' And they clinked glasses and poured another one.

Outside on the mudflats seals barked, slithered their blubbery bodies against each other, revelled in simply being.

The following day, somewhat the worse for wear, Ferdi and Wallace went out to the old glove factory. It had closed its doors for the final time five years before. Cheaper gloves were made in China now and sold at a discount in Evans' Department Stores. Their father hadn't been able to compete.

'I lost my virginity in that office,' said Wallace, pointing. 'Dad's secretary. I was fourteen and she was thirty-eight, married, had three children. Her husband was the copper who came to the school and told us to watch out for perverts. The things she used to make me do... And all under that blasted portrait of our father. No wonder I turned out a daft sod.'

It was eerie walking around the deserted factory. Ferdi kept expecting the machines to start up, or his father to appear, barking out orders.

It was as they went up and out on to the roof that he had his idea. It came to him because of the sea – it was just there, out past the mudflats, slipping and surging. Why go so far away when there was so much water so close to home?

'What do you think about turning this place into an aquarium? Me and you. I've got the experience. You've...'

Wallace attempted to light up a cigarette, the wind blowing out match after match.

'Just imagine what our father would have thought of his huge rooms filled with fish tanks. He'd have hated it!'

A match finally stayed alight and the cigarette caught.

'The building belongs to both of us now. And what else are you going to do? Do you want to work on that sleeper for the rest of your life?'

Wallace stood still for some time, his face blank. He took a final puff on the cigarette, flicked it so the butt performed an arc, fizzing down to the beach below.

'It wasn't me that made you queer, was it? When we were kids, walking around in the nuddy, always tossing off. I was your big brother, but I was an arse.'

A seal barked somewhere. Distantly another seal, or a dog, perhaps, barked in return.

'I'm pretty sure it wasn't that,' said Ferdi, suppressing a smile. He tapped the side of his head. 'It was in here. It was always in here.'

Wallace nodded, returned the cigarette packet to the back pocket of his trousers.

'Right then. This aquarium, I think it's a grand idea. As long as we can have those nippers that look like zebras. You know the ones I mean, black and white stripes?'

'I know the ones,' said Ferdi, and he smiled.

Setting up an aquarium is not an easy task, even for one with both the experience and money, quite an inheritance, and it was seven years later when they introduced their first residents – seals, as it happened, although strictly speaking seals were not fish but aquatic mammals.

'Pinnipeds. Carnivorous. Fin-footed. Related to bears, red pandas, weasels.'

Nemo stood proudly by the side of the enclosure, which he had designed himself. There was a plunge pool, scrabbly rocks, a sliding area. A home away from home.

'What's that you're saying?' asked Ferdi.

Appearing behind Nemo, he put his arms around him.

The years had been good to Nemo – his waist remained slim, taut, and his mental health had improved. The aquarium wasn't a kraken, but it *was* a project, a huge one, something for Nemo to be passionate about, pour his love into, and if he still thought about capturing the mighty kraken he didn't talk about it.

'Seals,' said Nemo. 'They're related to red pandas. Not a lot of people know that.'

'We'll put that in the brochure. Now come on, you can't spend all day mooning over our new beasts – we've got several mountains of work to do.'

'Oui, mon capitaine,' said Nemo and he gave a mock salute.

In the days after the seals came the taxonomically correct fish. One by one the glass aquariums were filled, and although not yet a rival to that marvel in France it was a beginning.

A good beginning.

To save money they had made their home in the loft of the factory – three converted rooms, echoing Ferdi and Nemo's days high above the *Gare du Nord*. Sometimes at night, while the others were asleep, Ferdi would go and stand outside the front of the building.

Where once had been letters spelling out Sheldon's Gloves, now different letters, ordered from Art Granger's Neon Lighting for All Occasions, burnt The Saltburn Aquarium into the night sky.

It was important to Ferdi, that erasure of the family name, Sheldon. For life, he believed, wasn't about a name, traditions, but what you do, the person you are, the things you create.

Two weeks before the grand opening Nemo, Wallace and Ferdi made a tour of the local schools.

The children loved to hear about the fish, especially enjoying the section about the sharks – hammerheads, great whites, tigers. The three of them had become quite a team over the years, and they conjured up such grotesque and brilliant images of underwater killing machines, Wallace acting out the jaws, Ferdi showing how they sliced through the waters like Robin Hood's arrows, Nemo making their noises, that on the day of the Saltburn Aquarium's grand opening there was a long eel of a queue outside its doors, children clutching at the hands of their equally expectant parents, all staring in wonder not just at the factory building itself – it was an imposing structure – or at the bright neon letters, but also at the huge fresco Nemo had done on the former front wall of the glove factory: a gigantic kraken rearing up out of a stormy sea, grasping and pulling down and snapping asunder a three-masted sailing ship with its mighty tentacles.

The money from their father's estate having only gone so far, one hundred huge glass tanks costing the Earth, money was tight in those first few years. No new clothes were bought, no fancy restaurants were dined in and, for one whole year, having received a particularly hefty electricity bill, Nemo, Wallace and Ferdi had turned off all the lights in the building, and on dark days guided the guests around with large oil lamps attached to the end of pool cues stolen from the table at the Jolly Fisherman.

This, however, had only added to the aquarium's allure and reputation. For there was something dramatic about the way a cod could loom out of the gloom, its big eyes bulging, its mouth open like it was screaming.

In short, they were a success.

In 1966 the Saltburn Aquarium featured as a 'Top Ten Attraction' in *Letts Guide to the North.* They were two places below the Foetus Museum, but two above the Poulton-le-Fylde Lido where, ironically, the statue to Ferdinand Magellan stood, from whom Ferdi has gained his nickname.

By this time the aquarium boasted two dolphins, a sting-ray pool and an extensive sea-otter colony. To Wallace's disappointment they had yet to acquire a blue whale, but Nemo was confident that one day this would come to pass – not housed in the aquarium itself, but they would make enough money that a boat could be acquired, deep-sea tours arranged.

The aquarium's five staff – ten in the busier holiday periods – were made up of students from the art college in the neighbouring town of Redcar. These students would arrive to work in clothes they had made themselves: Minnie Mouse ears and shorts, a bean bag with holes cut for arms and legs, cling film wrapped around and around the body.

One girl, Freya, wore nothing but tiny little hats, hundreds of them, fixed cleverly in place. She didn't sleep in a bed, she joked, but on a hat stand. 'You try taking four hundred hats off at night!'

They were one big happy family, and things could have been perfect, except, like during the war they had previously endured, dark clouds were beginning to gather.

On a rare day out, quite forgetting themselves, Nemo and Ferdi had walked hand in hand around the perimeter of Poulton-le-Fylde Lido. It just so happened that this was the same week Joe Orton, the playwright, had been bludgeoned to death by his lover, Kenneth Halliwell, in their tiny flat in London. Stories of men living together, performing unnatural acts, were all over the newspapers. Passions were high.

Within just a few days letters of complaint about handholding between men in public places had been written and appeared in *The Town Crier.*

Evans, a young and up-and-coming businessman, son of *the* Evans who owned all the Evans' Department Stores, and owner himself of the Poulton-le-Fylde Lido, saw the scandal as an opportunity. It had irked him more than a little to be ranked two places below the aquarium in the *Letts Guide* – surely his business should be number one.

He enlisted the help of a friend at the *Alnwick Examiner.* 'I want you to focus on the fish. Get rid of the fish and we'll get rid of them. Do you see? They co-exist.'

A petition was started and readers were encouraged to write in.

Pushing aside his kipper, Nemo held up the paper. 'It's like those letters we used to get,' he said, and read aloud: 'The fish are treated no better than animals. My Billy was shocked to see them crammed into row after row of glass cages. They could barely breathe. And it's unnatural. Who's heard of a rainbow trout? It's against nature.'

Nemo rubbed his eyes, somewhere between laughing and crying.

'It's signed "Outraged of Boosbeck".'

One morning Ferdi and Nemo woke to find a protest outside the gates. 'No more fish!' and 'Free the cod!' had been hastily daubed on T-shirts.

'It's a bloody joke,' said Nemo, looking out of the window as Evans rolled up in his limousine and handed out steaming cones of chips, bags of cockles, fried scallops, lobster tails, whelks, prawns, winkles. 'They're talking about saving fish while they're eating them. Or their relatives.'

Another morning one of the art students was abducted on her way to work. She was found weeks later working in the kitchen of a North Sea ferry that went between Hull and Rotterdam, drugged and with little memory of what had happened.

The message was clear: Evans was prepared to play dirty.

When Ferdi saw what was to be the first in a series of letters sent to the *Alnwick Mercury*, he wasn't even surprised. This 'Concerned Citizen of Poulton' claimed to have seen cigarette burns on the flippers of one of the dolphins. In the next letter this same citizen had been a 'first-hand witness' to perversion in the octopus tank.

'God created Adam and Eve, not Adam and Octo-Steve.'

'I mean,' said Nemo, kicking over a chair on his way out to see the dolphins, 'who the fuck is Steve?'

They had never had children, but Nemo loved these beasts as much as if they had been his own, and for their part, when they saw him they came over to the side of the pool and chirruped while he rubbed their beaks.

'I won't let you go,' he said. 'I won't. They'll have to tear me asunder first.'

A team of inspectors from the government's Fisheries and Aquariums Department arrived one morning without warning. One by one they examined the tanks, and on each one they placed the same sticker – red, and with a black cross through it, and the word CONDEMNED.

Ferdi, Nemo and Wallace were given seven days to find the fish 'a stable home in a suitable environment'.

The night after the fish had gone Ferdi and Nemo cried in each other's arms. And the night after that. And the night after that.

What were they going to do? And what about poor Wallace? He had come to love the fish as much as they did.

On the fourth day after the fish had gone, Ferdi, Nemo and Wallace were woken by sounds coming from the aquarium below.

It is an unacknowledged fact that pain can be infinite, but goodness never loses its capacity to surprise.

Going down the stairs the three broken men found the art students gathered, dressed in swimming trunks and wearing aqualungs. Next to them, and in the same get-up, were most of the local fishermen, Ginny from the arcade, the proprietor of Delicious Gifts, his two sons and a group of their friends. Each of them was holding a large black sack.

'Watch this,' said Freya, the art student who was usually dressed in all tiny hats. Climbing up a ladder propped against the nearest tank, she dived in.

'Oh my goodness,' said Nemo, putting both hands up to his face.

In the water the black sack she had been holding opened out and unfurled behind her so that it appeared she was being followed by a shoal of glorious fish. Their bright, stripy bodies swam gaily between the fronds.

'It's a miracle!' said Ferdi.

It was more than a miracle. One by one each of the students and townsfolk climbed into a tank, and soon here were sting-rays, there an octopus, there a happy, barking seal.

'And you haven't seen anything yet,' said Freya, putting her head out of the tank.

Ferdi, Nemo and Wallace were beckoned outside to where a group of four art students and four fishermen were standing. On the count of ten, they jumped into the pool together.

Moments later the massive shining body of a blue whale appeared. It swam around and around, getting faster and faster, before it launched itself into the air and did a backflip through a suspended plastic ring.

The crowd that was gathered – the rest of the townsfolk of Saltburn-by-the-Sea, those either too elderly, too young, or those not able to swim – went wild. It was a miracle.

Cod(a)

In 1969 the Aquarium appeared in first place in the *Letts Guide to the North* list of attractions. The same day the guide was published Nemo put the book in a protective plastic bag and went out to his newly purchased boat, the *Nautilus*.

There was a full moon. He had a flask of coffee and a bag of ham and sardine sandwiches.

The distance was not great, but it took him some time, as he was continually pushed back by the sea's swells.

'Easy, baby,' he said under his breath. 'Easy.'

Finally, happy he was in the correct place, he dropped the sea anchor and, leaning out over the prow, made a deep, brassy sound in his throat.

It took only a few moments for the two noses, beaks, to appear.

'Hello,' he said, 'hello.'

He showed his dolphin friends the book, and how they'd made number-one attraction.

After they had calmed down – for they were joyful, these beasts – he told them his dream. Not the South China Sea. Not the Straits of Magellan. Not the kraken. But to walk down the aisle and marry his loved one, Ferdi.

'My Ferdi.'

He had screwed up their wedding all those years ago, on the ship to New York. But this time he would get it right. It was love.

A PIECE OF ASS

Consenting Adults

Back then, this time I'm thinking of, Corey's mom read fortunes from a small tattered tent on the Clacton-on-Sea seafront next to the little kids' sandpit. The sandpit had been closed down the previous year after one of the little kids had fallen, knocked themself unconscious and suffocated in the sand.

Corey's mom had witnessed all this, tried her best to help. But still, the kid had died.

Tragedy all round, and you would have thought it couldn't get any worse – but then when the kid's parents had come to grieve, plant a commemorative cactus and sit shiva (the kid had been Jewish), Corey's mom, part out of guilt, part out of something she couldn't vocalise, had flown out of her tent, crystal ball in one hand, tarot deck in the other and, fluttering her eyelids like she did during a seance, had proclaimed that she could see a bright future – very bright, more children, a flourishing business, bagels – and little Elijah (that was the kid's name) gambolling merrily around heaven somewhere.

It took six philosophers, thin wiry men with freckles, thick-soled shoes and bad BO to pull the parents off. Angry? Those parents had been incandescent.

If you're wondering about the philosophers – where six philosophers came from out of the blue like that – I can tell you they had been there that whole summer season, parading up and down the seafront with their placards: *Nihilism! When do we want it? Never! Not in this lifetime. Or the next. Which we don't believe in!*

'But what did I do?' wailed Corey's mom that night, back home. 'I was only trying to help!'

In truth, far from being the victim, she had fought back like a tiger, still had the skin of the mother's neck under her nails, the torn-off shirt collar of the father balled up and bloody at the bottom of her handbag.

'I didn't kill the freakin' kid! Did he fall, or was he pushed? That's what I'd be asking. And cross my palm with silver and I might've given them the answer.'

Incandescent herself now with the thought of that day's lost earnings – she could hardly have gone back to work with a split lip and a ripped bodice – she slammed the pan of SpaghettiOs against the hob and told Corey she just wished his dad was there once in a while of an evening so they could talk through their problems like any other family.

'Jeez,' Corey said. 'We both wish that but sure as eggs is eggs we know that ain't going to be happening any time soon. Dad, he's a no-show – he's always a no-show.'

Back then Corey's father was absent just about seven nights out of seven, bussing tables at !!!Moustaches¡¡¡, and even though he pulled in eighty-plus hour weeks, still they struggled to make ends meet.

But hey, Corey thought, they didn't have it so bad. Other boys he knew didn't have proper homes. One boy at school lived in an abandoned air-conditioning unit, another in a tree house.

Some of the other boys were jealous of tree-house boy, tree houses generally being thought of as being as cool as mustard. Then tree-house boy slipped from a high branch while taking a shit, spent three weeks in hospital and now lived with an iron lung. He pushed this lung around the school on a trolley, and was often late for lessons, which got him black looks from the teachers and after-school detentions. And of course, having an iron lung in tow and struggling to climb up to his tree house, sometimes he slept in a drainage ditch with actual excrement in it.

If there was one thing Corey knew, it was that shit happens.

But all that is nothing. This is what I'm telling you – *this* is the story. It gets worse, believe me.

One morning three lithe shaven-headed boys in black Bovver boots, bunking off from Clacton's Technical College, had seen Corey's mom's sign outside her tent – Fortunes Told Here – and thought it would be a good prank to make off with it.

Two of the bunking boys had never wanted to go to Technical College in the first place, and the third only wanted to surf. It was his bright idea to use the sign as a bodyboard.

By the time Corey's mom saw them they had stripped to their pants and were down at the far end of the beach. Then they were in the water. With the sign.

'I wasn't going in the friggin' sea after them – not in my ermine robe,' she said to Corey's father later that evening as he was about to set off to his shift at !!!Moustaches¡¡¡, which wasn't the best timing. Twelve hours of work ahead of you – you tell me if you'd be in a good mood?

Pots got tossed to the floor; Corey's dad beat himself with the wooden spoon, dripping sauce from the SpaghettiOs, then lifted a pile of bills in red envelopes from the table, held them over his head and, half-weeping, half-yelling, demanded to know how the hell could they afford a new sign.

'Make me out to be the bad guy, why don't you!' said Corey's mom. 'No sign, I know, but at least I've still got my tent.'

Then the next day there was no tent.

Do you remember the huge storm that year? You know the one – they even gave it a name. Treena or Tabatha or some shit like that.

Well, that Treena/Tabatha day, as Corey's mom left her tent for her daily cappuccino and petit Chinois, declaring no goddam blinkin' storm would get the best of her, a strong gust of wind whooshing in the flap she'd just left open lifted the tent up like a balloon, and off it went who knows where.

Even the Climate Change Deniers couldn't help. They'd been out petitioning on the seafront that day. A couple of them had grabbed on to the bottom of the tent and they had been swept off too.

'Deny that,' said Corey's dad later, his face grim. He knew what no tent meant.

'At least you've still got your job,' said Corey's mom. 'As long as you've got your job we'll make ends meet.'

Corey's dad didn't make at !!!Moustachesⅈⅈ what he used to make at Consenting Adults, even though most of the time at Consenting Adults he had just tended the desk or replenished the stocks – genuine 1930s merkins, cock rings used during the British Raj, snippets of hair cut from Errol Flynn's butt crack and sold on in little presentation bottles with a fondling cloth.

Consenting Adults was listed in the *Green Pages* as a retail establishment, but for five pounds couples who had completed the obligatory questionnaire could take Corey's father into the back room and do with him as they wished. Some dressed him in flimsy pyjamas and then cut them into squares while he was still wearing them. Others would make him slip on a nappy and crawl on all fours while making baby noises, or use him as a love seat, heavy petting across his sagging back.

Corey's mom said it was degrading, but his father said five cold hard bucks were never degrading when they could put a spatchcock chicken and half a kilo of Brussel sprouts on the table.

But then all that New Puritanism had started, and Consenting Adults had been closed down, and that was when his dad had got the job at !!!Moustachesⅈⅈ. It was supposed to have been a stop-gap, but that had been years ago now.

'I started out as the door opener,' he liked to say, 'and look at me now. Bussing tables. Mister Success.'

And now we *are* really getting to it, I promise you – the whole freakin' point of this thing I'm telling you about. It's the saddest story you'll ever hear.

Two weeks before Corey's mom's tent blew away on the seafront, a new manager had started at !!!Moustaches¡¡¡.

Dwayne, this new manager, a former marine, so help them all God, prior to the restaurant opening each evening had instigated what he called Boot Camp.

A haunted look in his eyes, Corey's dad would describe it as a friggin' crazy circus gone wrong. Waiters had to slalom blindfolded and at speed between empty tables, five plates stacked on each hand, while the chefs were made to juggle knives usually meant only for cutting the livers from deadly blowfish.

And it was worse for the dishwashers and kitchen porters – they had to strip down to a kind of marine underwear supplied by Dwayne, the crotch cut out so that their willies dangled free, and then dick-slap each other vigorously until the last man standing begged for submission.

It wouldn't have been so bad, except Dwayne had set up a live feed on the dark web. Between 5 and 6 p.m. anyone could tune in and watch the spectacle. And they did.

Footfall in the restaurant was up, and rumour had it Dwayne was going to get all the staff to do the dick-slapping live for any diners who signed in triplicate a disclaimer that they wouldn't report it to the New Puritanism authorities.

'What about those who haven't got dicks?' This was from Fanny. She was one of the female waiters. She didn't take shit from anyone. She had once beaten a complaining diner with a lobster claw.

'Don't worry,' said Dwayne. 'We'll get you dicks.'

Things were coming to a head.

To round off Boot Camp each day Dwayne did what he called his 'How High?' competition. He would cry out, 'How High?', and all the staff, lined up, would have to jump into the air. The one that jumped the highest got an extra one per cent of that evening's tip share (minus tax and administration costs).

The previous week, Maurice's wife (Maurice was the sommelier at !!!Moustachesᵢᵢᵢ) had left him for a junior car salesmen and taken his two kids, Franny and Zooey. Then the bailiffs had turned up. It turned out the wife hadn't been paying the mortgage with the money Maurice been earning at !!!Moustachesᵢᵢᵢ, but had instead been spending it on vitamin supplements for her toy boy, the junior car salesman.

Now, as well as losing his family, Maurice was going to lose the house. This was why he was so desperate for money – even that one per cent tip share (minus tax and administration costs). So when Dwayne shouted out 'How High?' Maurice had scaled one of the adult-sized high chairs for overweight babies and leapt.

Everyone heard the snap of his ankles.

'Don't worry,' said Dwayne. 'We'll get you a wheelchair for the service. I'll push you to A&E myself later – or get someone else to do it.'

That's when Corey's dad stepped up. He knew what it was like to be humiliated.

One time at Consenting Adults he had been forced to eat porridge oats urinated on by a bank teller from Phoenix, Arizona and then zapped to high heaven in the microwave. It wasn't that it even tasted bad – it was the principle of it.

'Come on, Maurice,' he said, and lifted him up over his shoulder. Then he put him down again – Corey's dad not being the fine specimen of a man he had once been – and fetched Big Andy from the grocer's across the road. Big Andy could lift a sack of spuds in each hand while balanced on a beachball, also while being blown off by the two buxom blondes who worked in the laundromat next door. It was a party trick still talked about all across town.

The queue at A&E was eight hours long. When Corey's dad got back to !!!Moustaches!!! Dwayne was waiting for him. He said he would never work in the bussing industry again – 'or its ancillary services.' Then he asked for Corey's dad's apron, notepad and pens. These things didn't grow on trees.

Two months later, when Evans, their landlord, came for his annual visit, Corey's parents ushered Corey outside. They tried to keep things from him, but he knew his mom and dad weren't working and money was scarce – and besides, wasn't it him who had to go to the food bank with his dad every week and carry back those bulging carrier bags? All they'd eaten for seven weeks were tins of sardines. Corey had developed an oily skin and a certain smell lingered around him. The other boys had started calling him Fish Flaps, and made sea noises whenever he went near them.

On the street outside their house Corey found a sleek silver car and a man in a tight uniform leaning against it smoking a thin cigarette. Evans' chauffeur, he supposed.

On seeing him the chauffeur ushered Corey to the back of the car and, without any other introduction, unzipped his flies and asked Corey if he'd like to fondle his underpants for five pence.

'Who's paying?' asked Corey, but he didn't mean it. He had been warned of such men by his mother and told not to accept anything less than a one-pound note, and so he said no and went and sat in Mr McGinty's, their elderly neighbour's, porch. But once he was there he regretted turning down the fondling because he thought of all the things he might have bought with five pence – a gobstopper, a single sock from a charity shop, last week's Saturday supplement from the *Daily Record* (which had a feature on Corey's favourite basketball team, the Clacton Coldhearts) or a thimbleful of coke.

The corner shop had started selling soft drinks by the thimbleful. Some kids would save up all week and then would keep the sugary drink in their mouth for hours.

It was a new thing – the art of not swallowing. Legends were made of it.

When his parents finally called Corey in from Mr McGinty's porch, the sun had gone down, the neighbourhood cats were out on their nightly prowls and Evans and the fondle-my-pants chauffeur had gone.

'I've made you your favourite meal,' said his mom, and his father pushed a plate with one sardine on it towards him.

His least favourite meal was two sardines – which, by default, made his favourite meal one sardine.

'We think it's a wonderful opportunity,' said his father.

On his father's face was the look he had when he talked about that one time he'd had to shove a whiskey bottle up his ass for a client at Consenting Adults. It wasn't pleasure; it was pain.

'It's this or skid row,' said his mom.

'And we don't want skid row,' said his father. 'No siree Bob.'

He had always dreamt of being a hero, and even had the uniform – an acrylic jumper with numerous Velcro straps and a rubber mac he had found behind the cistern in the cinema toilets during a midnight viewing of *Citizen Kane*. Despite the other kids at school calling him Condom, or Rubber, the uniform made him feel like someone. Someone powerful. One day an old woman would be in need, and he would be there to help her with his plastic mac and Velcro straps. She would be out in a heavy storm without a hat, for example, and would need some kind of waterproof covering and to be lashed to a lamppost. These Velcro straps are as strong as iron! Then what would those other kids say? They'd be in awe of him.

'Sit yourself down, kid,' said his dad, while his mom stifled a sob.

Then they explained. In short, Evans owned a string of casinos. The croupiers in them were all teenage boys. The boys were trained at Evans' own Swiss Card Sharp Summer School.

'The thing is, buster,' said his father, 'Evans will train you up, and then there'll be a job waiting for you at the end of it. It could be anywhere in the world. You'll make a fortune.'

He handed Corey a pack of cards. 'Now get practising. All of our futures depend on it.'

All the French Singers Have Bum Postcards

Corey consoled himself with the thought he would be going abroad. Swiss Card Sharp Summer School – Switzerland. You do the math.

He had never been on an aeroplane, although once for a birthday treat his parents had taken him to Stansted Airport and let him look through the sturdy chain-link fence.

They had been there for a good two hours before a burly security guard rocked up in a sleek four-by-four, flashing lights, siren going. Getting out, swinging his legs like he had a dildo up his ass, he'd told them it was a restricted area and if they didn't move on he would have to take them down.

Corey's dad had called the guard a jerk under his breath and wanted to punch him, but Corey's mom said it wasn't worth the effort and, besides, she'd had enough of watching other people fly off to places she would never go. There was only so much envy she could handle.

Seven days before he was due at the card-sharp school Corey ducked out of his Civics in the New Puritan Society lesson (How to Spot a Refugee and What to Do Next!) and made his way down to the town's library. Smashing a window around the back, he climbed in.

Despite a twenty-four hour charity whist drive to raise funds, and although several elderly ladies chained themselves to the collected works of Catherine Cookson, hardback and large print, the library had closed thanks to a cut in its funding. The closing ceremony had been presided over by a semi-local New Puritanism politician, spouting some guff about one door closing, another one opening, etc., but where this door was opening he wasn't specific.

Flicking on the torch he'd taken from the kitchen drawer for when they had power cuts or couldn't afford the electricity, Corey went up and down the aisles until he found the only decent book on Switzerland that hadn't been stolen or sold out front from wobbly trestle tables by the soon-to-be redundant librarians.

Slipping *Switzerland, Our Castles, Our Souls* down the back of his trousers, he made his way home.

Up in his bedroom, in anticipation of his flight, Corey built a conning tower out of old sardine tins and eight rolls of Sellotape. Broken Moulinex mixers scavenged from the tip stood in for the kind of Boeing he would soon be flying out on. Holding a wooden spoon up to his mouth, balled-up dirty sock attached to its end to resemble a microphone, he practised being an air traffic controller.

At night now he dreamt of Switzerland. Lush green fields, crenellated chateaux, creamy chocolate and cowgirls – a step up from the lewd dreams he'd recently been having about Darren, the portly man who collected the pools money.

One morning when Darren had nipped into Wilma's Bakery and Café to relieve himself, Corey had found himself fondling Darren's still warm bicycle seat, feeling something stirring down below. And Darren wasn't even a looker! He'd overheard Madge from the mini-mart refer to him as No Marlon Brando, but Corey had caught a glimpse of Darren's bare ass in the lido changing rooms the previous summer (strictly against New Puritanism regulations: Darren should've been in a locked cubicle), and ever since Corey hadn't been able to get those perfect orbs out of his mind, mooning over them on an almost nightly basis. So that was that. As well as being poor he was a freak.

The morning before he was due to leave, at breakfast, half a sardine balanced on four Cheerios, his mom pushed a limp woollen thing towards him.

'I've picked apart your father's winter underpants,' she said, 'and made you a hat. Sorry about the colour.'

Pee-stained yellow, thought Corey. 'I love it,' he said, 'and the Swiss'll love it. We'll take it in turns wearing it on the poop deck of the chateau.'

In his mind, thanks to his book, he was under the impression that everyone in Switzerland lived in a chateau, but he saw a look pass between his mom and dad – like the one he saw that time they had joked they'd sold his older sister to the highest bidder but 'had got a very good price' and then it turned out they weren't joking.

'Swiss?' said his mother. 'As in Switzerland?'

'That's the baby,' said Corey, already feeling the dread rising in his stomach.

'You're going up north,' said his mom. 'To Saltburn-by-the-Sea.'

'Where the Swiss Card Sharp Summer School is currently located,' said Corey's dad. He pulled his lips back to form a kind of grimace. 'You didn't think... Oh blimey. A Swiss Card Sharp is a thing,' he said. 'Not a reference to the country.'

'Have another sardine,' said his mother. 'Apparently there are seals in Saltburn. They'll like you. All these sardines you've been devouring. Why, you practically look like one!'

'Arf arf!' said his father, comically clapping his hands together.

For the trip to the station his mom dressed in the feather boa and pair of enormous dark glasses she used to wear down to her fortune-telling tent. She thought she might pick up some work on the train concourse – a seance for one of the wealthy families heading off to the southern resorts or a tarot reading for a businessmen in a suit and at a loose end between meetings. But a down-beaten station worker in a coolie hat and thin shoes checked their ticket and pointed to a dark-looking arch with rainwater dripping from it, lights flickering on and off.

'All platforms south and to the Capital City are in a restricted area. Yours is that way... If you'd like to hurry. Your train is about to leave.'

The waiting engine pumped thick smoke up and out into a misty morning.

'I got you this,' said Corey's mom as she helped him up into the carriage. She passed him a toilet roll.

'It might look like just a toilet roll,' she said, 'but I've jazzed it up.'

For the previous eight nights she had sat up embellishing each of the sheets with a single inspirational phrase – 'Be the best you can be', 'Every journey begins with the first step', 'After darkness always comes the light'.

'Every time I look at it I'll think of you,' said Corey.

'You'll be sitting on the toilet,' said his mom.

Then, although he said he wouldn't, Corey started to cry, big tears forming in the corners of his eyes and rolling down his cheeks.

'My son,' said his mom. 'Me and your father, we're done, washed up. Our time has passed. Sure, we've made some mistakes. I should've taken a notice of the weather warnings – I might still have a tent. And your dad should never have shoved that whiskey bottle up his ass. He still can't take a bartender asking him if he wants it straight up. And whiskey *was* his favourite drink. But we did what we had to. And let's be honest, we made a clusterfuck of it. That's life. That was our life. Now we're depending on you. Be strong our little brave man. You're our only hope. We love you.'

Corey awoke to landscape scudding past outside and an old man, wiry hair sticking at ninety degrees out of each ear, leaning over him, arm outstretched. The man was pawing at his rubber mac, his superhero uniform, in the area of his inner thigh.

'Whaddayehthinkyerdoin?' belched out Corey, sitting bolt upright.

'For you,' said the man, 'very good price.' And with that he opened both wings of a voluminous tweed jacket and gave a bow of his head. Pinned there, to the ragged inside lining, were grimy blurry postcards of an insalubrious nature. French singers: Serge Gainsbourg, Sacha Distel, Charles Aznavour, Johnny Hallyday, Maurice Chevalier, Yves Montand, Alain Barrière, Philippe Clay, naked as the day they were born but at a certain angle, peering coyly back over their shoulders, full arses on display.

'Shall we say,' said the old man, 'two Gainsbourgs and a Distel? Forty-seven pence.'

Corey had heard of things like this at school. One boy had been expelled for having a grainy photocopy of Eric Cantona's buttocks, obtained while on a strictly supervised holiday in Normandy, Blu-Tacked to the inside of his locker. Now this boy was working under curfew at a chicken plant, and the rest of them, the boys who'd seen it, had had to attend a three-hour workshop on New Puritanism.

'I don't want your blasted French arses!' said Corey to the old man. He stormed off indignantly to the toilet, and spent the rest of the journey locked in there, ignoring the increasingly loud knocks at the door and the curses of an angry crowd, wondering why the old man had picked him to sell his illicit postcards to.

Was it written on his face? Unnatural perversions. Enter here.

Corey's first impression of Saltburn-by-the-Sea was that it was a desolate place. Outside the desultory station was a boardwalk from which the sand crept painfully down to a tumbling sea. On poles, dotted along the seafront, were a series of signs: No Ball Games! No Nudity! Beware Seals! There was even a seal there – or a statue of one – staring mournfully out to that tumbling sea, a huge cock graffitied on its proud chest.

With three hours before the scheduled Introductory Meet and Greet, Corey wandered along the front.

There were penny arcades, chip shops, boarded-up guests houses with peeling signs in their windows advertising long-gone pier-end shows, Mephisto the Magician and his assistant, Fanny!, Sideshow Steve, the Funniest Man in the North-East!, Saddam the Mind-Reader, He Knows Your Innermost Thoughts! But there were no people.

Past a souvenir shop, Delicious Gifts, its door firmly closed, but a rack of once brightly coloured plastic spades and buckets rattling in the fierce wind, half-deflated inflatable crocodiles and turtles rope-tied to its weathered frontage, Corey came across something that made him stop dead. It was a baby, made out of papier mâché, a steel rod up its bum, slowly rotating, puffy arms and legs folded towards its torso, its large head clumsily painted with large blue eyes and red lips coming around again and again to leer towards Corey.

What the...?

Behind the baby stood a dark, open doorway, above it a crackling and fizzing neon sign, some of the letters on the wonk, but still spelling out The Foetus Museum.

Corey's feet took him inside, whatever his mind may have wanted.

At the end of a long entrance corridor, dimly lit, images of half-formed babies adorning its walls, was a staircase whose every step creaked, and which had a sign on a pole in the shape of a pointing finger at the top of it: Teratology: the study of human deformity. This way.

Corey sucked in his cheeks and stepped into the room.

Each exhibit was in a huge glass jar – babies, he supposed, but not like babies he had seen before. Some of these floating creatures had two heads, or no arms or legs, or greatly enlarged heads that dwarfed the bodies below them.

Both shocked and intrigued, Corey explored the maze of rooms. In one was displayed the development of a baby, from single sperm to a fully formed infant in a mock-up of a womb, a lascivious smile on its face, like the one that chauffeur had had as he unzipped his flies.

Was there no escaping his desires?

In a panic, emotions already heightened, Corey started to run, entering one room, exiting it, knocking over a sign, losing himself, finding himself, until he was several stories up, on a roof terrace, which also was home to a gift shop.

Here, in the diffuse sunlight, were aisle upon aisle of goods. Corey, trying to get his breath back, found himself going past the same foetus key rings, postcards, pencil ends, snow globes, brochures, stacks of a book called *A Foetus through Time*, before he came to the cash desk, which was manned by an elderly lady wearing a see-through plastic mac with an inappropriately figure-hugging dress beneath.

Behind her stood another one of those fizzing neon signs, this one saying EXIT, and there was a winding staircase leading its way back down, Corey hoped, to the seafront.

'We don't get many single boys in here,' said the woman. 'Nor courting couples either, for that matter. They tend to go to the Saltburn Aquarium, or queue for the guided tours of the nuclear-power station across the mudflats. Can I help you with something?'

'I'll take this knob-end,' said Corey, using the word he and his schoolmates would use for the fancy ferrules they placed on their pencils.

'That's seven pence,' said the woman, and as she bagged up his purchase she leant across the counter and asked if he were a runaway.

Corey pushed his tongue into the side of his cheek and imagined that he was.

He could get a boat. Start out afresh somewhere, in another country. He did not want to spend his summer enclosed with other boys. They would bully him – make him do unspeakable things after lights out.

Then he remembered his parents. They were relying on him.

'I'm here for the Swiss Card Sharp Summer School,' he said, and the woman looked at his cumbersome hands sceptically.

He looked at them sceptically too. His mom had once told him he would never be a vet. 'You'd never get those things up a cat's behind.'

'My sister,' said the woman, 'she sometimes takes in boys for the summer. To help out with the slots. Ginny's Palace. You can't miss it – just along the front. If it all goes wrong tell her I sent you. Mable from the Foetus Museum. She'll know who I am. Here, take a card.'

An Introduction to Card Sharping

Corey was last on to the waiting minibus, the only seat available right at the front next to a driver who told an endless stream of dog jokes, slantwise, from the thick sides of his mouth, throughout the whole journey.

'Did I tell you the one about the Dalmatian? Most people spot the punchline a mile off. Did you hear about the round green dog that was always sadly chasing sheep? He was melon-collie.'

Looking surreptitiously behind him Corey eyed up the other boys. As expected they were all bigger boned than him and, in the way they laughed and joked, confident with it. Like the cool older boys at school they sported the brightly coloured shell-suits and fine slicked hairstyles made popular thanks to a recent reality TV show, *Refugee Down!*

In this show a group of rich teenagers put a group of refugees through a series of humiliating tests, the prize being, for the refugee who abased themselves the most, a six-month residency visa and a quarter share in a pushbike.

Somewhat overawed, Corey turned his eyes from the boys and instead fixed them on to the backs of gardens, the broken bikes, the tumbling sheds, the days-old washing clinging to sagging lines.

'My dog's got no nose. How does he smell? Awful!'

The Swiss Card Sharp Summer School, it turned out, was in a prison – or rather, an erstwhile one – the guard towers, the double chain-link perimeter fence, the barred narrow windows, making its former use immediately obvious.

They were met off the bus by two impossibly muscular men, dressed in tight sleeveless T-shirts and badly ironed shorts. They were told that as they had arrived late there would be no supper, that if they wanted to be top card sharps then this was the kind of suffering they would have to endure.

Then they were assigned rooms. Cells.

Corey, whose name was picked last out of the box, was to share with Kurt and Eli – Kurt gorilla-sized, Eli not so much.

Corey hadn't seen Eli on the bus, and now he wished he had. Eli was not like the other boys. He had a delicate chin, long eyelashes and was wearing a T-shirt with a single dove on it, soaring into the sky.

Having reached their designated cell Corey hauled himself up on to one of the narrow bunks, turned to face the wall and pulled his copy of Hammond Innes' *The Lonely Skier* from his bag. He had only read a few pages – Neil Blair is demobbed from the army and hired to go on a trip to the Dolomites to sniff out hidden Nazi treasure – when the book was snatched from his hands and Kurt, the gorilla, was saying, 'Good, glad to see you have brought me some top-notch bog roll.' He stomped off, presumably to the toilet, with the book.

'Don't mind him,' Eli said kindly. 'His bark's worse than his bite. What you have to do is blend in. Toughen up.'

'Grrrr,' said Corey through clenched teeth, and both boys laughed.

The instructors were a pair of former semi-professional boxers, famous for fighting dirty. Throughout the day they shouted out motivational phrases gleaned from watching old episodes of *You Can Beat It!* on a battered VHS player in their rec room.

Corey could just remember the show, evenings spent with his mom and dad leaning towards their old Binatone TV, teas on trays on their laps, braying in glee as *welfare scroungers* were helicoptered to a tiny Scottish island, stripped of their clothes and possessions and left to forage in the wild for twenty-eight days, all the while being filmed by hidden cameras.

Every three days, during the peak-time live shows, new hazards were introduced to the island – a plague of frogs, wildfire, a simulated tornado – while the studio audience, whipped into a frenzy, screamed out the show's title and catchphrase.

You can beat it! You can beat it!

The show was cancelled after one notorious episode in which the Amazonian candiru fish, also known as the toothpick fish, infamous for its ability to swim up urethras and cling on, was introduced into the water supply, and seven of the welfare scroungers, in extreme agony, ripped off their penises on live TV.

The New Puritanism party had had a field day, marches had been organised, banners waved, and a new Director General of the state TV channel had been put in place.

Now it was all baking shows, carol services, programmes about sensible lifestyle choices. Not a ripped off penis to be seen.

Or any penis, for that matter. Or a boob. Buttock. Vagina. Arse crack. Bumhole.

It was if these body parts didn't exist. The New Puritanism party, Corey's dad used to like to say, believe they are protecting you from arseholes, but the truth of the matter is that they are the arseholes, bumholes, fannies, butts, arse cracks, penises – the whole damn lot of them.

Every morning at the card-sharp school, after the designated prayer time, taking place in the former prison chapel, designated shower time, each of the boys carefully ushered into their own double-locked cubicle as per the national edicts, and the designated breakfast, eaten while sat on bum-numbing wooden benches, an almost inedible combination of green eggs and watery tea, the boys congregated in the cleared out sports hall.

Here was rigged up a mock casino. Think of it like a boxing ring.

Bobo Knuckles, *the fiercest, baddest man you'll ever have the displeasure to meet*, had decorated the walls of the sports hall with enormous peeling posters of his long-dead boxer heroes – Sixto Escobar, Kid Chocolate, Frankie Klick, Baby Casanova.

Under the gaze of these looming giants, for eight hours each day, the boys would practise routines – the three-card monte, the bottom deal, the Saltburn shuffle, the Monte Carlo cut and many, many other sleights of hand.

For Corey it was torture.

While the other boys could seemingly easily slip a card up their sleeve, cut a deck so the facing card was always the two of hearts, flip and switch while throwing an inverse wink, Corey could never do any of these things. Not even nearly.

Sometimes Eli, his roommate, would take him aside, offer encouragement, try to help him with his moves, but it was useless: he couldn't do it. And that Eli was taking pity on him made him feel even more humiliated. How would this boy ever return his admiration when he was so inept himself?

At night, wrung out and exhausted, his nerves shredded, Corey dreamt of the cards come to life, bleeding hearts, blood diamonds, clubs with nails in them piercing the heads of seals, the spades of gravediggers dropping soil down on to him. And his mom's face – telling him he was their only hope.

Only he wasn't. He was a big fat failure.

At the end of week one, An Introduction to Card Sharping, a mock yearbook was produced (below Corey's name some joker had written 'Most Likely to Fail') and a party was organised.

Brad, who had been using roll-on deodorant since he was eleven and who sported thick stubble as resplendent as a lion's mane, was sent into town to purchase the alcohol and, from

Delicious Gifts, a selection of 'blow-up birds', where they had been spied, desired and remembered: pink plastic women inflated through a tube and sporting all-in-one swimsuits that still remained somehow revealing.

By the time Corey got to choose (there was meant to be one 'date' for each boy) there were no 'birds' left, only an inflatable sheep – which actually he preferred, having already coveted from afar the sheep's cosy, almost smiling, visage on the cover of the packet the inflatable came in.

The blown-up women were scary, their heavily made-up painted faces reminding Corey of the women who had lined the street outside his home on Friday and Saturday nights, leaning into the windows of slowly moving cars, catcalling, caterwauling, adjusting suspenders on withered and ungainly legs.

'Shameful', his mother had called them; but then, sleepless one night, he had peered through a chink in his curtains and seen her there, boobs propped impossibly high, a cigarette in each corner of her mouth, an ascendency of smoke floating towards the lamplight. 'Would you like to see a lady, sir?'

The party, for secrecy's sake, was held on the crenellated rooftop of the prison. There was evidence of a riot having taken place there once – bits of broken chair, bloodstains, a barrier made of wooden toilet seats and plaintive demands daubed on the bare white side of the huge air-conditioning unit in salmon pink paint.

EARLY RELEASE FOR CARTER! HE NEVER DID IT!
WHAT DO WE WANT?
SOFT TOILET PAPER!
WHERE DO WE WANT IT?
ON OUR ARSES!

Corey quickly downed one bottle of warm fizzy beer and then another. He had never been drunk before, but his parents had once taken him for a day out at a wind tunnel, and it felt something like that – buffeted from all sides, a feeling of sickness and yet a certain thrill just the same.

As the night progressed there were fireworks in milk bottles, a table full of pickled snacks diminishing, a Binatone record player playing Jacque Brel's 'Ne me quitte pas' again and again, someone having accidentally pressed a butt-cheek against the repeat button.

Towards midnight, sprawled in an inebriated circle, a game of Truth or Dare was started, and when it came to Corey, fearing the Truth – about his innermost feelings about Eli (his crush had grown stronger and stronger throughout the week), about his mom, his dad, their jobs as a fortune teller and bus boy respectively – said Dare.

He guessed he might have to remove his shoes and socks and walk barefoot across a broken bottle, do a handstand and sing 'Joe le taxi' while chewing on a pickled egg, or perhaps even eat one of the other boy's curling juicy bogies, but Kurt, drunk on three bottles of Greedy Goblin, drew himself up to his full height and, pointing, said Corey had to kiss Eli's bare ass.

Had he guessed? And what even was he asking?

The National Football Team, fondly formerly known as the Clangers, were now in a prison somewhere in Cambodia, seven years hard labour, thanks to their backsides having appeared on an illicit calendar that was destined, supposedly, only for close family members, but which had gone viral.

'Ass,' proclaimed Kurt again, belting out the word like Ethel Merman in *Anything Goes*, and all the other boys, caught up in a collective hysteria, took up the call, shouting out, 'Ass, ass, ass!' while clapping their hands together.

It was a fait accompli. There was no way out.

And so as Kurt held a wriggling, fighting Eli around the neck, backing him up to Corey like a dump truck, Corey didn't struggle a jot, merely watched agog as four of the other boys, two holding Eli's legs, two working on the garments, first lowering Eli's jeans, then his outer pants, then his secondary pants, then his final back-up pants with the protective layer.

As the bare buttocks came nearer, Corey saw his whole life flash before him, saw his mom, dad, Darren, Eli. He was damned if he did, damned if he didn't. So he puckered his lips for a kiss and closed his eyes – and that was when he heard the shout, 'Fuck! New Puritanism patrol alert! Ditch the naked guy. We're sprung!'

A scuffle, a commotion, the tread of heavy feet.

Corey felt the pressure of naked flesh on his face – they must have dropped Eli, who, unable to right himself, must have fallen.

Corey wanted to say sorry, to apologise for something that wasn't his fault; opening his mouth to do so, that's when someone accidentally (or on purpose) stood on Corey's balls, causing him to clamp his mouth down in agony.

There was the sound of a curdling scream, the taste of blood, then nothing.

Corey woke in the cleaning cupboard. There were snails crawling down the walls, empty industrial-sized vats of Dettol, broom handles with suspicious stains on their ends.

For hours he had heard gruff angry men calling his name, somewhere in the background, sobbing – Eli? – and the high-pitched sounds of the other boys' voices.

He could imagine them. *It wasn't us. It was him. The freak. We knew he was weird by the way he looked at us.*

In his hand he was surprised to see he was clutching, his fingers curled around it, a rather large piece of flesh – spongy, slightly bloody.

He knew where it had come from. Eli.

When his mom did her fortune telling there were always people coming to her wanting to make contact with a lost loved one.

'Bring a piece of them,' she used to say. 'Something close to their skin.'

She'd tell stories to Corey over the dinner table – how she'd had prosthetic limbs, false teeth, once even an eyeball.

'But touch those things and close your eyes and, you know, I sense them.'

What had his mother called it? A feeling.

'You just know,' she said. 'It's all there in your head, like a moving picture.' Her voice had wavered, stuttered. 'They call me a fake but I'm not. Your mom's a psychic! And maybe, just maybe, one day you will be too.'

Closing his eyes, concentrating, letting the images come, abandoning himself to them, Corey closed both hands around the piece of ass. Slowly at first, and then quicker, he saw it all:

That Eli's full name was Elijah – he was named after his Rabbi grandfather and the prophet and miracle worker from the Hebrew Book of Kings; that Eli had lost his virginity at the party following his bar mitzvah: that it had been to one of his drunken mother's friends, and although she had breasts that sagged and an afternoon gin habit he had loved her a little and had written her thirty-four love notes, all unanswered; that Eli ate his own cum after masturbating, and he promised himself the next time would be the last time he would do it, but it never was; that Eli had a dog called Rockie and, although he was stern and manly with him in public, secretly he let him into his bedroom every night so he could sleep on the bed on his feet; that he loved that dog – he loved all dogs; that he dreamt of being a good man, but he easily slid down the path of deceit, like that time when he had once followed through on a fart in a biology class while dissecting a rabbit's eyeball and he had blamed the smell on Ronald, who wore pink glasses and was fat, and who all the boys teased; that two weeks later he had asked Ronald to slow dance with him at the school disco, and although he told the other boys he was doing it for a dare he had got a stiffy; that after the dance he whispered in Ronald's ear that he was quite the little mover, and he sent Ronald secret Valentine's cards even when it wasn't Valentine's Day; that one day he was

going to marry Ronald, even if he didn't shift the weight; that
the marriage would be on a mountaintop, and doves would caw
(if that's the sound doves make); that he knew he was a stupid
boy who nobody would ever truly love and that made him sad;
but he couldn't tell anyone that, and that was that.

At dawn, sensing all at last was quiet, Corey made a break for it.

He bum-hugged walls, static sparking from his hair, slipped
down the stairs, holding his breath as he opened the door. He
only paused, finally, at the gates, spinning around, bold now, to
stick out his tongue and give the whole lot of them the Vs.

He wasn't going back.

Finding a phone box on the front, the distant doggy faces of
seals just visible out across the flats, he dialled the number for
home.

'I've graduated,' he said, 'with honours. Being sent to Monte
Carlo. Who'd believe it?'

He promised he'd send his parents money just as soon as he
could, and then he told them he loved them. It was only after
he'd put down the receiver that he said he hoped they could
forgive him.

Although it was not yet seven there was already an elderly
man outside Delicious Gifts, involved in carefully attaching
the partially inflated inflatables, dinosaurs, donkeys, frogs with
their tongues out, to the netting on the façade. If the man was
surprised by Corey's request for something in a jar, something
cheap, he didn't show it.

Strawberry jam, twelve pence. That would do the trick.

Corey ate it with his fingers, sitting on the kerb. It was sweet,
filled with little seeds, and it felt, he thought, like moist shit.

The Foetus Museum, he remembered, was next door to
Delicious Gifts. It wasn't open at this hour – he hadn't expected
it to be – so he crept up the fire escape and, first pulling off and

then wrapping his jumper over his hand, he punched the glass out of one of the windows.

Inside was lit with dim out-of-hours security lights. It made the unborn babies even more eerie, if that was possible.

For his plan he wasn't precious about which exhibit he used, so he went to the nearest. The baby-to-be inside seemed to glare at him as he prised open the lid of its final resting place.

'I'm sorry, but my need is as great as yours – greater, perhaps!' he said. 'And the small volume I require won't hinder your rest.'

The strawberry jam jar he had licked and fingered clean. Now he dipped it into the baby's preserving fluid, submerging it so it filled to the brim. Then, taking it back out, he held it up, admired it, dropped in the piece of Eli's ass and reaffixed the lid.

For two long weeks Corey lived on the streets.

There was an Italian restaurant, Gino's Place, out of the back door of which the fat chef would throw scraps of food at the end of each service. Corey would fight the local dogs for them, baring his teeth and pressing himself against their warm, steaming bodies.

At night he slept in the waiting room of a former bus station and in lieu of a bedtime story he would run a finger down the faded timetable, mouthing the name of each town, imagining himself heading north to the mountainous region no longer served by the buses.

He missed his mother and father, but how could he go back? He was penniless, outcast.

On the thirteenth day, searching his pockets for a piece of foraged change, he came across a card, dog-eared; he remembered now – it was given to him by an old lady at the Foetus Museum on his first day.

Ginny's Palace
We've got a slot for everyone!
Come over and chance your luck!

It came back to him: 'My sister, she sometimes takes in boys for the summer. Here, take a card.'

He called from a phone box smelling of urine, plastered with hundreds of tiny illicit cards displaying images of women in high heels, tight leather skirts, wielding whips above their heads, and as he spoke he imagined men calling them, arranging ten-pound meetings, while they came up with excuses to tell their wives.

The waiters wore lobster tails and prosthetic claws, which made it difficult to handle the slick, black trays.

Ginny was waiting for him at a table near a window, looking serene and regal. She scowled at the waiter as he attempted, time and again, to get their glasses upright and on the table.

The food was delicious; Corey opted for crab cakes and a mountain of the bottomless chips. Lulled by the security of a full belly, he found himself telling Ginny everything: his parents' financial troubles, being sent to the card-sharp school, living on the streets. The only thing he left out was the contents of the jam jar and how it had got there – the piece of ass he was going to keep close to his chest.

'You really have been through the wars, haven't you?' said Ginny.

Although apparently old, her skin was as smooth as a scampi's tail. She'd had a cigarette in her hand all the time he'd been eating. Now she lit it, thrusting puffs of smoke towards the sign that said smoking was not allowed.

'You've seen Ginny's Palace, of course,' she said, a proprietary gleam coming into her eyes. 'It may not look like much, but there's always things to be done. And I know a good worker when I see one. Just one thing.'

She leant across the table, leaving a trail of smoke behind her.

'You don't mind mermaids, do you? Some people have an aversion to them.'

Mermaid

Ginny's Palace sat between a shop that sold huge sausage rolls and a children's ball pit. Over the years every single one of the balls had been stolen, so now the pit was simply a square, walled hole in the ground.

But as it was free and sea-facing, and had a rickety old bench, parents still brought their children to play there, and while their offspring crawled amongst the detritus gathered within the pit – used condoms, sardine tins with sharp serrated edges, bits of seaweed, old rain-soaked editions of the town's newspaper, *The Crier*, with its stories of serial rapists, bus-shelter closures, raffles and coupons – the parents would stare desolately into the distance, taking in the seals and mudskippers out on the flats, over towards the domes of Saltburn-by-the-Sea's nuclear-power station, wondering what in life had brought them to this sorry place and how in hell they would ever escape.

Corey's job in the Palace was mainly to sit behind a bullet-proof square of plexiglass and hand out the change for the slots, the bright, flashing fruit machines with audacious names like The Ambassador, The Arcade Bomb, The Ship's Gantry, Tiger King, The Heart of Luxor, Zebedee's Delight. Ginny didn't like Corey to make up the 1ps and 2ps into ready towers totalling a pound or fifty pence; she said it looked more professional if he counted out the coins for each transaction there and then – and besides, making the punters wait created a queue, which in turn made the shop seem busy.

Each night Corey's fingers smelt of copper, tin and zinc, and he was haunted by dreams in which he slowly turned to metal. For the most part they were not nightmares, though – not like when he'd been at home and his mom and dad were arguing about his dad's antics at Consenting Adults, or when Corey'd been at the card-sharp school and was fearful he'd wake with a huge moustache drawn on his face. Here he slept well, in the basement of the slot machine arcade.

'It's only full of old crap,' Ginny had said on his first day; and, enlisting the help of several of the idle fishermen, the crab boats grounded due to inclement weather, Ginny had said that whoever cleared the most junk would get five minutes' free run on The Queen of Sheba and a pot of her best herbal tea.

The Queen of Sheba was the latest slot machine to arrive, and it had caused something of a stir, featuring as it did a life-size plexiglass model of the Sheban Queen herself sitting atop of it, her ruby lips glistening and her bosom swelling.

Some of the fishermen claimed she was the most beautiful woman they'd ever seen, and if they weren't already married…

'You can do with it what you like,' Ginny had said to Corey once the basement was cleared. 'A home's not a home until you've made it your own.' So on his first afternoon off Corey went out collecting, and returned some hours later with a box of discarded ships' lightbulbs scavenged from the bin outside Greb's Boat Chandlers, a voluminous pair of *Starsky and Hutch* swimming shorts, left bodiless on the beach, and many dozens of cockle shells, also from the beach, which he liked the shininess off, the feel in his hands.

His most treasured possession, though, remained the piece of Eli's ass.

He only had to lay his two palms around the jar that it swam within to find out what was rushing through the inner sanctum of Eli's mind:

That his father was disappointed with him after he got caught with his dick out behind the synagogue following his cousin Isaac's circumcision ceremony, as they compared battle scars; that he didn't want to attend the synagogue at all; that he thought the Rabbi was a doofus and that religion was a doofus too; that he didn't want to join his father's accountancy firm when he was older but wanted to be a writer; that he had recently read *Animal Farm* when they did it as a set text in English and he had loved it and that he had checked out *1984* from the school library and thought it even better than *Animal Farm* – actually he was *amazed* by it, the words, the language, the story; that he had read *1984* again and then again, and then had returned to the school library and hunted out other similar books – *Brave New World, I, Robot, The Sirens of Titan, Little Women* – which wasn't that similar, but he had cried when Beth died, and he had got an A on the English assignment written on it – *Little Women and Me!* – and when Kurt had found out about it, because the teacher had told him to stand up and read out his 'wonderful essay' to the whole class, Kurt had called him a *poofter* and he had lied and said he had copied it off Fat Ronald, and Kurt had laughed at this and said it was all right then, and then that after school Kurt had told him to set fire to the assignment and laughed when it went up in flames, and Eli had laughed too, but later that night in bed he had cried about it because he had been proud of that assignment; that he didn't know where he fit in any more in the world, although he also knew that it was easier to go through life just pretending that he did; and that when it came down to it life was one big fucking joke.

The post office not only sold stamps and all sizes of envelopes and Jiffy bags, but also pears in syrup, buckets and spades, vintage postcards with a view of the shoreline pre nuclear-power station, flip-flops of every colour and size, tiny bags of wipes to remove sand, bibles in twelve different languages, sunscreen in a variety of colours (lime green, tulip red, thunder-storm grey), racks of discounted VHS cassettes (every other one of which was *ET* or *Poltergeist*), individually wrapped grapes in cellophane, accompanied by a grape-related inspirational phrase – *Be the best grape you can be!, Best grape forward* – tiny wounded tin soldiers with a variety of backdrop dioramas that could be bought separately – Napoleon's invasion of Russia, the Charge of the Light Brigade, Crassus at the Battle of Carrhae, Meccano sets whose enclosed instructions detailed how to construct flea-pit motels, garages run by cowboys, seedy massage parlours with names like Hands On!, and Oil Yer Bits! – jars with built-in spider houses, colourful bleach blocks for domestic toilets, charity biscuits in support of three-legged children and other things like that.

Every Tuesday, on his day off from Ginny's Palace, Corey went to the post office and telegraphed eighty per cent of his wages to his mother and father. Afterwards he telephoned them from the same phone box he had called Ginny from.

Monte Carlo was a hoot, he would say – the sights, the sounds, you wouldn't believe! To add veracity to his ramblings, in the background he would play croupier noises he had prerecorded on a Memorex C60 cassette from the ancient Binatone cassette player Ginny had lent him along with a selection of cassettes (Jacques Brel, Charles Aznavour, Sacha Distel, Edith Piaf and so on).

Having no friends, after his visit to the post office, for the rest of his day off Corey would tag around town on his own. Sometimes he would go to the library and check out classic adventure stories – *The Riddle of the Sands*, *King Solomon's Mines*, *The Prisoner of Zenda* – and if the weather was clement he would take his book out to the mudflats, where he would read amongst the basking seals in the lee of the nuclear-power plant.

But if the weather was not clement, and these were his favourites days, he would go to the Saltburn Aquarium and stand with his nose pressed to the tanks as aquarium staff in embroidered wet-suits and painted aqualungs mimicked the graceful underwater movements of a porpoise, a manatee, a killer whale or smaller fish. Transfixed, Corey's heart beat with joy as whole shoals of clownfish, cichlids, gourami and tetras went gliding by.

It was remarkable.

The only other member of staff at Ginny's Palace, Peggy, was a mermaid. Each morning Peggy swam out to the rocks and regaled the fishermen with her siren song. She said that she was using her beauty and seductive voice to entice these sorry fools to fall impossibly in love with her, but all the fishermen knew her, as they were amongst Ginny's Palace's best customers, and were always telling her to leave off with her terrible singing.

The fisherman came in every afternoon when their boats were safely back in harbour and their catches had been put on ice and sold down at the fish market. Then they would turn their hard-earned one-pound notes into 1ps and 2ps and gamble their futures on the luck of the slots.

They were always dreaming of that one big win – one that would rescue them from a life of fishing – although as the biggest win to date had been the thirteen-pound jackpot on the Days of Thunder machine, Ginny exchanging the coins into one-pound notes, counting the notes through clenched teeth, money which Juris Jansons said he was going to use to buy his wife the hairdryer she had always wanted, but which he had gradually changed back into 1ps and 2ps over the following weeks and frittered away, who knew what they were really dreaming.

But that was gambling for you. It was an escape, and in a penny arcade nobody got hurt. Fortunes were neither lost nor made. And that is the best that can be said about anything.

When Peggy was on duty she worked behind the plexiglass while Corey did front of house.

He swept cigarette butts from the floor, wiped fingerprints off the front of the machines, intervened when any customer attempted an unauthorised rocking of the penny-drops.

Every two hours he would make a tour of the establishment with a tray around his neck, from which he sold light refreshments. These Ginny made herself in the back room: tiny herring roll-mops, paper bags of glistening winkles, along with a pin to extract them, and something of her own invention: seaweed wigs. Most of the men, she said, were bald, and in the advertisements she posted around the arcade she highlighted how a seaweed wig would heighten a man's attractiveness to women. As a kind of promotion she made Corey himself wear one, despite his protestations that it made him look like a *tool* and he didn't care for the smell of seaweed.

Despite this, he enjoyed working there. The only blot on his horizon was that he was sure Peggy was plucking up the courage to ask him out on a date. She was forever dropping hints about how they would be married one day, and how they would create other little people *just like themselves*. She was only waiting until he was eighteen and became a *real* man.

He hadn't the heart to tell her he *was* eighteen. He had celebrated the night in question on his own in the basement, his hands around the jam jar. As the images flashed through his mind he repeated softly, 'Oh Eli, Eli, Eli.'

Then, for the first time, 'I love you.'

Ginny must have intuited it, this official change from boy to man – or more likely found the eighteen candles Corey had fixed to oyster shells and then discarded in the garbage – because one morning she turned up with a large *I am 18* badge and a page ripped out of *The Town Crier* with that night's film times on it and suggested he finally ask the girl out.

What could he do?

Peggy read out the film's synopsis in the stage whisper she always adopted when she was being serious. 'Backward Steve – an inspirational story about a man who can only walk backward. Four stars.'

'It's part of a trilogy,' said Corey. 'I've seen *Forward Steve*, and I think the last one's going to be called *Stand Still Steve*. Actually, that one's more of a photograph.' He was joking but Peggy didn't laugh.

There had been a fire at Dave's Picture House the week before and, as over sixty per cent of the seats had been charred beyond appropriate seatage levels, they had to stand. During the interval Brian, the owner (Dave was long gone to Florida to work as the site manager of a crocodile attraction), walked along the aisles with an electric fan in each hand, attempting to disperse the residual smell of burning.

'Isn't it romantic,' said Peggy, squeezing Corey's upper shoulder, 'the film on the screen, the wind in our hair.'

She was wearing a quilted bodice and spectacular high heels so Jago Barnacle, the fisherman standing directly behind them, kept asking if she wouldn't mind crouching down a little.

Corey didn't find it romantic, although he did have a certain erotic relationship with picture houses. The plastic mac he always wore hadn't been found behind the cistern in the men's toilets as he told his mom; it had been given to him by a policeman called John Strange during a matinée screening of Bill Murray's *Stripes*, in return for Corey allowing John to roughly massage his inner thighs.

PC Strange had come to the school shortly after to give a talk on Stranger Danger, and pretended he didn't know who Corey was, although Corey had only just had to lie to his mom when she spied the finger marks on his legs.

But that was life.

After *Backward Steve* Corey and Peggy walked along the front, past the lobster café, past the shop which only sold enormous sausage rolls, past the children's ball pit, recently cleaned out by a group of green-jumpsuit-wearing volunteers, but full again already with rubbish. When they reached the pier they stopped.

In the last government's final round of public funding, the pier had been converted into light industrial units – a bottle-top factory, a moped-repair garage, a manufacturer of plastic gloves – but soon, thanks to economic conditions, all these businesses had folded, and the units remained forlorn and empty, windows caved in, walls daubed in graffiti (mostly huge dicks, which the fishermen said they could see from over a mile out, although Ginny always said fishermen were liable to exaggerate).

Under a broken street light, empty chip papers blowing past their feet, Peggy bent towards Corey – she towered over him in her heels – and said he could kiss her.

The only person Corey had ever kissed had been Eli. They had done it one night when Kurt was asleep, leaning across the open space between their bunks. Eli had told Corey he needed the practice, that there was a girl he loved back home. His mouth had tasted of the Lancashire hotpot they had had for dinner, and little bits of mashed lamb kidney had passed between their mouths.

It was funny how things could shine retrospectively.

Corey stuttered, said it wasn't Peggy, it was him. Then he bit the bullet.

The inspirational quote on the piece of toilet paper he had used that morning – he was rationing them – had quoted his father's favourite roll-on deodorant advertisement, *Be all the man you can be. Today and every day.* He wasn't going to get anywhere by lying.

'I like boys,' he said to Peggy. 'Or rather, men – you know what I mean.' He felt like a weight had been lifted.

Peggy took it better than expected. Nearly all the mermen were gay, apparently, or had leanings that way, which is why the merpeople were a dying species and why so many mermaids came up out of the sea. But she didn't resent them for it. That was just how they were. It was nature.

Corey and Peggy sat on the beach all night talking. He told her about all the other lies in his life: how he had run away from the Swiss Card Sharp Summer School after biting off a chunk of another boy's ass; how he had this piece of ass preserved in fluid he stole from a dead baby; how he could *read* the ass – the most intimate details of its former owner; how he had lied to his parents about graduating; how he had told them he was working as a card sharp in Monte Carlo; and how he had said to them he ate croissants for breakfast each morning, had an even tan and a French girlfriend called Fabienne who he was going to marry.

'You've got to come clean,' said Peggy. 'A life built on lies is no life at all. Believe me, I know.'

And as the seagulls were waking, as the seals and mudskippers were beginning their daily stretching out on the mudflats, Peggy marched Corey directly to the phone box on the front.

'They'll never be up at this hour,' Corey protested. 'Dad still keeps ¡¡¡Moustaches!!! hours and is never up before midday!' But the phone was answered on the second ring. He could hear the tears in his mom's voice right away.

'It's Evans,' she sobbed. 'The filthy money-grabbing bastard. We've got three weeks to come up with all the back rent we owe or we're out on the streets. Corey, darling, can't you steal some money from that casino of yours or something? We're relying on you to save us.'

The Sugar Plum Fairy

The first Corey knew of the circus was when, opening up Ginny's Palace one morning, he saw the flyer gummed to the outside of the window.

Stephen Blackpool's Circus
Elephants and Acrobats and Tumblers
Genuine Wild West Stage Show
The Fattest Man in the World
2 nites only
Concessions Available
Tickets on the door
All Welcome
No pets

Out on the mudflats was the tent, framed by the tumbling sea and the towers of the nuclear-power facility, and just for a moment Corey recalled his mother's fortune-telling tent, which had been similar, if not so grand.

The previous night Corey had tossed and turned on his truckle bed. Two weeks had passed and he'd yet to come up with a moneymaking plan.

Last time he'd spoken to his mom she'd said she was considering setting up a fortune-telling stand in the no-go area behind the train station where the gangsters and pimps hung out. And his dad was thinking of going back to Consenting Adults, which had opened up again (but underground now). Apparently it was thirty-per-cent-plus tips in the Jerkatorium! Corey said he didn't want to know what that was, but his mom said it was basically a huge beer barrel with slots in the side that guys could put their dicks through. 'And your dad would be right in the centre of it all!'

Even touching Eli's ass hadn't helped soothe his mind, because Eli wasn't in a good place himself. Last time he checked he was planning to run away to the Capital City, where he had heard young men of a certain disposition could get jobs on reality TV shows and build up huge followings of young women who would bank-transfer all their savings for a wink and promise of a walk along a moonlit beach. It sounded too good to be true, so probably wasn't.

'Maybe I can disguise myself, get a bludgeon from somewhere and steal the takings from the circus,' Corey mumbled, only half-aware he was speaking out loud.

'From a slot machine to a bandit,' came a voice from behind him. 'One small step!' Peggy was filling the Queen of Sheba, 1ps and 2ps cascading noisily down the metal chutes.

Friends now, she came and placed her arms around his waist.

'Or we could just *go* to the circus. Please. I've never seen an elephant.'

'Me neither,' said Corey, although this was another lie.

One summer, when he was five, his mother and father had broken into Colchester Zoo and enticed Merlin, their prize African forest elephant, out of his enclosure with two bags of peanuts and a boot on the end of a boat hook. His mom believed she could charge double, probably triple, giving fortunes off the back of an elephant. And she *had* been doing a roaring trade on the end of Clacton Pier until apprehended by the local police.

She was lucky to be let off with a caution, his dad always said. 'Not many people hijack an elephant and get away without a spell in the slammer, but that's your mom for you – she has the gift of the gab.' His eyes always went misty, and he ended, 'And that's one of the reasons I fell in love with her.'

By seven o'clock that evening the circus tent was full. Corey and Peggy were in prime seats, five rows back.

The elephant opening the show walked slowly around the ring swishing its tail while two slender children played a duet on a Hammond organ and sang an uplifting version of 'Pie Jesu'. Then there were clowns, then a trapeze artist.

Corey's favourite part of the evening was the acrobats. With their muscular, defined, bending bodies they made him think of Eli.

Earlier that afternoon, seeing the lack of sleep in his eyes, Ginny had told him to take sixty minutes, and he had gone down to his room and touched Eli's ass. He learnt that, not having run away yet, Eli had joined a secret ballet society; that he had heard that they met in a former snooker club and performed pirouettes on the green baizes, which were ripped and torn with age; that for his joining audition Eli wore his brother's cricket cup, his grandma's slippers stretched tightly over his huge feet and a tutu he had made by scrunching up bits of toilet paper and gluing them to a pair of his mother's butchered tights; that dressed like this he had thought he looked somehow magnificent, but when the other ballerinas had seen him – lithe young women with pointed narrow toes and hair in perfect buns – they had told him that he had joined the wrong sort of ballet club, and that he wouldn't be joining theirs; that having spent all his money on bus fares he had had to walk all the way across town to his home, pas de chat, pas de chat; that Kurt had driven past him in the old Ford Capri he had bought from the money he earned working nights at the abattoir; that Kurt had got some mates together and taken Eli down to the quarry and beaten him with sticks; that afterwards Eli had been found by a dog walker, who had called the paramedics, and Eli had been taken to hospital; that when he woke up the doctor had told him he had lost an eye; that the doctor had shown him the eye floating in a glass jar; that the eye had been skewered on the end of a stick; that one of the paramedics had found it and brought it to the hospital, said it was his if he wanted it, but he didn't; that the whole thing had been filmed and put on the Internet; that his dad had seen it; that his dad said that he was having no son of his parading around town in a *fucking pink tutu*; that he said that the tutu wasn't pink, but that wasn't the point; that his dad had gone mad and thrown him out; that Eli was homeless; that he had made his way to the Capital City, the place he had been intending to run away to anyway; that the cushy job on a reality TV show hadn't come to fruition – *who wants to look at some freak with one eye*; that Eli was living in a station toilet cubicle; that he was turning tricks to make a living; that some men liked to put their dicks in his empty eye socket; that to blank out the pain he had started injecting; that he wanted to forget everything; that life can really fuck you in the ass. And in the eye.

Towards the end of the evening the lights in the circus tent went out and came back on again and Stephen Blackpool, the ringmaster, was there, announcing that now they were going to see the Fattest Man in the World.

'A man so fat he will take your breath away. And then eat it. A man so fat you had better hold on to your seats, for the very ground will shake in his presence. A man so fat he eats an elephant every day for breakfast. A horse for lunch. A hippopotamus for dinner!'

Then the lights went out again.

Peggy nudged Corey in the side as the lights came back on, revealing there in the centre of the ring the fattest man in the world. He had a fat head on a fat neck, fat fingers and a fat nose. Fattest of all, though, was his fat globe of a stomach, which looked as big as a planet in the sky. But it was the hair sticking out at ninety degrees from his ears that made Corey sit up straight, lean forward.

He had seen that hair before. And it came to him – 'For you, very good price' – the encounter with the man on the train: the one who had the bum postcards of the French singers tacked to the inside of his jacket.

But how had he got so fat?

This question was answered almost immediately when the boy in the seat next to Corey – perspicacious, or maybe simply recalcitrant – leant forward and, picking up one of bows and arrows mistakenly left behind by the Genuine Wild West Stage Show, took aim and fired.

The arrow performed a perfect parabola through the air before embedding itself in the fat man's side.

For a second the fat man looked shocked, like he really had been shot, then he gave the arrow a double-take and that shock changed to panic. He grabbed at the arrow, but it was too late. The air was filled with a high pitched *faaarrrrrttttttiiiinnnnnggggg* sound as slowly, slowly, the fat man was revealed to be not so fat after all, but simply wearing a fat suit that was deflating.

Like everything else in the circus it had just been a show, a sleight of hand, a performance.

In the early hours of the morning Corey knocked on the door of the caravan where he knew the man was staying. He had hung around after the circus, watched the performers as they traipsed off to their respective lodgings. He wanted to ask something.

He banged on the door. 'Hello! Sir!'

He knocked again and called out, said he wasn't going anywhere, not this evening, not the next, and when the door finally opened he put his foot in the crack.

'If you were selling bum postcards,' he whispered, leaning into the gap, 'then there must be a market for them. Bums. Willies. Boobs. All that can't be shown in public. It's human nature. Tell me. Where do I go? I need money, and I need it quick.'

Corey told Ginny he needed forty-eight hours. She was decent about it, said he could take as long as he wanted, and then, motioning for him to wait, went behind the plexiglass and very deliberately counted out two pounds and fifty pence in 2ps.

'On top of your wages,' she said. 'That should get you somewhere.'

Checking his rucksack was firmly closed, that the jam jar was inside it, Corey set off towards the station.

Grapefruit Moon

Poulton-le-Fylde was a place that paid visible tribute to the gilt accoutrements of soulless commerce, branded monuments to men and women who lived and died on the exchange of a cold, hard buck.

Under multi-bulbed street lights, long turned off in other towns to save electricity, rattled jam-packed trams, overflowing horse-drawn omnibuses, the stretched limos of the fabulously wealthy, sleek, sporty town cars and the ubiquitous green-liveried taxis driven furiously by men sporting fabulous beards, cabbies so intent on the notion of making a living they pissed one-handed into Evans' Cola cans to avoid taking a break and therefore missing out on the next fare.

The pavements themselves were no less crowded, boardwalks of crushing desire filled with surging crowds of people who looked like they wished to be moving faster than they were, elbowing for position, sighing and stomping in their pursuit of movement, stopping abruptly and without due care, only to enter one of the many enticing doorways: steaming saunas with hot-sounding names like HEAT!, SWEAT!, BURN!, tanning shops, nail bars, fast-food restaurants, bookies, chandlers, haberdashers, pet stores, barrel makers, candle-sellers, card shops, bath and tap showrooms, funeral directors – Let Us Send Your Loved One on Their Next Journey – travel agents – Let Us Send You on Your Next Journey – and so on.

It was Evans' heartland, this, his alma mater, the place from which he sprang, and it was impossible to turn a corner, take a side street, without being confronted by large neon tubes spelling out his name.

EVANS' CARS, EVANS' TOYS, EVANS' PHARMACY. EVANS!

He was a man who indulged your every sin, and his own, and, so it was rumoured, bathed in sackfuls of gold coins and the milk of a thousand yaks.

Ginny had booked Corey a room at the Moon Hotel, where all the rooms, she said, were named after phases of the moon. His was Waning Gibbous, but still he was surprised to find the curtains, the bedspread, even the wallpaper adorned with the moon in this diminishing oval state.

He slept badly, every few minutes being disturbed by the elevated tram rattling past his window, by the calls of the call girls circling the street down below, by the drunken football songs sung by drunken yobs;

Evans United,
We're the dogs,
Evans United,
We're the dog's bollocks.

He took it from this that the team had won. Or lost. He wasn't exactly a football person.

Before retiring Corey had gone to the top floor of the hotel where the Moon Bar was situated.

The barman wore an old tired spacesuit, its elbows patched with Band-Aids, a rocket launch emblazoned across its chest. He greeted every single customer with the same wearily delivered line: 'This place, huh, got no atmosphere.'

Taking his drink Corey had gone over to the jukebox, where he flicked through the records – *Moon River, Moondance, Blue Moon, To the Moon and Back, Fly Me to the Moon, Bad Moon Rising, Man on the Moon, Walking on the Moon, New Moon on Monday* – before settling on *Grapefruit Moon* by Tom Waits, and then he had gone to the centre of the dance floor, where he put his arms out, imagined Eli within them, and slowly rotated alone until the song came to an end.

Having finished his breakfast (a moon-shaped poached egg served in a crater of toast), Corey went out into the street. There was one of the gaudy red tram stations right in front of him – EVANS' TRAMWAYS. 'Taking you there. And back!'

He purchased the ticket with a pang in his heart, the machine reminding him of one of upright machines he tended at Ginny's, and as he waited for the tram's arrival he thought of all the gifts he would bring for Ginny and Peggy on his return – a jar of pickled onions, a swan's feather, a bow tie.

In reality he did not know if he would be going back.

According to 'the fattest man in the world' Corey needed the Red Tramline in the direction of the far-north terminus, which meant he had to change twice. As he headed north the crowd thinned out, bodies disembarking at ever more abandoned-looking, desolate stations, until he was left with a nun curved over her book, a busker with a broken ukulele and a pregnant woman with a sign around her neck saying God Loves Propagation.

When he saw the sign for Acme Traction Machines (For All Your Traction Needs) he pressed the bell for the tram to stop and descended to the platform.

'Every Tuesday', the fattest man in the world had said, 'that's when the auctions take place. Don't be fooled. The sign is just a front. And ain't that a kick in the ass? Right in Evans' own heartland, these guys are meeting and doing their deals.'

The password he had written with a red biro on to Corey's outstretched palm, leaning over it in the same fashion Corey's mum had done when she was practicing her fortune telling.

Before he had left the caravan the fattest man in the world had given Corey a final warning. 'Watch your back. That's all I'm saying. These are serious bananas. So watch your back. And your ass. Your back and your ass. Watch them both. You hear me?'

Opposite to Acme Traction Machines was a café, Groucho's. As Corey entered a stout man in a leather tuxedo banged a gong and all the staff and customers turned towards the doorway.

'Entrée!' they all said together, and Corey was momentarily startled by the sea of identical faces, horn-rimmed glasses, bushy eyebrows, bulbous noses with luxuriant moustaches beneath them.

'It's one helluva day,' they chorused, before going back to whatever it was they were doing – drinking tea, making their way slowly towards a toilet, carrying drinks on a tray.

'Please,' said one of the staff members, a tall thin Groucho with a club foot, indicating a basket where the Groucho make-over sets lay, 'we're all Groucho here. Now, what can I get you? Today's special is duck soup.'

Corey took a table next to the window, the better to keep an eye on the factory entrance, ordered prawn toast, and by the time it arrived he had already spotted his first mark.

A shifty-looking man in a Homburg hat pulled down low over his eyes went sauntering past the factory once, twice, and then, on his third pass, exchanged words with a hefty guard sat in a security hut and disappeared inside.

Five minutes later, same kind of guy, same kind of hat. This one did five passes and walked with the assistance of an ivory cane designed for a much shorter person, but the set-up was identical.

Arrive. Password. In.

Corey called one of the Groucho staff over, paid his bill and went back out the door and crossed the road.

The security guard was wearing an ill-fitting suede cardigan, had a large mouse-shaped wart above his left eye. He didn't look up from the worn copy of *The Hound of the Baskervilles* he was engrossed in as Corey whispered the password. Turning a page, tongue sticking from the corner of his mouth, the guard pointed towards a doorway with a porthole window and a pink handle.

'Enjoy yourself, buddy, and spend wisely. No refunds. That's what I'm saying. My tip for the day.'

Inside the building it smelt of sweat, old bodies, urine and Artemis aftershave. Corey moved his rucksack from his back to his front, hugged it, looked around.

High, crumbling brick walls were painted green and covered here and there in black mould. There was a stage some distance away made from old planks of wood sat on tractor tyres. On the stage sat an extremely skinny man wearing vintage swimming goggles and a stovepipe hat.

'Is this the bum auction?' asked Corey of the fragrant smell-ing man in a lime-green jumpsuit standing next to him.

'Shhh,' whispered the man ferociously. 'They're about to start!' He moved away.

'Lot 56 is an impression of Rudolf Nureyev's derrière taken from a banquette in the upper stalls of the Kirov Theatre circa 1953. Who will start the bidding at 56p?'

The words boomed out around the cavernous room, and Corey thought there must be a microphone somewhere – there was no way such noise could come from such a slim man.

'40p!' shouted someone, and all the men, mostly shabby men in suits carrying calfskin briefcases, shifted forward, elbowing each other for position.

'Fifty-five,' shouted someone else.

'And we're off!' said the man on the stage.

After money had exchanged hands, the purchased object placed in the winner's calfskin briefcase, the next lot was wheeled on from stage left by another man in vintage swimming goggles and a stovepipe hat.

'A bit of a unique one, this,' said the auctioneer. 'A collection of Chinese Ming era pornography. Very rare. Twenty-six penis-shaped units. Let's start the bidding at five pounds. Now, who'll give me five pounds?'

Corey had seen enough. Excusing himself as made his way through the crowd, he went over to a door marked Toilets.

Inside was a long silver urinal, a row of wooden cubicles covered in stickers advertising long-retired end-of-pier comedians – *Little Johnny Ramsbottom, Greg Tooley and his Bugle, Jeff Finch – now he's a conundrum!* Corey locked himself in one of the cubicles, put down the seat, opened his rucksack and took out the jam jar.

Oh baby.

For one final time Corey closed his eyes, placed his hands around the glass, and with the same whoosh, the same sudden lurching, he saw everything:

That Eli had contracted gonorrhoea of the eye socket and that another man who had put his dick in the socket had caught the gonorrhoea and had come back and found Eli and taken him to an alleyway and beaten him with an iron bar; that Eli had been found by a young woman called Mavis who was on her way home from her shift at Burt's Wholesome Burgers; that

Mavis had come in the alleyway to pee, but when she found Eli she had helped him up and taken him home; that Mavis lived on the top floor of a tower block with her elderly mother; that her mother was Vietnamese and Mavis was half Vietnamese, the other half being an American soldier in Oregon or Michigan or some goddam place like that; that Mavis' mum was used to patching up the Viet Cong, and had seen worse wounds than this; that Jimmy Rabbit on the floor below sold knock-off penicillin; that they got Eli some penicillin for the gonorrhoea in his eye; that Eli broke down in front of such kindness; that he sobbed and sobbed; that he said he had seen too much and didn't know if he could carry on any more living in a toilet and selling his body; that Mavis said, because Dave, her colleague at Burt's Wholesome Burgers, had been nicking from the till and giving his mates free burgers, he was going to get canned and there was probably a job going if Eli wanted it; that Eli wanted it but thought he looked like a freakin' freak with his freaky eye; that Mavis and her mum made him an eyepatch out of an old pouffe cover that they didn't like anyway; that to make the eyepatch look trendy they stencilled an image of downtown Portland on it; that they had wanted to do New York but it didn't fit; that Mavis had said New York was a cliché anyway; that Matt Groening, Courtney Love and Gus Van Sant were all from Portland; that her dad might be from there too; that he might be a schmuck, that's what she thought; that Eli was nervous when he went to the interview with Burt, but Burt was really nice; that Burt drove a Harley Davison and had *Don't Mess With this Shit* tattooed on the backs of his hands, but he was a big soft bear with twin baby girls, Edith and Edna, and they were the apple of his eye – apples; that Eli got the job; that he really liked flipping burgers – he really flippin' liked it; that Mavis said after his first shift that he she would go with him to collect his stuff from the toilet cubicle where he had been living and he could stay with her and her mum until he got on his feet; that she said, Is that all your stuff? when he came out of the toilet cubicle with a single plastic bag; that he said he liked to travel light; that they had laughed; that he hadn't laughed in weeks; that he woke with a jerk on his first night staying in Mavis and her mother's apartment and, seeing that the stars were out, he had climbed off the sofa that was his bed and had gone quietly out of the apartment and up the stairs and on to the flat roof of the block and had looked out across the Capital City; that the lights twinkled like Christmas lights or the lights of the night fishing boats out on the sea in that town where he had studied at the Swiss Card Sharp Summer School; that he still remembered that night when he had leant across the bunks and made up a story about having to practice kissing a girl and he had kissed that strange boy Corey; that Corey was a man really; that Corey was big and strong and handsome; that Corey had beautiful eyes; that he liked Corey's plastic mac and his jumper with its Velcro straps; that it made him, Corey, look like a superhero – one who would one day save him; that he wondered where Corey was; that he wished Corey were with him here now; that they would dance together here in the moonlight; that his favourite song would be playing; that it was *Grapefruit Moon* by Tom Waits, with his beautiful gravelly voice.

In the cubicle Corey took out the knife he had borrowed from Peggy, the one she used to clean under her scales. Then he lowered his trousers and pants.

He had marked out the place on his buttock with a pen that morning in his room at the Moon Hotel.

It looked bigger in the harsh light of the toilet cubicle.

A pound of flesh. An eye for an eye. Early bird catches the worm!

'£10.21! £10.22!' Even in here he could hear the booming voice of the auctioneer. 'You've got to be in it to win it. There's no time like the present. Make your move!'

Clenching his teeth, bracing his feet against each side of the cubicle, Corey thrust the knife into his buttock and cut in a circle. He pushed the knife in and out, in and out, until there was a dull thud as the piece of flesh fell to the floor.

Then, lid off, *quickly, quickly*, he bent, retrieved the bloody lump, placed it into the jar, where it floated, sank, met Eli's piece of ass, formed a kind of ball.

Yin and yang. Two pieces of ass together.

Corey closed his eyes.

'£12.99!'

He could see it all. This time he didn't need to touch.

'£14.50!'

He would hand in his jar at the booth.

'£18.36. Teenage. Genuine. Buttocks. £23.15! With psychic potentiality. £27.12! In the right hands. LOT 86. A once-in-a-lifetime opportunity. £43.50!'

Corey placed a Band-Aid across his wound.

'£56.10! To own this piece. Pieces. £61.20!'

He wrapped a bandage over the plaster.

'£68.20! Star-crossed lovers. £72.01!'

Around and around himself.

'£75! In a specimen jar. £81.60!'

Pulled up his pants. Jeans.

'£85.03! That formerly held jam. £92.86!'

Buckled his belt.

'£93.86! Let's start the bidding at… £100!'

A gasp from the crowd.

'£105. Do we have…? £120!'

A shuffling of feet. A press of bodies. Move close. Move closer.

'£240. Did I hear…? £270!'

And so much pain. So much bleeding. Seeping through the bandage. Is it worth…?

'£320!'

And he would take this money. Oh yes!

'£380.'

Gladly.

'£450!'

Willingly.

'£520!'

Pockets bulging he would sit, or stand, on the train.

'£580!'

Walk from the station. Run the last bit… Home.

'£640'

'Mom! Dad!'

'£730!'

How much is that rent?

'£830!'

Tears of joy. Bundles of money. Pounds and pounds.

'£980!'

'We've got plenty left over. '

'£1050!'

'Let's tell Evans to shove it up his…'

'£1500!'

'But there's something I've got to tell you.' He can't hold it in.

'£1700!'

'There's a boy – a man – I love. There it is!'

'£2109!'

'And he's waiting for me on a rooftop. Dancing to *Grapefruit Moon*.'

'£2300!'

'So go to him, darling!' (His mom.)

'£2700!'

'Go…' (His dad.)

'£3100!'

'…To…'

'£3500!'

'HIM!'

'£4200!'

'Because you can't put a price on love.' (His mom, putting her arm around his dad, smiling.)

'£4500. Going once.'

And so he goes.

'£4500. Going twice.'
And so he goes.
'£4500. Going three times.'
And he's gone.
'SOLD!'
Bowled over. In the clover.
'To that man there.'
Me.

Yes me.

And this is the story I was telling you – the story about how I got this jam jar in an auction. About how when I put my hands around it there was this whole other story inside. This story, the one I've been telling you. The saddest tale you've ever heard.

Only it isn't. Even now I only have to put my hands around the jar and I see it – them, these lovers, these happy lovers – dancing for ever under that grapefruit moon, and the whole world seems well... you know, you've read it...

Better.

STICK OF ROCK

Buggers

' I 've got buggers in my rock.'

The man, face angry like that of the red leaf monkey Harry had once seen in a documentary on wildlife and foliage devastation in eastern Borneo, had entered the shop forcefully, clattering the bell above the door in an alarming manner. Harry, reassuring himself with the realisation that the anger must have issued from another source, not him or his shop, Delicious Gifts, smiled and placed his hands reassuringly on the counter.

Harry thought himself a good judge of people. Before becoming a shopkeeper, in his distant youth, he had taken a series of psychology courses in a bleak northern European university, where he had attempted, and failed, to sleep with a number of slim women with bowl haircuts and thick black glasses. Mary, Harry's eventual wife, was dismissive of such esoteric matters as psychology. Her passion was not the mind but knitting. A customer to her was a customer, and she treated everyone the same, except for sizing them up, wondering how many balls of wool it would take to make them a decent Aran sweater, a pair of gloves, a snugly fitting willy warmer.

Having now reached the counter the angry man slammed his stick of rock down, breaking it into pieces, several of which he began waving around like Animal with his drumsticks. After Scooter, Beaker and Bunsen Honeydew, Animal was Harry's son's favourite Muppet, along with all the other members of the show's house band, Dr Teeth and the Electric Mayhem.

'Bugger. Bugger. Bugger. I've got all these buggers running right through my rock.'

Harry, reminded of the old joke about the fly in the soup, wanted to say to the man that he should stop going on about his buggers because then everyone would want some, but restrained himself and said simply instead that it was his wife who usually dealt with complaints, and she wouldn't be in until 7 p.m. He should come back then.

It was only after the man had gone that Harry picked up two of the pieces of rock the man had left on the counter. The public ends were all in order – 'Ginny's Arcade' clearly written there, the letters pink and jagged against the white, this particular rock having been made to advertise another of the local businesses. But on the broken inner ends, in the same pink lettering, was the word 'bugger'.

'Bugger,' said Harry.

He lifted the counter flap and went out on to the shop floor. He prided himself on knowing every item in the shop and its exact price to the nearest penny: a pair of lambswool socks (89p); a snow globe depicting Dr Frankenstein's dash across the ice (56p); a seal's paw key ring (15p); twenty sheets of Saltburn embossed writing paper (32p); a miniature plastic bucket and matching spade (6p); ninety-six custard-flavoured condoms (sold individually, 5p each); a signed and laminated photograph of Bob Monkhouse (looking slightly startled, taken when he came to open the Foetus Museum, 99p); the fossilised wing of a seagull (12p); itching powder (33p); twenty-eight willy warmers, each with a popular name knitted into them – Andrew, Paul, Royston and so on – Mary made these and, if given two hours' notice, could run them up to order (85p off the shelf, 96p bespoke); a pack of seven postcards featuring (1) the nuclear-power station, (2) the beach on a stormy day, (3) Ginny's Arcade, the Foetus Museum and the Saltburn Aquarium in three windows, the fourth window declaiming *Welcome to Saltburn!*, (4) Harry and Mary themselves, standing outside Delicious Gifts with their arms around each other, smiling a little tensely at the camera (their son Sven had just told them he wanted to be a soldier and to go off to fight in wars, but the photographer had been booked and it was too late to back out now), (5) two seals apparently kissing, (6) an aerial view of Saltburn taken at night, unfortunately on the night of the power cut, so it was impossible to make out anything except tiny plumes which, it was discovered later, were from some boys on the hill engaging in a fart-lighting competition, (7) the Saltburn Pier before it had been blown away in a storm (70p); a King Kong baseball cap (88p); a pair of sunglasses, the arms of which were lime-green crocodiles (50p); an old hardback copy of *Swallows and Amazons* (£1.50); a Michael Jackson backscratcher (99p); a yellowing paperback copy of Hammond Innes' *The Lonely Skier* (£1.25); a green towel (£2); a rattan beach mat (£2); an inflatable rubber ring (£2); a thermal cover for a regular cup (43p); an inflatable beach ball (£1.25); a travel-size bottle of factor-twenty-five suncream (£5); a doll whose eyes opened when she was sitting up, closed when she was lying down (£1.05); a nose-hair plucker (22p); a silver teaspoon with the town's crest at the end of its handle (£3.12); a Kenny Everett rubber (4p); a box of fifty fun snaps (99p); camel-print flip-flops (77p); toenail clippers with the name of the town stamped on them (48p); a pink thong (£1.12); a seven-inch single of the Human League's *Electric Dreams* (£2); eyeliner, hair glitter, rouge, twenty different shades of red lipstick, eyebrow pencil (75p each); a Tiny Tots toolkit (64p); a tin of corned beef hash (65p); a head the size of a golf ball fixed to a small plug which you could put up your bum to make it look as if a person was crawling out of your anus (£2.50); a pair of feet attached to a plug, etc., etc., the reverse of the aforementioned (£2 – the price less as the coming-out version was more desirable than the going-in); a Painting With Nancy watercolour set (23p); a small triangular flag of the United Arab

Emirates on a plastic stick (15p); a jigsaw of the nuclear-power plant (500pcs, £2.01); a red penknife (45p); a black biro (8p); a red biro (8p); a blue biro (8p); a green biro (10p); an itsy-bitsy lime-green polka-dot bikini (£1.67); a blue bikini with a padded bra (£2.50); a yellow beach umbrella (£2.22); an inflatable dingy with optional pump (£25 without, £26.25 with); a set of body paints (79p); a plastic flower with hair grip (12p); various sticks of rock, over 300 in total (25p each or five for £1).

Harry stopped by the rock display, picked one up after another. They all seemed in order. But still... Picking one up at random, he broke it in two.

'Saltburn-by-the-Sea' on the outside, and there on the inside, 'Saltburn-by-the-Sea.' Nothing to worry about.

Noticing the time, Harry flicked the sign hanging on the inside of the door from 'Open' to 'Closed for a moment' and went outside.

There was a seal on the promenade, barking angrily. Two seal volunteers, in the navy-blue jumpsuits the volunteers wore to identify each other, were standing with bright red and blue paddles trying to encourage the seal back towards the sea. The paddles had been donated by Saltburn Airport after it had gone into administration. Evans, the industrialist from over in Poulton-le-Fylde, had purchased it at a knockdown price, and much to the chagrin of the town, and had turned the runway into an exclusive overpriced golf course, the conning tower into a set of luxury apartments.

At the bank as Harry stood in the queue with his two five-pound notes, ready to swap them for bags of 1ps and 2ps (due to the pricing structure the shop seemed to get through an awful lot of change), when he felt a tug on his arm.

Duncan from the canning factory was there, smelling strongly of potted meat. Across his forehead was an impression of letters – E V A N S – still visible from the time he had fallen into the stamping machine; most strangers, and even his friends and family, called Duncan E V A N S, pausing dramatically between each letter.

Duncan was dressed in an old purple ski jacket, faded green John Amaechi basketball shoes and a pair of Pirelli jogging bottoms, on which the waist elastic had snapped, so he always had at least one hand in a pocket to hold them up. There was a meerschaum protruding from his lips, unlit.

'Day off, is it?' asked Harry brightly.

'My wife,' said Duncan. 'Any news?'

'I'll meet you at the seal,' said Harry, under his breath. '7.15 p.m. I'd rather not do it here.'

Several months previously Harry had put a card up in the window of Rose's Roadside Café: 'Gumshoe for hire'. He had bought himself a burner phone and put the number on the card under 'Reasonable rates. No job too big'.

Mary was in the dark about his gumshoe business; although she had her willy-warmer sideline she was averse to them taking on any extra work. Not that there had been much extra work. Duncan was his first big case. Missing wife. Where was she? That was the question.

Having collected his change Harry was making his way back to the shop when he became aware of a loud banging, the cause of which soon became apparent.

Standing at the door of his shop was a muscular youth with lips pulled fiercely back from a set of jaunty gold teeth. From the hand not involved in the banging of the door protruded two broken ends of a stick of rock.

'Not another bugger?' asked Harry apologetically, jogging up.

'It was a present for my girlfriend,' said the muscular youth, before letting rip with a real haymaker.

When Harry came around on the pavement, his left eye throbbing – he was going to have a proper shiner there – with his good eye he saw the two broken non-public ends of the rock staring back at him.

'Slag', they said.

The mystery deepened.

Wanker

Duncan was early. As Harry came up he jumped from the pedestal of the seal statue and pulled from his pocket a dozen tins of potted meat. 'Not here,' hissed Harry, and pointed down the alley by Chippy Chips.

Duncan's wife had gone missing the previous week. She had gone out to work as normal and never come back. Harry had already checked out the Saltburn hospital, gone door to door along the front where all the B&Bs were, holding up a picture of Duncan's wife, asking if any mysterious new guests had checked in, and had even scoured the beach, looking for a body – body parts, even; a hat. Duncan's wife Mo was famous for her hats – extremely tall, or wide, shipped in on a monthly basis from a hatters in Poulton-le-Fylde.

Harry was serious about the body. Mo, famously small, appearing as orphan Annie for a record fifteen years in a row in the Saltburn Players' annual Christmas production of *Annie: The Panto*, was a prime target for the seals.

Sometimes seals took lone children, dragging them far out to the mudflats, playing with them before slowly eating them alive. There would be a fuss for a while, brawny men, their blood up, going out to cull seals under a full moon. Then people would forget, and everything would go back to normal.

'So have you found her?' asked Duncan plaintively.

'I want you to walk me through the scene of the crime,' Harry said, scratching his forehead thoughtfully – a tic he had picked up from watching reruns of *Van der Valk* over and over on VHS. 'A reconstruction, so to speak.'

Mo had sold ice-creams and balloons from a cart Duncan built out of old meat tins. It was still there on the front, but the police had put tape around it. The ice-cream, melted, was giving off a meaty smell. The balloons, helium expended, were lying flat on the ground, their strings still attached. It looked like a place where a clown might have been murdered.

'I suppose you've asked in Ginny's Palace?' Harry asked, nodding towards the door just visible at the end of the alleyway, half open, from which drifted the sounds of Michael Jackson's 'Thriller' and coins falling into slots.

'I have.' Duncan took out his meerschaum and fingered the zip of his old purple ski jacket sadly. 'Nobody saw anything. You know what it's like. People are busy nowadays. Busy or sad. Both of which kind of blind you. Except when you're at home. When you're in your own home, that's when people want to watch you. Like that TV show that's all the rage – *Big Brother's Brother's Brother*. Answer the questionnaire, be anatomically pleasing to a trial studio audience and they'll fix up a series of cameras in your house and put you on the show. Woohoo! Here I am boiling an egg! We've developed a kind of inverted privacy. And me and Mo should know, living where we do.'

Duncan and Mo lived in the Panopticon, a social housing experiment designed by an architect from the Capital City, built in three short months on the front where the old container docks had been. Although it was a spectacular eyesore, shaped like a cock and balls dropped from a great height, the locals liked to say, it had won several awards. There were fifty flats in the block, situated at such an angle that all the flats overlooked every other flat and nobody had a sea view. The architect had famously said, 'The sea is our mistress, not our master. I wanted to reflect that.'

In the first year six of the residents had committed suicide, eight had discovered voyeurism and ten exhibitionism.

'One morning,' said Duncan, 'while I was eating my corn-flakes I saw one grown man doing something unrepeatable to another. The one doing the doing saw me looking and shouted out if I wanted to meet him for a pint down the Jolly Fisherman later. There's communal living and there's communal living.'

Duncan took out a folded-up photo from his pocket, unfolded it, let out a sob. In the picture he and Mo were standing in front of the canning factory. Or Mo was standing, Duncan was down on one knee, proposing. In the background was Evans, the industrialist and owner of the factory. He was looking at his watch, and even in the picture you could hear him tutting.

'I miss her,' Duncan said. 'Please bring her back to me.'

Having found nothing at the scene of the crime, Harry asked if it was OK if he searched the flat.

'There might be something you've missed. You never know.'

While Harry was doing his search Duncan put on an LP, Serge Gainsbourg and Brigitte Bardot's 'Bonnie and Clyde'. He said it reminded him of Mo. Serge Gainsbourg and Brigitte Bardot were her heroes.

All the flats in the Panopticon were the same – one room with a bed on pulleys that could be let down from the ceiling at night. For those with children there were trundle beds that slid out from the baseboards of the kitchen units, two in each apartment. If you had more than two children they had to double up. Some of the flats had two adults and four teenagers all in the one room.

Duncan shook his head, watching as Harry pulled out first one of the trundles and then the other.

'Me and Mo could never have children. That's why she had her hats – something to love, take care of, nurture. I don't think she's run off. Look.'

From a stand in the corner of the room Duncan lifted a hat. It was in the shape of a miniature Eiffel Tower, and it had a bust of every President of the Fifth Republic affixed to it.

'She was going to show this at next week's Boosbeck Hat and Fascinator Fete. She couldn't wait.'

Harry was getting up from his knees, having checked under a jaunty occasional table holding Duncan's long-service award from the canning factory, when he noticed something long and pink sticking out from the bedstead above his head.

'What is it?' asked Duncan, noticing Harry's face going pale.

Harry reached up and pulled out the thing. It was as a feared: a stick of rock.

Without saying anything he broke it across his knee, and there it was in the middle. Plain as day.

'Wanker.'

Cunt

The old lighthouse had been converted into a barracks for Saltburn's army cadets.

Harry nodded to two of them as he strode past. They were sitting outside playing cards on a paste table and smoking, the ashtray on the table overflowing with spent butts, and the scene made him think of his own son fighting in a war somewhere.

All Sven's postcards ever said was that he was getting on OK; the men in his unit were treating him well, but it was hot as all holy blazes. He always ended his postcards with, ironically, 'Wish you were here,' and an exhortation, 'Please don't worry about me.' But Harry did worry. He'd read about wars in history books – young men been sent off to kill folk. It used to be about who got to put a crown on their head, then who had rights over this bunch of people or land, but more lately it was difficult to work out what it was all about. What Harry thought was, wait long enough and the problems would sort themselves out in the end. Take this missing wife: she would probably turn up. And if she didn't turn up, well, he would get paid anyway, and Duncan would find himself a new wife.

As well as working at the canning factory Duncan was employed by a company that made humane rodent management videos. The one about wood-mice infestations had gone viral after Duncan had mistakenly taken both hands from his pockets and his Pirelli joggers had descended to his ankles. In the following weeks at least two women and one man had tracked Duncan down, probably thanks to the stamp on his forehead, and asked him to elope with them to Leeds.

So Duncan would marry again, and when he did die, finally, this new wife, or husband, would visit the grave, drop flowers, cry a bit, until they in turn found a new husband or wife, and so it would go on.

That was life.

Having a son living away, a wife he hardly saw, thanks to them working opposing twelve-hour shifts, Harry had become cynical. Existence wore you down.

Past the lighthouse was the old industrial estate. Most of the units were abandoned. Some had been taken over by seals, others used by local teenagers as hangouts, each gang, or group of youths, plastering the walls with posters which signified their allegiances – to Jacques Brel, or Patti Smith, or Kurt Weill, or Robert Mapplethorpe. This last, Mapplethorpe, a New York photographer, was Sven's favourite, his images plastered all over his bedroom walls. *Please God let him be OK,* thought Harry. Not that he believed in God. God was as much of a nonsense as war. Probably more, because God was often a reason for war.

The last of the units had a railway sleeper outside its open door, a sign propped against the sleeper, 'Stick of Rock' spelt out in a circle like the letters that appeared inside the sweets. The owner, Ronald, was sitting there listening to Maurice Chevalier quietly playing on an old phonograph, the scratch of the needle almost as loud as the record itself.

Ronald was used to visitors coming to see how the rock was made – groups of Japanese tourists all in the same little hats, or lads on stag dos, putting the sticks between their legs and waving them around like penises. But Harry was more than a visitor. Harry was one of Ronald's best clients. Delicious Gifts sold upwards of five thousand sticks of rock a year, and at 25p a stick, five for £1, that was no small bananas.

'All right, mate,' said Ronald lifting himself up, holding out a hand. He could see Harry looked troubled.

'I've had some buggers,' said Harry. 'A slag and a few random wankers. All in my rocks. I've come to check on the production. If that's OK?'

Roland's unit had low ceilings, except for its associated tower, where the rock was stretched. That was what most of the visitors came to see. It was quite a spectacle.

Ronald made Harry put on a badge – JUST VISITING – for health and safety reasons, and sat him in front of the educational video running on a loop in the visitor centre, a couple of dozen orange plastic chairs in front of a Binatone black and white TV.

Harry sat watching the grainy images. Men in white suits stretching the boiled sweet on a kind of loom. In the background an orchestra was playing. Sun came through the window at an angle. It all looked very wholesome. Not the sort of environment where an expletive would feel at home. But you couldn't be sure.

When it came to the crucial part, how the lettering was made, Harry leant forward, squinting his eyes, and watched intently as thin strips of white and red sweet stuff were cut to length by nimble fingers and fitted together one by one so the visible ends formed a letter.

Harry thought of the pieces of rock lying as evidence under the counter of Delicious Gifts, a sly 'bugger' beaming out from each side.

'You haven't had any other complaints, have you?' he shouted over to Ronald.

'It's an age-old process,' shouted back Ronald. 'You've heard of the rock of ages? That's us. My father made rock. My father's father made rock. It's in our blood. We don't make errors.'

Once all the individual letters were formed they were assembled into a single stick and wrapped around a huge central slab of white sweet. The whole thing, according to the voiceover on the video, done by Gloria Wingbottom, former star of Cakes of Yore, a show in which she replicated cakes from throughout history (cancelled when she did her infamous 'Neolithic Man' episode – basically bugs and twigs – after which two viewers died choking on a twig), weighed two hundred hundredweight and was three foot six inches thick.

'I'll show you the next bit in person,' said Ronald, coming over and standing in front of the TV. 'It's the best bit. The stretching.'

Ronald turned the sound down on the TV and handed Harry a postcard of the Queen of Sweden posing with a group of white-suited workers outside the front of the unit. In a promotional stunt the Queen of Sweden had a stick of rock horizontally fitted through the tall bun of her hair.

'If you've got any doubts about the quality of work, as you can see for yourself, we've got royal approval.'

Ronald led Harry through the unit to the tower. Harry had been here before, but it amazed him every time. Looking up the length of the tower was like looking along a tunnel. It seemed to go on and on for ever, a tiny patch of light at the end.

'If it was down to me,' said Ronald, 'I'd make this tower one of the wonders of the world. I'd take it over the Colossus of Rhodes any day.'

On the tower's floor was a huge stick of rock, like the one from the video. It had a chain wrapped around one end. The other end of the chain went up into the tower, looped over a pulley, before hanging back down.

Ronald made a signal and a group of five or six white-suited workers grabbed the dangling end of the chain and pulled and pulled, lifting the end of the rock attached to the chain higher and higher into the tower while the rock itself stretched and stretched.

'That's the miracle of rock,' said Ronald. 'From one big lump to one hundred and eighty yards of succulent sweet which can be cut into nine hundred and sixty six-inch sticks not much wider than a walking stick.'

He turned to Harry grinning, obviously pleased with the show. 'There's no room for messing here. Our rock is solid. Rock solid.'

Harry was sitting outside with Ronald, listening to Maurice Chevalier sing 'I Remember it Well' when a green van, spanking new, hubcaps shiny enough to see your face in, pulled up.

A sombre-looking man with a flat nose and eyes too far away from each other for common decency got out, opened up the back of the van and stood with his arms folded. He scowled, lips a line of discontent, while the same five or six white-suited workers from the unit loaded the newly made rock into the back.

'Who's he?' asked Harry after he'd gone.

'Don't you recognise him?' said Ronald. 'He's brought the last couple of batches of rock to your shop. He's our new delivery driver.'

Ronald stood up and put a hand up to shield his eyes as he watched the van disappear into the distance.

'Hard worker. But a strange bloke. He's from Poulton-le-Fylde.'

'Cunt,' said Harry, suddenly seeing the whole thing.

Arsehole

A hard rain was falling and Harry had to fight his way through the umbrella sellers gathered outside the station. The sellers all had their umbrellas up, lashed together, the better to show off their wares – even after two sellers had been caught up during Storm Treena and carried away. One had fallen into the North Sea, and had been rescued by prawn fishermen, slightly cold but otherwise uninjured. The other, not so lucky, had landed on the deck of a Russian trawler, actually a spy ship, and having been drugged and indoctrinated, was now an assassin-to-order for a rogue section of the former KGB. She was known as the Wheelchair Killer. Landing on the deck of that ship, she had irrevocably smashed both ankles.

After several near misses, and a couple of actual umbrella strikes, Harry made the station concourse. He spied the delivery driver right away, standing in line at the ticket kiosk, his lips in an O now, apparently innocently whistling.

Harry had followed the driver from Stick of Rock to the Top Rock Emporium, to Dave's Picture House, to Terry's Videos. This pursuit hadn't been easy, as Harry had been on foot, the driver in his van, and it gave, Harry supposed, plenty of opportunities for the driver to swap the 'decent' rock for ones filled with bad words.

Tit-Wank. Knob-End. Bum-Fucker.

Harry had broken and examined the sticks he had purchased from each of the establishments as soon as the driver left.

Checking these sticks were still safe in his pocket after his jostling outside the station – they were evidence, after all – Harry took up position in the queue behind the driver. Close up he smelt of anchovies and cream cheese, a slightly off-note baguette. He was skinny, but his bright-blue jacket had huge shoulder pads sewn into it and an acutely tapered back, so from behind it looked like an upside-down triangle pointing to his behind.

'Arsehole,' mumbled Harry.

'Excuse me?' said the train-station employee behind the glass window of the ticket office.

Without realising it Harry had reached the front of the queue.

'Blue jacket,' he said. 'Where's he off to?'

'Poulton,' replied the ticket seller. 'But if it's Poulton you want you're going to have to run. The train's about to leave.'

The train had a single carriage, and despite it being almost full Harry managed to get a seat behind his quarry. The rest of the seats were taken by a group of lads each wearing the same livid-pink T-shirt, the words 'Larry's Stags' blazoned across them.

As the train pulled out of the station one of the lads gave out love-heart Deely bobbers, then they all broke into a rendition of

Black Lace's 'Agadoo', standing to do the moves that went with the song.

At the next station a doctor got on. His scrubs had a number of banjos and other stringed instruments hanging from it. The doctor's face was pinched, his white coat spotted with blood. He had the appearance of a man beaten down – one who hasn't slept, who has witnessed terrible humbling things and now just wants to get home for his tea – but as the train pulled off he went along the carriage trying to sell his instruments. The dedication!

Two of the stags bought a banjo each and one a miniature harpsichord. When he reached the end of the train the driver looked at him from over his glasses and told him to piss off.

'So he's not a supporter of our National Health Service,' thought Harry. 'That's the kind of guy he is.' And he took out his notebook and made a number of detailed notes.

Harry had come to Poulton with Mary for their honeymoon thirty years before. They had stayed at the Ritz, marvelling at its onion-shaped domes, its intricate metal railings, how all the rooms had a sea view at some point during the day, thanks to the hotel rotating slowly (more quickly if you fed one-pound notes into the designated slot – which meant when someone fabulously rich was staying, the hotel spun as quickly as a merry-go-round).

Harry and Mary's personal waiter, Edmundo, recently arrived from the town of Tarapoto in Peru, had slept on a trestle table in a tiny annex, and at opportune moments had appeared to spray them with a refreshing perfume. Each morning he had removed the pith from their breakfast grapefruit and, as a matter of delicacy, gone for a brisk refreshing walk when they had wanted to make love. Which was often.

'Those were the days,' thought Harry.

But since those days Poulton-le-Fylde had become what the Reverend John James, leader of Saltburn-by-the-Sea's ecclesiastical community, had referred to in *The Town Crier* as a 'modern-day Xanadu of iniquity'. What once was elegant and suave was now both brash and seedy, a sinkhole of sleaze for any ready money.

Harry followed the driver out of Sir Christopher Wren's magnificent station, its concourse filled with potted meat sellers, carts containing live crabs, oysters, mussels, prawns, lobsters, crayfish. There were even seal pups, tethered, available for purchase, their faces upturned and crying for their mothers.

Outside the station the surrounding canals were packed with party barges, their decks thronging with bare-chested young men, tattooed and muscular, trying to woo huge Botox-lipped women with eyelashes so long they had supporting cables affixed to their foreheads so in profile they resembled tiny suspension bridges.

Harry followed the driver across elevated walkways, down underpasses and into the town centre.

Here a group of elegantly dressed youths sat smoking cheroots in the window of a Kinko's. Xeroxing was in fashion in Poulton, a cult. Andy Warhol, their god and guru, had been right: art is simple mass production; and so the youths made copy after copy of their faces, mailed them to acquaintances, performed daring guerrilla skirmishes and took over billboards, advertising nothing but themselves, the big I Am.

After the Kinko's came sardine shops, an oyster bar, a place where you could have thin cords attached between you and a loved one. A line had formed outside a peep show, the elderly performers leering suggestively from posters outside. A sign for a bowling alley promised heavily permed women performing karaoke on roller skates; another showed a very large man with an erotic novel tattooed in tiny letters across his upper back on slender stilts serving shots from the holes of the bowling balls. At the Tunnel Club you could put your eyes to a pair of binoculars and watch a series of women performing the cancan in the distance. Lost homeless boys sold donuts outside the orphanage, and at a club with a sign depicting a single large enamel tub you were served drinks while fully immersed in water. Here also were human candleholders, their bodies painted the colour of dolphins.

As they reached the badly lit car park of a tall building displaying 'The Atrocity Exhibition' in neon letters above its doorway, a sweaty overweight barker outside this door shouting over and over, 'Live autopsies performed here daily!' the driver stopped and lit a cigarette. He looked up and down the street, glanced at his watch, tapped the glass impatiently.

Crouching in an adjacent alleyway, Harry waited. It was just five or ten minutes later that the driver was joined by one man, then another, and another. Each was dressed in the same kind of jacket – triangular, blue, tapered to a point, pointing to the behinds. It was a uniform.

As Harry spied a fifth and a six man – same uniform – approaching from his side of the street this time, he ducked further back into the alleyway, worried that he would be seen. When he resurfaced the triangles had gone.

'Oh blast,' he cursed. 'Now you've done it! Just when you had them in the palm of your hand.'

Then he spotted them ascending a hill in the distance, heading towards a building the size and shape of a fortress, its crenellated towers lit by forks of lighting, large Hollywood-style letters jutting from its roof clearly visible against the night sky, spelling out a single word: 'EVANS'.

A storm was gathering.

Bum-sucking Son of a Bitch

Harry stood outside the high perimeter fence. He had watched the men enter through a gate, greet the guard there with a nod, disappear inside the building via a large wooden door. Once everyone was inside the guard had released two growling Alsatians, which set off at a run around the side of the building.

Moving a safe distance from the guarded gate, Harry activated the timer function on his Casio digital watch (£5.99, or £8.99 with a built-in calculator). It was twelve minutes before the dogs reappeared. Then another twelve minutes after that.

Waiting until the dogs began their third loop, Harry hauled himself over the fence and landed with a thump on the other side. As a young man he had been Saltburn's monkey-frame champion three years in a row. His favourite superhero being Spider-Man, he had collected spiders in a matchbox, releasing them into his bed at night in the hope that they would bite him and he would wake with special powers. He only stopped this practice when he was twenty-three and he met Mary.

'It's the spiders or me,' she had said.

Of course, he chose her.

An single oblong of light spilt from a window in the side of the building. Channelling his inner Spider-Man, thinking himself that seventeen-year-old boy again, full of hope and dreams for the future, before they had been beaten out of him by the cold, hard realities of life, Harry sidled up to the window and pressed his nose against it.

The scene before him was like the one he had seen in the rock-making room at Stick of Rock, only on a much bigger scale. The vat where the sweet was boiled resembled an Olympic swimming pool, and the table where the letters were formed was medieval in size and length and had at least fifty women lined up on each side. Harry was horrified to see the women were shackled at the feet, a thick metal ring on each ankle, connected to the woman on each side with a heavy-looking chain. Standing guard, each holding a bludgeon, were more of the triangular-blue-jacketed men.

Harry was about to pull away – the dogs would be back any minute – when there was a kerfuffle at the far end of the table and a stick of rock was knocked to the ground. As the woman bent to retrieve it, Harry caught a good look of the woman's face.

He would know it anywhere. She was always coming into the shop to stock up on Painting With Nancy watercolour sets (23p), red penknives (45p) or sets of the postcards (70p), which she used to write to her childhood pen pal Birgit in Malmo.

It was Mo. Duncan's wife.

The following morning at seven o'clock, when Harry went downstairs to take over from Mary, she said he looked tired. She looked tired too. It was a tiring life.

'To earn some extra money,' she said, 'I've been sewing turnips into men's trousers. I'm going to sell them – £2.15 a pair. I heard down at the market that turnips are going to be all the rage this year.'

'It's "turn-ups",' Harry started to say, but didn't have the heart to disillusion her.

'And look, we've had a postcard from Sven.'

Harry took it from her. On the front was a vista of sand stretching for miles and miles under a burning sun, and on the back, written in Sven's distinctive large letters, 'Today we are going to do some cultural engagement. Show and tell with the locals! I'm taking my *Hong Kong Phooey* pyjamas. Wish you were here!' Then at the bottom: 'Don't worry. I'm OK. Muddling through.'

Harry felt a tear form in his eyes – for between the gaps in those words he could see bombs crashing into the sand, exploding, limbs flying, bullets piercing the night air, boys crying out for their mothers. And fathers.

It was a long day in the shop with few customers, thanks to the heavy snow falling outside. This was almost a relief. For every time the bell did go Harry worried that it would be another customer returning with a complaint about their rock. When it wasn't he would cross himself and look over to the empty shelving where formerly the rock had been. Until this whole thing was cleared up he couldn't risk selling any, and that was going to affect profits. There'd be no holiday again this year, and they would have to cut back on meat. Or he would. Mary loved a pork chop, and it was a sacrifice he was willing to make.

When Mary came down at 7 p.m. for her shift she asked Harry what he had in his rucksack. Harry looked at her; this was the woman he loved, who he had never lied to.

'It's nothing,' he said, and walked quietly to the train station in the still falling snow, leaving fresh footprints and his guilt behind him.

At the station a funeral was taking place for one of the workers from the Boosbeck Butterfly Farm. The worker had entered the butterfly shed at feeding time, and the rest was history. Eaten alive.

Evans had said the signs, 'Beware the Butterflies', were unnecessary, and had had them removed as a cost-cutting measure when he had taken over.

The station master did the service over the tannoy, interrupting the eulogy here and there to say this or that train was going to be early or late, or that today the café was doing a special on egg-and-cheese sandwiches. Several young men from the butterfly farm stood and wept, which caused confusion amongst the commuters.

'There's nothing special about those egg and cheese sandwiches,' Harry heard one of them say. 'Nothing to cry over, anyroad.'

Harry was alone on the train this time.

In case he died on his mission he had brought his and Mary's scrapbook with him. In 1972 Mary had wanted to climb a mountain, so he had built one from old suitcases he had found washed up on the beach. There she was, sitting on the summit, ice crystals in her hair, her breath coming out in puffs of smoke. Then there they were when Sven was born. Harry had bought a ukulele from the midwife in celebration.

He was interrupted in his reverie by the conductor appearing. He was pushing a trolley from which he was selling warning signs – 'NO SMOKING', 'PLEASE KEEP YOUR FEET OFF THE SEATS', 'DANGER! DO NOT PUT YOUR HEAD OUT OF THE WINDOWS'.

Harry bought a 'NO SMOKING' and 'IMPROPER USE OF THE COMMUNICATION CORD WILL RESULT IN A FINE OF 85p'. The signs came with a card to say all the money raised would go towards food for the station dogs and emergency track maintenance.

It was still snowing when Harry arrived in Poulton-le-Fylde. The hustlers and hot-dog sellers who plied their trade around the station had tiny snowploughs fitted to their feet so that they cleared the sidewalk as they went. This was a city ordinance – as was keeping your shoulders free of snow. If they spotted any snow on your shoulders a Poulton cop would fine you. It was easy money for the police force, and they used the money for beer, polish for their boots and trips to Amsterdam, where there were less strict rules regarding prostitution.

There was no queue outside the tanning shop today, but the Kinko's was full. It was free entry if you were wearing a spectacular hat, and many youths were sitting there in seasonally inappropriate clothing and huge statuesque hats, their eyes completely dead. Suddenly it dawned on Harry: the copy fluid was a drug. These were licensed drug dens, and he knew who would be behind them.

Evans. He had his fingers in too many pies.

Retracing his steps from the day before, past the car park, up the hill, Harry snuck by the guard station and stopped at the same spot on the perimeter fence and undid his rucksack. He had filled several of Mary's willy warmers with corned beef hash (65p), along with a good dose of Mary's sleeping tablets crushed to a powder (£2.50 from Pete's Chemist). He threw the laced willy warmers over the fence, and while the dogs were distracted he clambered over.

Reaching the window, he knelt and watched the women at work. Adjacent to where the letters were formed was the packing station. As sticks came along the conveyer belt the women stationed there put stickers on them, wrapped them in shiny paper, twisted and scrunched the ends. Two hundred an hour. Three hundred. Evans had quite the production line going here, and, so Harry surmised, once the rude words in the rock had ruined the local rock-selling businesses Evans would be ready to take over the world. The rock-selling world, at least.

Reaching into his bag again, Harry took out a Michael Jackson backscratcher (99p). Inserting it into the spot where the window met the frame, he leant his bodyweight against it and, with a dull pop, the window lock buckled open.

Waiting a moment to confirm he hadn't been heard, Harry lifted the window and rolled inside. The smell of the sweet was overpowering. As was the sound – rock-making machines heaving and pounding in a cacophonous din.

On his hands and knees, Harry crawled over to the nearest woman. Her brown hair was long and oily. She had a tattoo on her left ankle: a piece of cheese with an arrow through it. Then Harry realised the cheese was a love heart, faded and distorted with age. He undid the shackle using the screwdriver from the Tiny Tots toolkit (64p) – not easy for a layperson, but Harry had had years of practice from when his son Sven was a little kid and liked nothing better than to build replicas of the Cheddar Gorge with old lollipop sticks and half a Meccano set someone had returned to the shop even though it hadn't been purchased there. Once he'd got the shackle off Harry whispered up to the women that she should arm herself with something and wait for his signal.

The next woman had fatter ankles, and the shackle had chafed her skin. The ankle after that was knobbly but slender, like a golf ball in a sock over the end of a golf club. The ankle after that sported a fat, throbbing vein – ideal for an elderly vampire bat that was no longer able to fly, Harry couldn't help thinking.

For years afterwards Harry would dream of nothing but ankles. There were two hundred and fifty-two in total, which made one hundred and twenty-six prisoners if you assumed that all the women had two ankles (and Harry didn't remember otherwise and was pretty sure a one-legged woman would've stuck in his brain).

As the last shackle fell to the floor Harry gave his signal. This was a whole box of snaps (99p), which he threw into the air. As they landed they caused many tiny explosions, which was enough to distract the guards. The women were on them with sticks of rock. (When he said 'arm yourself', what else were they going to use? Talk about hoisted by your own petard.)

At the bottom of the hill Harry stopped to watch the factory burn. Not his idea, but some of those poor women had been subjected to who knew what. One had called Evans a bum-sucking son of a bitch – a phrase Harry was sure they would struggle to fit inside a piece of rock. But if they wanted revenge, who was he to stop them? He'd had a job to do, and he'd done it. What those women wanted to do was up to them, but he wouldn't like to be in Evans' shoes. He doubted they'd stop at just the rock factory. Somethings things come back to bite you on the bum. And deservedly so.

It was only as they got to the road outside the train station that he stopped to take in Mo, Duncan's wife. Her hair looked dishevelled, and the rings on each of her fingers had become tarnished, thanks to all the sugar in the rock – but he imagined Duncan's face when he saw her again. Happy, and a bit goofy – no, a lot goofy. Families should be together. He thought of Mary and what he would do if she became a victim of human trafficking, and he took out his scrapbook and flicked through their pictures. The very last one was a picture of her and Sven standing outside the entrance to the Foetus Museum. It had been taken on Sven's eighteenth birthday, the day before he went off to war, and so as a treat he had been allowed to wear his *Hong Kong Phooey* pyjamas outside. They were his favourites. He and Harry used to watch the cartoons over again and again. That was where Harry had got his idea to become a detective. If a mild-mannered janitor could do it…

The station was all closed up for the night, and the snow was still falling, heavier than ever.

Mo put out her hands, let the snow build up on her palms. Then she started singing a Christmas carol. 'Hark the Herald, the Angel sings.'

Her voice soared up into the night. It was beautiful. So beautiful.

Jeez, what had he been doing with his life? He worked twelve hours in the shop; Mary the other twelve. His son had gone. His dear daughter was dead.

It was all very well rescuing other people, but what about himself?

He made a resolution. When he got back to Saltburn in the morning he would suggest to Mary that they reassess the shop's opening hours. And if their son ever came back from the war, they would love him and love him and love him.

That was what was important. Not money. Or fighting. But love.

Love. Love. Love.

Stick that in your rock and eat it.

GINNY

Ginny's father dived into a cup for a living. The cup itself was rather larger than the one that appeared on the mimeographed promotional fliers Ginny handed out in the summer months to the hordes of day-trippers descending in their droves upon Saltburn-by-the-Sea from Poulton-le-Fylde or one of the other nearby urban conglomerations.

On the fliers, upright, steadfast, Ginny's father looked the spit of Cary Grant from his masterpiece *Bringing Up Baby*, black hair brilliantined, wearing a fur-lined bathrobe, chin as square as the turret of a Matilda World War II tank.

In real life he was red-faced, wizened, as thin as one of the moray eels Ginny sometimes found out on the mudflats, wriggling and writhing in the brackish water on the windward side of the nuclear-power-plant works.

But despite this anomaly, between 'as advertised' and 'in the flesh', Ginny loved his father, and was never prouder than when, the time of the show approaching, the Most Stupendous Cup-Diver Ever Known to Man etc., etc., pulled on his tight hand-knitted trunks, hooked around his ears the tiny streamlined goggles and ascended up the towering ladder 'a thousand feet above the naked ground!' to take his pre-dive pose above the cup.

What did it matter that this act, purely high theatrics, a big splash in a small pond, made Ginny a laughing stock at school?

What did those doofuses know? Ginny's father was a legend. Hadn't his face, before Evans opened the canning factory and replaced the visage with his gurning own, appeared on the side of all the locally sold tins of corned beef hash? 'Dive into a side of pure beef!'

Ginny still had one of these, kept under his bed along with his other precious things, a scrimshawed tooth found on the beach, a postcard with Jacques Brel's autograph on the back, one of his dearly departed mother's snowdrop pearl earrings. God bless her little soul. Not that he believed in God. No. If there were a God, then where were the miracles?

Ginny and his father lived above the fishmonger's on the seafront. *Prawns are our specialty! Caught daily!*

As well as selling cockles and winkles from a pier-end handcart and giving lessons in fish prep for beginners, Ginny's mother had run the fishmonger's until her death the month before.

The whole time she was ill Ginny had made his way daily to the hospital, trudging up past the many gift shops that filled the first and second floors of the building, then the food franchises on the third, then the bowling alleys on the fourth and fifth, then the music school on the sixth, before finding his mother on the seventh.

On his first visit the doctor informed Ginny there was a five per cent relative's discount in Flip-Flops, the second-floor gift shop that specialised in rubber shoes. Or he could choose free bowling-shoe hire on level four, and, right throughout July, a twenty-five per cent discount at the music school.

The doctor himself had a number of banjos and other stringed instruments fixed by straps across his body, each with a price tag dangling from them like a Christmas tree bauble.

On his mother's final day, as the doctor reached across to close her eyes for the last time, these instruments crashed together, performing a mournful cacophony, the sound barely concealing Ginny's sobs.

Placing a hand on Ginny's shoulder, and as if he were reading the words from a card, the doctor advised there was a once-in-a-lifetime discount on harpsichords for the recently bereaved.

Times were hard. His mother and her income from the fishmonger's gone, Ginny's father had to take on a second job.

Five nights a week now he made his way down to the cemetery, where he worked the night shift digging graves, the thick trousers and gloves a far cry from the miraculous outfit he wore for diving.

'Now, you be good when I'm gone,' he would say to Ginny each night before he left, respectfully knocking and then poking his head around the door. 'Don't get up to stuff. A teenage boy alone, believe me – I know about these things.'

But how could he know this?

It was on the first night of his father's new job, two weeks to the day after his mother's death, staying up late to play his mother's Jacques Brel LPs over and over on repeat, that Ginny discovered on the stroke of midnight he had turned into a girl. Winky gone, breasts bulging out, the whole lot.

Although the sensation was unpleasant, it was not like the violent change scenes he and Charles had cooed and awed over in Guy Endor's *The Werewolf of Paris*, reading the passages out to each other over and over. No. This was seamless, the click of the fingers, a snap of an elastic band.

Had it always been on the cards, genetically predetermined from birth? Or was it a new thing? Proof of the God he didn't believe in?

Ginny's best friend Charles lived with his father in an extremely narrow and dilapidated house situated between Saltburn's lifeguard station and the school for the blind.

Charles' father worked as a professional map-maker. In a fit of self-promotion, several years previously he had changed the family name to Atlas. Overnight Charles Johnson had become Charles Atlas, like the Italian-American bodybuilder with the fabulous body who in turn had named himself after the statue of Atlas on top of a Coney Island hotel.

It was the tossing of a gauntlet.

Boys drunk on Bullshot (a heady mix of vodka, beer broth, Worcestershire sauce) would come in packs to Charles' house, and hang outside smoking pendulous roll-ups until Charles made an appearance. Then they would take it in turns to knock him to the ground and declare themselves the defeater of Atlas, the bravest of the brave, the strongest man in the universe etc., etc.

But what Charles lacked in brawn he made up for in brain. He was the cleverest person Ginny knew. At just twelve years old he had taught himself both German and Russian from library-borrowed primers, and he regularly shamed their history teacher Mr Richards with his knowledge of ancient Greek and Roman history; and so it was to Charles that Ginny went, the day after making his shocking discovery.

'What – an actual girl?' asked Charles, pushing his thick spectacles up his long nose. 'Like Judy Garland in *A Star Is Born?*'

Although a confirmed homosexual, Charles had a thing for certain Hollywood actresses – Marilyn Monroe, Grace Kelly, Kim Novak, Doris Day.

'An actual girl,' repeated Ginny. 'Twelve hours later I'm a boy again.' He grinned. 'Or a man, with my humongous wanger. Meet me on the mudflats just before midnight – I'll show you. But tell anyone you've seen me naked and I'll bash you worse than those Bullshot high boys.'

And so it was later, out on the mudflats, Ginny standing naked, legs astride two rocks, moon behind him, 'humongous wanger' dangling – and then not, as the stroke of midnight struck – that Ginny said that if Charles could help him with his problem he would get Charles twelve pairs of worn underpants. (Underpants were Charles' thing.)

Earlier that summer Charles had developed an obsession with the Stasi, the East German secret police. Scouring their records, he had come across numerous articles regarding their collecting and storing of underpants in glass jars in underground bunkers, and had come to the conclusion that, if he collected a pair of underpants from everyone in town, he might be able to track, through his acute sense of smell or that of a suitable sniffer dog, where anyone had been at any given time.

'Just think how useful I'll be to the police. Any crime or anti-social behaviour takes place – by smell alone I'll be able to pinpoint who was responsible. And if words gets out I won't get boffed so much. Everyone in town will be sucking up to me big time so I don't put the finger on them.'

Two days later Ginny approached Lenny 'the Lynx' Lomax at Rose's Roadside Café.

Lomax, six foot two, once declared winner of Best-Dressed Cowboy at the Poulton-le-Fylde annual hoedown, had hoped to go into cowboy impersonation as a profession, but now worked with Ginny's father on the same graveyard shift at the cemetery. He was also the coach of Saltburn-by-the-Sea's basketball team, the Saltburn Stranglers, and this was where Ginny's interest lay.

'You,' said Lomax, and he looked down at Ginny as if he might be seeing a tiny dot at the end of a telescope, 'want to be in team?'

'You can leave me on the bench,' said Ginny. 'Or on the bus. I'll tidy. Get in some refreshments. Whateveryouwant.'

'We're a basketball team. You get it? To win the game we have to get an orange ball through a high hoop more times than our opponents. And that means no space for short-arses.'

'I know about the stockings,' whispered Ginny, leaning in, playing his trump card.

In one of their weekly 'share sessions', instituted after the death of Ginny's mother, Ginny's father had told his son how one night he had come across Lomax digging the graves dressed only in a pair of sheer black stockings and a blond wig, listening to Dolly Parton's *Hello, I'm Dolly* on an old gramophone.

Bridling, Lomax shoved a whole iced bun into his mouth. 'We leave from Chippy Chips at 4 p.m. on Friday. If you really want to join the Stranglers, be there. But I warn you, you may have got one over on me; the lads on the team are their own beast.'

Ginny had always been scared of the Stranglers, long-legged kids with self-cut hair and and home-made tattoos. On weekdays after school they hung out under the pier and shoved cold chips up their noses and made zombie-like noises at the tourists from the neighbouring towns walking the boards above them.

There was just one genius amongst the Stranglers, Brains, named both for his knowledge and his resemblance to the character in Gerry Anderson's latest hit TV show, *Thunderbirds*.

Brains formulated the team's tactics on the backs of Lucky Strike cigarette packets. He could smoke one of those slender sticks with his anus, puffing out perfect rings while whistling a theme tune of your choice. That he did this on the team bus while formulating the tactics made him something of a legend.

As the bus set off, keeping a low profile, Ginny peered out from his front-seat window. Secretly, he was staring at his own reflection.

His mother had called him her beautiful boy and saved his long eyelashes when they fell out in an old humbug tin. She'd had a fascination with eunuchs, hermaphrodites, books about men who had been born without their private parts, or who chose to have them removed in expensive Swiss clinics. She liked to watch the Olympic Games on television, but was only interested in the Soviet teams, pointing out the athletes who had undergone hormone treatment or something she called 'its opposite'.

'Did she know?' thought Ginny. 'Was she just waiting for the right time to tell me, and then she died?' Troubled, he closed his eyes and continued the imaginary conversations he'd recently been having with his mother. After the initial shock of discovery, its surge of revelation, he'd come to despise his transformation, the way it threw him bodily from perceived social norms. So *Mum, am I a monster? Mum, am I a monster? Mum, am I a monster?*

was the litany he repeated until the noise of the other boys around him indicated they were entering Poulton-le-Fylde.

Although it had been bright when they left here hung a dense cloud of smog, the chimneys of Evans Industries' factory buildings pumping out thick smoke twenty-four hours a day.

The game was to be played in a stadium that was shaped like a goldfish bowl. The car park was full of brightly coloured Standard Vanguards, Humber Hawks, Vauxhall Crestas, all with flame designs on the bonnets or half-naked women with impossibly large bosoms bursting out from bodices. Programmes (2p) were available from carts on either side of the entrance, along with rolls of wallpaper featuring a basketball-player design (£1), replica basketballs with the name EVANS stamped on them (3p), key rings in the shape of slick sports shoes (21p), tiny plaster busts of Evans (£1.01), team stickers (5p each), opera glasses (66p), T-shirts with an image of LeRoy Dwayne Lefebvre, Poulton-le-Fylde's most famous player (89p), snow globes (23p), fridge magnets (5p), rattles (15p), maracas (12p), paper cups (2p), notepads (31p), 'crack' scratchers (2p), a set of ten tokens for Evans' Tramways (17p), maps of the stadium (1p), kazoos you could put up your bum to make your farts melodious (26p), hand-knitted willy warmers (17p), sets of commemorative postcards (8p for 6, 10p for 10), stink bombs (33p), LeRoy Dwayne Lefebvre face masks (14p), commemorative bangles (33p), visitor guides to Poulton-le-Fylde (99p), a history of Evans' Industries (£3), a collection of Arthur C. Clarke short stories (8p), a quasi-religious powder you could put on your willy to make it glow in the dark (23p), inflatable basketballs (50p), a basketball board game (£1.56), Evans odour eaters (30p), Evans china teacups and saucers (£2.50), a guide to Japanese World War II aircraft (12p) and so on and so on.

Having been led to the away changing room by a small woman with tightly permed hair and a touch which she used erratically, they were left to get ready for the game.

As the other boys removed their clothes Ginny sidled over to where Lomax was putting Brains' tactics on a blackboard with a piece of blue chalk and said he had taken a turn for the worse.

'I'm going to have to sit this game out.'

Lomax shook his head sadly and took out a handkerchief shaped like a kipper.

'I've got a pony riding on this one. So to be honest I wasn't going to put you on anyway. Five foot nothing short of a donkey's arsehole, what were you gonna do?'

As the other boys disappeared down the players' tunnel Ginny sat alone on one of the changing-room benches and waited until he heard the roars for the home team, the boos for their team and the whistle that meant the game had started. Then he went around the changing area and collected all the underpants. As instructed, he placed each pair in a separate paper bag. This, apparently, was to stop cross-contamination.

There was a scene after the match when the boys discovered their missing pants. Some of them only owned that single pair.

'You had one job,' growled Lomax. 'Guard the kit.'

Ginny was both outraged and ashamed. *That* had never been his job, but he was guilty of the crime.

'You're fired,' said Lomax. 'And if you think you're travelling back with us you've got another think coming.'

Ginny was still on the train when he felt himself turning. Was it midnight already? Squeezing past two hirsute soldiers playing gin rummy across the table, he went along the carriage to the toilet. He usually liked to be asleep when the change happened, because it wasn't a pleasant sensation – like being turned inside out.

After it was all over, having taken some moments to gather himself, Ginny took out the bags containing the underpants and held them up to the light fitting, one by one.

He was trying to see if he had any sexual inclination towards them. If he was a girl then he supposed he should. These pants had been worn by flesh-and-blood boys. Or maybe if he did like them that would mean he was a boy who liked other boys.

Weren't there boys at school who loved each other? All of a sudden they would pledge themselves to one another and turn up the next day connected by numerous lengths of string. And of course there was Charles – but he was not a yardstick by which to measure anything.

Ginny put his hand inside his shirt and felt his breasts. They were both soft and firm at the same time, and the feeling was not altogether unpleasant. One day, depending how things worked out, he might use them to breastfeed. That was a thought! And despite the knocking at the door he sat down on the toilet and considered what he might call his baby; Charlie, Sidney, Florence, Edith, Alan, Duncan, Thomas, Clive, Sally, Sam, Stephen. He mouthed the names on and on until he drifted off.

The following day, up in his room, Charles pulled a copy of *The Town Crier* from under his bed and held it up for Ginny to see.

The Stranglers' story had made the back page:

PANTLESS IN POULTON

The Crier's top investigative journalist had been assigned to the case, but so far no fingers had been pointed at Ginny.

'They all had to go home without pants,' read Charles, 'which was a first for the Stranglers, although not the first time they had been whooped. Who can forget last season's run of twenty-six games without a win? Or the time the bus had become stuck out on the mudflats? It seems bad luck follows the team... Any information about the missing pants will be gratefully received and treated in the utmost confidence.'

Charles was pleased with the underpants, and Ginny watched as he placed them one by one in the stoppered glass jars he had prepared earlier.

Ginny had the idea that they should throw them out to sea, where they would be found, like messages in a bottle.

'Do you remember?' Ginny asked. When he and Charles were younger they had started a small industry making messages in bottles and selling them to day-trippers to toss from the pier.

Inside they put pithy phrases: 'I hope you got your fingers stuck in the bottle while you tried to retrieve this message. That'll teach you to be nosy!', 'I found a bottle washed up on the shore and all I got inside was this lousy message.', 'I am stuck on desert island and so horny. Please come and rescue me. If ugly, bring handsome friend!'

One time they had managed to squeeze a complete copy of *The Pickwick Papers* into an extremely fat bottle, but no one wanted to buy that one, so they threw it into the sea themselves, watched it immediately sink, weighed down with heavy words.

After Charles had finished putting all the underpants into the glass jars, fixing a card on the bottle with the name of the boy the pants had belonged to, he reached under his unmade bed and pulled out a thick, wide book.

'To solve the mystery of yourself you need to go on a long journey,' he said mysteriously. He tapped the cover of the book. 'In here are described all the works of an artist called Man Ray, whose real name is Emmanuel Radnitzky and who is an American but who now lives in Paris.'

Puzzled, Ginny asked, 'But what's that got to do with me?'

'The first step to recovery is to find another person in the world like yourself. This book is full of weird and wonderful people. You'll see.'

Charles and Ginny stayed up all night looking at the pictures – weird, androgynous creatures, the likes of which Ginny had not seen before, and which caused tears to flow down his cheeks.

'I told you,' said Charles. 'People as strange as you exist in the world.'

Determined to have enough money to go to Paris, to meet Man Ray and to move in his fabulous milieu, Ginny bought himself an old slot machine, and each evening after college he wheeled it down to the front.

In return for some potato peeling and helping out with frying at peak times, the owner of Chippie Chips allowed Ginny to run a power cable from the slot machine into the shop. Every night, and all day at weekends, Ginny was there, and while the punters played, he devoured French books, marking the words he didn't know with a red pen, later transcribing them into his vocabulary book.

In those weeks he got through *L'étranger* by Albert Camus, *Quinze contes* by Guy de Maupassant, *Bonjour tristesse* by Françoise Sagan, *La Porte étroite* by André Gide, *Candide* by Voltaire, *L'Avare* by Molière, *Le Rouge et le Noir* by Stendhal, *Madam Bovary* by Gustave Flaubert and *Notre-Dame de Paris* by Victor Hugo.

He also learnt to love the sound of the 1ps and 2ps as they fell through the slots, the viscous buzz of frying chips, the slap of waves on the shore.

His eighteenth birthday came and went, and with it a new and constant horniness that couldn't be assuaged with any amount of masturbation or with the placing of suitable objects up his bumhole. 'Enough information already!' was his father's response at their still-continuing weekly share session.

Sometimes Ginny would attempt to flirt outrageously with the out-of-town girls as they changed their 10ps into smaller denominations, but in his bright green galoshes, his father's grave-digging trousers with enforced knees and a pink cagoule in case of a heavy downpour, his efforts were often met with derision. So he decided to chance his arm post-change with the after-hours fisherman down at the Jolly Fisherman.

His mother's clothes still remaining in her wardrobe (his father had not yet been able to dispose of them), Ginny dressed himself in a pink miniskirt that stuck out at ninety degrees from the tops of his thighs, a yellow jumper with short arms, a neckline too tight for his neck, and sprayed a gargantuan amount of hairspray on to his hair, having styled it into a kind of upright strato-spheric bob.

Ginny had been in the bar for only seven minutes when she was approached by Kasper Igorsson, the town's only Norwegian fisherman.

Having offered to buy 'the new girl in town' a drink, Kasper returned from the bar with a pint for himself and something pink in a tall, thin glass for Ginny. One drink became two, then three, then four, until, quite drunk, Kasper, who seemed to have fallen for Ginny, asked if she would like to come back to his home.

'I've never done this before,' said Ginny.

'I can be gentle,' said Kasper.

Ginny, quite drunk too, smiled. 'I don't know that it's gentle I want.'

They walked together under the moonlight along Saltburn-by-the-Sea's designated Romantic Mile Seaside Walk.

Coin-operated machines lined the walk selling artificial roses, pages of romantic verse, commemorative love beads encased in a kind of Perspex.

Other lovers formed orderly queues in front of these machines, no doubt dreaming of their life ahead – marriages, mortgages, children.

Ginny could only glance at them and shudder. The only dream she had was of a much nearer future: what would happen at midday tomorrow when she returned to being a man.

Kasper's home was a former fishing vessel that he had hoisted out of the sea and mounted on firm wooden struts. Once inside there was no messing about, no preamble. It was clothes off and straight down to it.

It felt strange to Ginny, being entered by a penis in the place where her own penis had recently been; but it wasn't unpleasant, and after that first night, they both being agreeable, she returned there on each subsequent night, but only after she had changed into a woman.

Kasper rose early in the mornings to fish, well before Ginny turned back, and on the seventh morning, Sunday, he went to the service at the Saltburn-by-the-Sea reform church, and spent his afternoon doing gardening work for several of the elderly parishioners.

Sundays were Ginny's favourite days because she could linger at Kasper's – there was no college to go to – and imagine that this would be her future life, her home and, when it came to it, for the truth always comes out in the end, Kasper would love her penis as much as he did her vagina, accepting her for who she truly was: both the one thing and the other. After all, she was still the same person.

Kasper had his own dreams. One day, he said, he and Ginny would run a garage, Kasper's Parts, on an A road together. They would be like the couple in *The Postman Always Rings Twice*. Ginny would work in the garage shop, providing light snacks to waiting customers, while Kasper himself would man the pumps, polish car windscreens, do repairs, change the oil, tyres, fix minor engine problems.

But then one morning these dreams came to an end.

They had woken to a storm, wind and rain lashing against the windows of the boat, and Kasper said he would not be fishing that day – 'Not for anybody's life, not even my own.' He ran a finger along Ginny's taut belly. 'For once you'll have your little Kasper in the morning, all day.'

'I better go,' said Ginny, later, as she saw the clock hands inexorably progressing towards midday.

Kasper grew petulant, said they had never had chance to spend the *all day along* together. Today was that opportunity. It could be a test run for their life together.

'I guess we have to do that some time,' said Ginny.

It was his hand that found it first. Unlike those attendees of the school for the blind, you didn't need to be a Braille expert.

Ripping the duvet from the bed Kasper was first surprised, then horrified. He paced their tiny bedroom, clenching and unclenching his fists while Ginny tried to explain.

'But I wanted you,' said Kasper finally.

'I am me,' said Ginny.

'You know what I mean,' said Kasper.

Ginny was heartbroken, but not surprised, when Kasper said he couldn't see him any more. He had read enough books about monsters to understand that before acceptance, or death, there was a period which involved being cast out, or dying.

Standing outside, looking up at the boat, his clothes packed hurriedly into a cardboard suitcase, he decided it was time he went to Paris. Man Ray was waiting, along with all the peculiar people like himself. Herself. Themselves.

Ginny in Paris

Upon his arrival in Paris Ginny spent many days in wonder wandering the wide boulevards and narrow streets of his new home town: Rue Lepic, Rue des Martres, Place des Abbesses, Rue Berthe, Rue des Trois Frères, Rue Chappe, Rue Gabrielle, Rue Norvins, Place Dalida, Rue Condorcet, Rue Milton, Champs-Elysées, Avenue Victor Hugo, Avenue Montaigne, Rue de Rivoli, Passages Couverts, Boulevard de Clichy, L'Esplanade des Invalides, Avenue de L'Opéra.

Those streets became a foreignness mapped in his heart.

Ginny found a room in a fleapit hotel near the Pigalle metro station. The owner, Gaspard, an extremely corpulent man who had a fresh live pig delivered every Tuesday 'for the benefit of the guests' also performed in a local theatre as a Man of Memory.

Each time Ginny entered the hotel Gaspard made a great show of remembering which key was his. Usually got it wrong.

In his sixth-floor hotel room Ginny had a metal-framed bed, a pot adorned with famous figures from the French resistance to piss in and a photograph of the Eiffel Tower in all its glory affixed to a sunless peeling-papered wall.

There was no window in this room, but Ginny discovered if he went up a staircase, up another staircase, climbed up and out on to the flat roof of the hotel he could see the whole of Paris. Dominating the horizon was the miraculous A frame of Eiffel's tower itself.

But Ginny, like many self-aware monsters, was scared of such huge constructions, their wide open spaces in which to be chased or attacked, and much preferred Paris' narrow doorways, dark alleys, bars you needed to descend to with waiters who would ignore you until, at the last moment, they would bring you a red wine and a tiny pot of fresh nuts.

There were many prostitutes who worked on the street outside the hotel, and often when they didn't have clients Ginny would sit in the *Café Pierre* with them and quietly talk about the works of Balzac, Zola, Rabelais, Dumas, Charles Baudelaire.

The prostitutes would put Edith Piaf on the jukebox, smoke Gitanes and feed each other crumbs of the tiny baguettes brought to them by the café owner, Claude.

Sitting there with them Ginny almost felt French by association, and this feeling was a better feeling than feeling like a monster.

It was the fashion back for prostitutes to have monumental hairstyles and colourful bustiers, and they all carried ornately carved wooden sticks.

For the most part the prostitutes' clients were the browned sailors blown in on fair winds from Martinique, Tahiti, French Polynesia, or the American beatniks, carting cardboard cases packed with their unpublished works of staggering genius; but their most desired customers, because they paid the most, were the rich out-of-town businessmen who would turn up in long black cars with dark windows.

These cars were hired from Victor, the hotel owner's brother, and the drivers of these cars, all of them Algerians, lived on the top floor of the hotel.

The Algerians owned one typewriter between them and were writing a novel, taking it in turns each day to write a single sentence each.

This novel, a roman-à-clef about a group of Algerian immigrants who pick up married men in hired cars and drive them to illicit rendezvous with monumental-haired prostitutes, they believed, was going to make them famous.

Sometimes Ginny would go to their rooms, and they would read out a section to him.

This man, he wants woman, you see? Paris woman, they on strike for the intimacy. Then a shot rings out in the dark. Hit the pedal Jack. A cloud goes over the moon. It is Tuesday. In Africa as well as in La Belle France.

Ginny's favourite place in Paris was the Aquarium tropicale de la Porte Dorée.

He went there at least twice a week, and would press his body against the tanks of exotic fish, watch his breath condensing on the glass.

With its dim lighting, moist warmth, there was something of the womb about the place, and he wanted to be reborn.

Take me for who I am! Neither man nor woman nor beast. Especially beast.

After three weeks in Paris Ginny's stock of 1ps and 2ps from his slot machine cash box was running out. All too soon there would not be enough money for his daily cheese, bread and wine or to pay the rent on his room in Hotel Dix.

He was considering becoming one of the prostitutes – a female one, after midnight when he became a woman; or a male one, joining the young, lithe men he had seen plying their trade below the bridges of the Seine. But then, out of the blue, Houd Abaoub, one of the Algerian drivers, was shot dead trying to rob an Italian pizzeria on the Bois de Vincennes – the money desperately needed to pay for a family business calamity back home – and Victor asked Ginny if he could step in and drive one of the long black cars with many windows.

Ginny enjoyed the streets of Paris at night, although he was not keen on the men he had to pick up. They were all made in the same factory – long drooping moustaches, fat cigars, dark glasses they wore halfway down their noses, as if the glasses were incredibly heavy or their noses incredibly slippery.

Before the meetings these men would be boisterous, splashing champagne into glasses, roaring with laughter, but afterwards they would become sentimental, sliding grainy photographs out of their wallets, thrusting them forward and saying they would do anything for their wives. Anything.

It was in August of his second year when Ginny found the second-hand shop in Montparnasse. Vêtements Vrais was run by two large Germans who, like those gay boys from his school years, were connected to each other with many pieces of string.

The Germans offered a Personal Design Service; and, because the shop was filled with many stray cats, fed and cared for by the proprietors, Ginny took these men to be kind, and so told them about his turning into a woman each night and how he wanted a single set of clothes he could wear in each of his forms – one that would appear feminine when he was a woman, masculine when he was a man. Or at least sit comfortably between the two.

Standing in front of the mirror afterwards was a revelation. There was his mother's beautiful boy again. Or girl.

He had never lost who he was, but now he had found it.

One night he was involved in an accident. Driving away from a rendezvous, the client in the back became enormously sexually aroused by Ginny's new clothes and started chewing at the seat cover. Turning to calm him, Ginny lost control and crashed into one of Paris' many cleaning carts and went flying through the windscreen.

The next day, not being able to work, Ginny decided to visit his old haunt, the Aquarium tropicale de la Porte Dorée. It was his first time there sporting his new clobber, and it was as he was looking at the rays that he was approached by a tall man with a drawn-on pencil moustache and buggy brown eyes.

The man placed one of his slender spidery hands on Ginny's shoulder and whispered into his ear that he would very much like to take his photograph.

'I can pay you. Your look. It is very unique.'

Charles, Ginny's old friend from Saltburn-by-the-Sea, was living in the Kreuzberg district of Berlin now, working as the music producer of guitar and drum bands formed in the area's dive bars and squats by skinny young men and women with sharp cheekbones and unobtrusive self-inked tattoos, dreaming of one day setting up his own studios.

In the last of his many long letters he had written, 'After a monster learns self-acceptance there comes a period of performance which leads to society welcoming that which is different, or not, casting it out so the cycle begins again.' He finished by asking, as he did in every single letter, 'Have you met Man Ray yet? I feel you are not trying hard enough. You are thinking about it too literally…'

'Are you Man Ray?' asked Ginny, recalling this letter, turning to the man who had touched his shoulder.

'I am a man,' said the man obsequiously, 'and that is a ray.' He pointed at one of the fish circling the tank. Then he pointed at the floor between them. 'In the middle, the emptiness, the truth lies.'

Man Ray lived in a small apartment above the aquarium. In it was a gramophone, boxes of LPs with faded, torn covers, dozens of umbrellas (all shapes and sizes), many hundreds of hats, fitted one on top of the other so they formed spooky leaning towers, boxes and boxes of old shoes, but hardly a pair between them, purses, prosthetic limbs, eyeglasses, belts, marbles, plastic combs, monogrammed handkerchiefs, socks, underpants, cufflinks, pieces of window putty, a gas mask, several battered teddy bears, piles of paperback books, many with racy covers displaying half-clad buxom women and titles like *J'ai besoin de vous* and *Le Branleur*, rolled-up newspapers, soiled wedding dresses, enormous home-made black dildos, gloves sorted by colour and size and, in a kind of crate, many thousands of letters, slit or torn open.

These items had been abandoned in the aquarium and found by Man Ray, carefully labelled with the location of where they were discovered and when.

'If they are not collected within twenty-eight days then they are sold. This is how I make my living. They think of me as a lost-property collector; I think of myself as a collector of lost souls.'

'Like me?' asked Ginny.

One week after that Ginny quit Hotel Dix and moved in with Man Ray. It was a purely business relationship. They would collect lost property together, and Ginny would have his, or her, photograph taken.

It was on that first meeting in the apartment above the aquarium, suffering still from concussion after his accident, that Ginny had blurted out the truth about themselves, half man, half woman, or maybe all of both, half the time.

Man Ray in turn told of his past. For many years he had been a seaside photographer in Le Havre. Couples parading along the front. Babies in bonnets. Fat elderly men sending inappropriate pictures to ladies in the east – 'I will give you a better life.' Then there had been a scandal. He had got a young lady pregnant. She was married. How was he to know? Or that her husband was a boxer. His camera had been smashed to smithereens. Threats made – 'Do not return here or you will pay!' And he had made his way to Paris, where photographers were two a penny. Or a franc. Hence the lost property.

'But with you my dear,' he said, 'I have found my muse.'

In one of the photographs Ginny was laid out under the bed, his legs dramatically spread like he was going hell for leather over a high hurdle; in another her feet could be seen sticking out from a pile of umbrellas; in yet another there were just his fingertips, clinging on to the window ledge, the Paris skyline looking radiant behind.

'I don't know what I am entering into,' wrote Ginny to Charles. 'It is all very well coming into an accommodation with yourself. An accommodation with others seems to depend on those others, and it is they who I do not trust. Paris is beautiful in the spring. But I think we are entering a new period. Both me and the city.'

One day May Ray said they were ready. The photographs were to appear in an exhibition taking place in the chimney of a former shoe factory.

Using a system of pulleys and a small crane Man Ray and his helper, Alice Prin, a thin-waisted woman with square, shiny hair who had made her name around the cabaret bars of Montmartre but had since fallen on hard times and now lived in a rather worn-out tent on the flat roof of a German charcutier's shop, had positioned all of the photographs around the top of the chimney.

On the opening night, when each of the guests arrived, they were handed a pair of binoculars by a monkey borrowed from the zoo at Bois de Vincennes and dressed as Oscar Wilde's lover Lord Alfred Douglas.

Ginny asked for a pair of binoculars himself, but Man Ray pooh-poohed the idea with a wave of the hand. 'A star is looked at,' he said, casting a hand up towards the chimney, 'not looked upon.'

So as Ginny was standing, being looked upon, there now being quite a crowd with the binoculars gazing up into the chimney, a man in a long forbidding hat in the shape of a Empire State Building leant into him. His breath smelt of garlic and aniseed.

'I want to see *it* disappear,' the man whispered, the tips of his lips brushing Ginny's ear. 'I hear you are... how shall we say it... available... these photos a calling card...'

Ginny waited until midnight. As a woman she felt more decisive. When her penis was present during the day she had begun to dress it in funny costumes made to order by the two fat Germans: an anteater, a fire hydrant, an elephant. Manhood was so much easier to deal with in disguise. There was an inherent theatre to it in the flesh; the way it rose and fell, demanded attention like a child.

'I'll be back,' she said to the man – to all these men – and then, locking herself in the toilet, she removed the wooden toilet-roll holder and smashed the tiny window with it.

'I won't be back,' she said, and, getting up on to the cistern, climbed out into the Paris night.

Gaspard threw his arms in the air when he saw Ginny standing at the door of the fleapit hotel. 'I have missed you like I would miss a third arsehole,' he said. 'You're back.'

'I have been nowhere,' said Ginny. 'Only to some poxy art exhibition.'

'Then we have a problem,' said Gaston. 'Your previous habitation is not available, and all the other rooms are booked to the brim.' Then Gaston rubbed his chin, smiled. 'But maybe not a problem. You have become a peacock, I see, in these months that I have been missing you. Perhaps this room can be shared. I think you two might get along. Let's say I can see it written in the stars.'

Jean-Louis le Baptiste was forty-three, and had a tattoo of a sea urchin on his left arm, a birthmark in the shape of a dolphin on his left. As a young boy he had dreamt of being an astronomer – something to do with the stars – but then his mother had died when he was twelve years old, his father when he was thirteen; now an orphan, he had turned to drink, thieving from shops, stealing cars, breaking into tabacs. There was a spell in prison, a spell as a waiter in a seedy bar, a long spell that was much of nothing except a series of ever more insalubrious rooms. Finally, after a disastrous suicide attempt in which he had thrown himself into the Seine, a nurse and her lesbian lover had taken pity on him and helped him turn his life around. Sober now for a number of years, he worked nights as a street cleaner and slept throughout the day. For a hobby – he needed something to occupy himself and keep him off the dreaded booze – he told fortunes, read palms, cards; he had even been known to pull histories out of a crystal ball if one was available.

He was, thought Ginny, impossibly handsome.

During that first week Jean-Louis le Baptiste and Ginny used the bed in shifts, standing meekly by its side as one either got in or out. Already by the second day they were leaving each other little notes on the pillow – *All Yours!*, *Sweet Dreams!*, *Enjoy your zzzzzzs!* – which Ginny interpreted as flirtation. It wasn't until the weekend they shared it together.

Having been down this path before, Ginny thought it best to bite the bullet before it was shot.

'So you are a man, you are a woman, who cares?' Jean-Louis le Baptiste reassured her. 'Cleaning the streets of Paris I see a lot of filth, and this is not filth. You, mon ami, are doubly beautiful. I see it in your eyes, and also in the stars.'

Ginny blushed at this. She had been right – it *was* flirtation. And so when Jean-Louis le Baptiste asked if she would like him to tell her her fortune she said she would. She held out her hand.

Ginny's Fortune

Having learnt a lesson from Man Ray about the nature of lost property, you will go to the Aquarium tropicale de la Porte Dorée each day, and you will collect all the books that have been unlucky enough to be parted from their owners there.

When you have enough books you will open your own stall on the Left Bank.

Your stall will be very successful, thanks to your English accent, your outlandish dress, the many copies of Jean-Paul Sartre, Simone de Beauvoir, Jean Genet and Jules Verne that you have for sale – people who attend aquariums generally having very good taste in books.

You will become both the husband and wife of I, Jean-Louis le Baptiste, on the second anniversary of our meeting. We will have a secret ceremony in the Notre-Dame cathedral, attended by two men who operate a barrel organ who we will co-opt to be our witnesses. Their names will be Simone and Gaston. They will be lovers. They will cry when I kiss you. As will I.

We will live happily in Paris in a small set of rooms above a bicycle-repair shop until, in 1981, we move back to your home town of Saltburn-by-the-Sea. This is initially to tend to your elderly father, but after he dies we will decide to stay.

You will open a slot-machine arcade called Ginny's Palace. Ginny, it will be assumed by those in the town, is a woman; you do not correct them. If people remember you they do not say. Only we know what you are, and we exalt in that.

I, Jean-Louis le Baptiste, will die in 1985 from cancer of the colon, a short illness discovered late, which spares both of us a long goodbye. It will be said at my funeral that I have been loved. As have you.

I will keep up, to my death, the habit started during our early courtship in Paris, of bringing back my best finds from the streets and presenting them to you as gifts.

These gifts will include a fountain pen engraved with the name Rothschild, a mahogany bas-relief of a Tyrannosaurus rex chasing a group of fleeing cavemen, a pair of silk pyjamas still in their presentation box, a Rolodex filing system containing the details of only one person – a certain Mr X, a street map of Toronto, a leather dog collar with a dog tag attached inscribed with the name Mr Pickles, a single leather brogue, a stuffed squirrel with each of its teeth broken in half, a tiny stethoscope with a missing earpiece, a complete set of Wild West Top Trumps, a personal journal written by a lady who was clearly being held prisoner in a tall tower, the final entry which reads 'I fear that this night he will ki—', seven single leather gloves, a 1976 *Carry on Camping* wall calendar, a set of false teeth, a 1983 *Wisden Cricketers' Almanack*, a book of tide tables, a pork-pie hat, a set of love poems. And so on.

These 'lost things' are the things you will remember me by. You will keep them in the attic of your apartment above the arcade. Sometimes you will go up there and spend time looking through these things. But you will not be sad. You will not be sad. You will not be sad.

You might be.

I cannot lie. You will be sad. Death is vicious and cruel, but it comes to us all.

SVEN GOES TO WAR

Warriors of the Wasteland

W hile their parents watched the actual war spin out on the
TV news programme, *Look North with Arthur Seagull and
Molly Splat*, the boys, and one other, being neither boy nor non-
boy, played war games down on the mudflats. Setting themselves
up into armies, Shirts vs. Skins, Terminators vs. Rambos,
Circumcised vs. Hooded (*Claws* in common parlance, as in, 'Are
you a Claw or Non-Claw?') they took up positions behind old
abandoned shopping trolleys, in forts constructed from for-sale
signs stolen from the overgrown gardens of long-derelict houses,
and in the abandoned crumbling concrete Martello, stinking of
tramps' piss and filled with sad-looking wrinkled used, sometimes unused, condoms. They were Trojans, all of them.

And these poor innocents, they would go at each other with
wild euphoric abandon.

Happy days. The country was never happier, more unified,
than when it was at war.

Except, just as in any war, there were dissenting voices.

Those who were not happy. Not exactly.

For Sven Tosier-Gumshoe, being the smallest, feyest and,
perhaps, because of his position as neither boy nor non-boy,
when the war games were coming to their nightly close, ragged,
careworn parents having started to line up like gulls along

the pier rail, shouting out that it was time for their respective charges to hurry home for tea *or there would be tanned hides all round*, was the one who was, most often, taken hostage.

A quick resolution was needed to finish the game.

'I'm Private Tosier-Gumshoe,' they would say. 'Fifteenth Seal Regiment. Identification Number 35654. I won't tell you anything.'

Usually then they would come at them with a used condom filled with sand, or a live crab with snapping claws, or the rusty speculum Aart Jansen had stolen from his doctor dad aeons before, telling them with faked horror that a speculum was something you used to look up buttholes.

'OK,' Sven would say, 'I give in. Our army is massed behind the seal fort... Plans are to advance at midnight... The password is Valkensteeg 17. Just don't hurt me. I'll tell you anything.'

This sequence of events had happened so often that when, on this particular day, a group of the boys, the Circumcised or Hooded, Claws or Non-Claws (Sven was not entirely clear on this point, having not seen their actual in-the-flesh willies), came at them, they went without a fight.

As Sven was dragged, one boy at each armpit, two more tightly gripping a leg each, towards the Martello, where they would be tied to the special hostage chair, they weren't overly scared, just put out. Like, Here we go again – get it over with, do your worst.

But on this day the Bones Brothers, Billy and Bunty (their father, Caged Bones, the wrestler, hoped the boys so-named would follow in the family line of man-to-man combat), had been experimenting with a new Minty Fresh fanny deodorant stolen from their mother's purse.

Airtight plastic bags fixed firmly over their flinty heads, they had been both sniffing and inhaling for the previous forty-five minutes in the bin alley behind Ginny's Palace.

And now they were bug-eyed. High as kites. And, what was worse for Sven, with boners to die for.

'Is yours?' asked Billy, with a taut twang of his stiff member in his silky Bret Hart Wrestling Buddy shorts.

'You bet it is,' replied Bunty, with a mighty twang of his own, his Hulk Hogan Breakout shorts filled to the brim. (Billy had his father's nose and cheekbones, Bunty his mighty endowment – always a bonus for any wrestler, to look *bulging* in a skin-tight leotard – as Caged Bones, their father, often quipped, 'Brings in the punters boys, showing off a tidy package.')

'This donger's ready to blow,' said Billy. 'Let's see if old papa's right.'

Just the night before, while backstage at Saltburn-by-the-Sea's Wrestle Madness Extravaganza and Showdown, held amid much uproar every Tuesday evening at the Civic Centre and never missed by the boys, both dreaming of their names up there on the advertorial posters one day, next to the whist drives and cake sales, bingo and aerobicise, Billy and Bunty had overhead their dad boasting to Captain Cornstacks about how the best blow job was one performed with no teeth, and didn't he have the truth of it. 'To cut a long story short,' he intoned, Charlene, kicked in the mouth by one of the pier-end donkeys as a child, and now a toothless, topless bar dancer at the Jolly Fisherman's Friday Night Free for All, had taken the whole of Caged Bones' 'mighty todger' down her gullet while on her knees in the bar's disabled toilets, two pound notes poking from her knickers. 'Shouldn't o' done it, but what can you do?' Caged Bones had guffawed, almost rattling his stage wig. 'Between you me and the gatepost, the best blowie I've ever had. If it's a choice between teeth and no teeth I'll go with the full gums any day.'

That explained why Billy and Bunty, diverting from Ginny Palace's bin store before rejoining the games down on the beach, had come equipped with stolen pliers and their mum's best gardening gloves.

'To protect us,' said Bunty, the brains of the brace, 'pre-extraction, against any biting.'

Poor Sven didn't stand a chance. They had lost four of their best incisors, Billy holding while Bunty pulled, before the other horrified boys, Clifford, Clarence and co., realising that tooth extraction was out of the bounds of typical game dynamics, could get the two not-so-little, whacked-out-of-their-faces wrestlers off.

Backbreaker. Powerbomb. Piledriver. Stinkface. The Bones boys utilised all of their best moves. If they had been performing, lights, camera, action, in front of the usual Civic Centre's pissed-up and braying crowd, their dad would've been proud. It was their most magnificent performance ever.

It was also their last, for two weeks later, after another Minty Fresh outing behind Ginny Palace's bin store, this time pre-equipped with an industrial-sized jar of peanut butter and the Bones' dog's plastic hollow chicken, a perfectly sized hole exactly where its butt should be, the Bones brothers jerked and sniffed to a zonked-out delirium, had been hit by Goran Alfson's dray horse outside the Jolly Fisherman. It wasn't the horse that killed them but the wheels of the cart behind. Weighed down by six huge barrels of Evans' Brewery's best ale, it had sliced their legs clean off.

PC Ivan Gorenski, two weeks into the job and 'just having a swift one', was first on the scene and, so the story went, it wasn't the severed limbs that made him puke his guts out ('At least two pints of God's Own Country Pale Ale and a battered saveloy with cheesy chips,' as one onlooker termed it), but how the steel-rimmed wheels had somehow circumcised both of the boys, to add insult to injury; which fact would've meant that, if the boys *had* lived and *had* partaken in any more beachside battles – and why wouldn't they? – then they would've batted firmly on the side of the No Claws; for which side you are on is often as arbitrary as that.

Private Life

Back in those days Sven lived in a narrow room on the third floor of a tall, thin building whose windows peered over the seafront with what a certain infamous sixties romantic novelist, visiting the town during the research period for his latest foray, *Saltburn Shrugged*, had described as having 'the mightily sombre and forlorn disposition of a bride who has been jilted for her dying uncle's manservant on the midsummer's eve of her most unwished-for wedding'.

Battered all the year round by fierce North Sea winds, the double-glazing on those windows had long since blown, and so Sven, who loved to gaze clearly and without interruption upon both the stars, *Antares*, *Pleiades*, *Betelgeuse*, and their beloved North Sea, had got into the habit of climbing out on to the fire escape. There, *Hong Kong Phooey* duvet wrapped snugly around them, they would sleep the whole night through.

During the dog days of the previous summer, a record canicule of oppressive heat which had swept in with it a swarm of ladybugs and bad tempers, this habit had so caught on amongst the other tenants strewn along the Victorian seafront – the tradesmen, the barfolk, and the employees of Evans' Canning Factory and Fishery – that on many nights the fire escapes and slender metal balconies common to this type of building had, for some, resembled those of New York's Bowery district, where, during the Roaring Twenties, the newly immigrant Jews would build up their sukkahs outside their too-hot rooms and lament the whole night for their old country before going off early the next morning, having hardly slept a wink, to their jobs as porters, railwaymen, bellhops, or to their burning benches at one of the many factories butting up to the infamous Brooklyn Bridge, home to many a desperate suicide.

Sven and his parents did not have so far to travel to work, for on the ground floor of this tall, thin building the family establishment sat squatly: Delicious Gifts.

The shop was, in theory, as the name implied, a kind of gift shop, but over the years, in the spirit of diversification and commercialisation, their parents had so branched out, branched back in again, made stunning miscalculations, misinterpretations of customer wants and needs, that the name now hardly implied to the impatient bell-tinkling customer what they might be in for.

It was Sven's father fault in the main. Harry Tosier-Gumshoe, the paterfamilias, was forever attending trade fairs, scouring the inky black back pages of industry magazines, searching for that one killer item that would bring in the big bucks and take all their family's cares away.

These *big bucks*, however, had never materialised, Harry somehow always swimming just behind the wave of fashion, or being completely capsized by it, and on many occasions when Mary, his wife, alone and sitting at the kitchen table, had finished the stocktaking and accounts, responsibilities that were hers alone, she would put her head in her hands and cry out forlornly, 'We are the kind of shop that sells everything (poorly) and almost nothing of worth (at all)!'

Then she would leap up like the Devil was in her – Sven had witnessed this in person, peering down at her through the bannisters when they were supposed to be asleep – and, with the look of Lady Macbeth in her eyes, she would take out her bunch of keys and one by one undo the padlocks on the many rooms in the multi-storeyed house that had long since been turned over for storage.

'What kind of commercially backward madness and fecundity is this?' she would demand.

Tears in her eyes, she would stand glowering at the racks of incandescent Koosh balls, at the stacked mounds of luminous jelly shoes, at the boxes upon boxes of Rubik's cubes, at the bin bags of leg warmers, at the many dozen sets of sew-in shoulder pads 'suitable for any occasion', at the Sony Walkmans with a Rolf Harris pictorial tie-in, at the stacks of Sea Monkey aquariums, with the picture of the boy in wonder on the front, and she would dream of what might have been – sales, in short, and not this pointless hoarding.

One consequence of so many rooms being turned over to storage was that, at fourteen years old, the time when they were beginning to sprout unwanted hairs in unusual places – and this *despite* the under-the-counter medication they had purchased – and develop an interest in previously boring Olympic activities, beach volleyball, gymnastics, Greco-Roman wrestling, Sven still had to share a room with his Dead Sister. Or rather, the ghost of...

Sometimes she would come to them in the early hours of the morning, sit on the end of their bed and insist, for old time's sake, they should go down to the shop *proper* and do some shopping.

Two ladies of leisure. Millicent and Maureen. (Sven had always been Maureen.)

So they would pull on a pair of their sister's panties, a pair of her Sunday best stockings, and the dress that would indicate they *were* Maureen.

She liked that one with the flowers on it, their sister would say, tight around the arse, her best feature, much better than the face, which had a tendency to be pursed and cranky and could cause a dog to turn nasty; and decked out thus they would do some shopping, each with a basket hooked in the crook of an arm, taking what they wanted:

- snow globes (48p a pop);
- tiny rubber animals (12p each or five for 50p);
- cherry lipstick (68p);
- a grainy black-and-white postcard of the nuclear plant (2p);

193

- a Mexican-style hat (£1.50);
- a magnetic spider – with magnet (18p);
- a pair of pink flip-flops (74p);
- a tin of potted Best Pig! (52p);
- a magnifying glass with a knife built into the handle to scrape crustaceans off rocks (99p);
- a super-high bouncy ball, pink (6p);
- a selection of cassettes – Michael Jackson's *Thriller*, *The Essential Patti Labelle*, The Beach Boys' *Pet Sounds* (£1.05 each).

'Millicent's a bugger for those snow globes,' their Dead Sister might say to them, gathering twenty in her own basket. 'Has them all lined up on her chimney breast, if you'll excuse my French.'

As a ghost she had a tendency to ramble on – which was odd, as in the flesh she had been noticeably terse.

'Lives in the hope Arthur Scargill will pop round one day. She likes a passionate man with a comb-over. Hopes he'll shake her globes vigorously, if you catch my drift. Oh, Maureen, you are awful.'

With tears of both sadness and joy Sven would pretend to ring all their selections through the till, bag them up, wish their sister a good day. Although of course she was dead, and now just a ghost – the presence of which they were ready to swear upon. 'Honest to God, wrap my genital regions in barbed wire and tug me along the seafront with a banana up my arse.'

Not that they could tell their parents about their Dead Sister's regular apparition, because they would go absolutely flippin' bananas, accuse them of making up stories again. But there *was* a mermaid who worked in Ginny's Palace. And Alexi Macarov *did* have two dicks. Sven had fondled one of them during Mrs Ginty's extremely long description of oxbow lakes in double geography and had had to appear before the headmaster, who had shouted, 'You're an outrage, Tosier! Tell me why I shouldn't call your parents right now. Right now!' And they wanted to quip, 'Because their phone was cut off after Dad squandered all our available cash on a boxful of genuine USSR cosmonaut suits,' but they didn't, because the head might then write a letter, and if their fondling of dicks came out – or, at least, one dick – then so might their biggest secret of all: that they loved being Maureen in the flesh – two pendulous boobs and a triangle of scratchy grass; that they wanted to be Maureen even when they were a man. Supposed to be a man. Although they didn't feel that way.

But then their nighttime jaunts had to stop.

It all started, or rather all stopped, when their mother and father sat them down at the kitchen table and explained that because of 'tough economic conditions' the shop was going to go to transition to twenty-four-hour opening hours – 'As many hours as there are in the day, and then when that day ends another will have started – or will start just then. And we'll still be flippin' open.'

Time and tide waits for no man. Their dad would do the day shift from 7 a.m. to 7 p.m. and their mum would do the night shift, 7 p.m. to 7 a.m., and they would meet in the middle.

On their way to school that morning Sven stopped and examined the new sign outside the shop – its appearance overnight mirroring that morning's confabulation.

Come On Over, We're Always Here!
Need A Spade, or Hair Gel!, at 3 a.m.
We're Where You're At
We also sell Potted Meat, Seasonal Fish Fingers, Handmade
Willy Warmers
Give Delicious Gifts a Try
Today
Or Tonight!
Open 24 hours
Every Day

What am I going to do if I can no longer dress as a woman? Sven thought. *I think I'll go bonkers and then they'll put me in the lunatic asylum up on the hill to be tended on by nuns, those Devil's brides.*

So instead of going to school they went and sat under the pier and, to mollify their winded happiness, listed their other favourite things which might remain: chips with tons of salt on them, watching and rewatching their dad's *Magnum, P.I.* VHS cassettes, visiting the seal colony out across the mudflats, sneaking into the Foetus Museum before it opened for the day, stripping off their clothes and then jumping from behind one of the jars to startle the unwary tourists who would take them for one of those poor dead half-babies come to life, sitting in the bus shelter on stormy afternoons and listening to the thump of the raindrops on the corrugated metal roof, going out to the abandoned train station and putting graffiti on the toilet doors, although they had got the fright of their life one time when a tall, skinny man sporting a colourful hat and a drooping moustache had put his willy through a hole in one of the cubicle walls, and, staring eye to eye with the willy, Sven was unsure who was going to make the first move, until they had bit the bullet and, grabbing the willy firmly in one hand, they had stretched it tight and written 'Supercalifragilisticexpialidocious-wanker' on it, which was the longest word they knew, even without the wanker on the end, and finally – *one final thing – I've started, so I'll finish – nothing for a pair not in this game* – they loved that their dad had become a gumshoe (hence the addition to their name – their dad had proclaimed, 'We're going to be a flippin' brand, like Pinkerton's detective agency or Inch-High Private Eye!'), placing a card on the noticeboard outside Rose's Roadside Café:

Cat gone missing? Lost a slipper?
Errant wife/husband?
Harry Gumshoe is your man.
Night rates only.
Ring 0800-GUMSHOE

After the start of their dad's new on-the-side profession, one of Sven's favourite things to do was to follow him when he was out on one of his assignments, looking for the missing cats (usually eaten by the seals), stray husbands (usually one of the fishermen – they were an errant lot), stray wives (usually sleeping with one of the fishermen), solving the occasional murder (mostly done by out-of-towners – shady, heavily tattooed folk from Alnmouth, Boosbeck or Poulton-le-Fylde, involved in murder-attracting professions such as people-trafficking, gun-running, midnight car-park drug deals).

Their dad was Philip Marlowe from *The Big Sleep*, Sam Spade from *The Maltese Falcon*, the mild-mannered janitor from *Hong Kong Phooey*. Or rather, Sven wanted him to be, dreaming of the one big case that would save them, make them famous and release them from their wretched lives. In fact, they had been dreaming of exactly such a thing when they had been apprehended by those Bones boys, dragged to the Martello and had their teeth forcibly removed in the hope of a blow job of a lifetime which the telling of our story started and appeared to have been done with. Except, except, except…

Summer Holiday

Having a Dead Sister, Sven understood it wasn't right to speak ill of those who no longer walk amongst us, so they had never told their mother and father who was responsible for making them so gummy. Standing at the Bones boys' funeral amongst all the other mourners, they had shed genuine tears.

So it was unfortunate that, when the bill from the dentist had dropped through the door of Delicious Gifts, their mother opened it right there in front of them – not even a drop of her nightly gin to soften the monetary blow.

'You're not going anywhere, child,' she uttered, firmly grabbing one of their protruding ears, 'until you've told us who did that to your mouth. That'll be 58p, sister.'

(Their mother was in the middle of serving one of the devout nuns from the lunatic asylum up on the hill. The devout nun was buying a tiny Jesus fixed to a cross – pull a cord on the back of the Jesus and it would recount one of the parables from the Sermon on the Mount. This Jesus was available in two versions: a clean one and a dirty one. 'A Bun and a Fish for your Son' vs. 'A Bum and a Fisting for your Son'; 'Hungry and Thirsty' vs. 'Hungry and Thirsty for your Love Juice, Baby'. The Sister, reluctant at the best of times, was buying the dirty version.)

Sven's father, roused from his bed by a wail up the stairs, was sitting on an upside-down plastic bucket, rubbing ruefully at his tired, red eyes.

'Four teeth at £8.66 a piece is not a smiling matter,' said their mother. 'Times are hard. We can't all be the next *Jaws*. What do you say, Harry? I think now's the time.'

'Mebbe,' Sven's father said cursorily. 'We'll see.' Then he had stood with a sigh and click of old tired bones and, going over to the door, had done something that hadn't been done for many days. He turned the sign over from 'OPEN' to 'CLOSED'. 'Go to you room,' he said. 'Me and your mother need to have a bit of a family conference.'

Sven had seen a family conference once on their favourite TV show, *Mrs Brady and Her Many Peers*. Little Tommy Brady had been hit by a runaway horse. The horse had sent him under a tram and the tram had run over his arm and the arm had come off. Then, while he had been lying there, helpless, he had been bitten by a rabid rat and become delirious. Over the following weeks he had called Mrs Brady 'an old coot', 'a varmint' and told her she was as 'ugly as a burnt boot'. The Brady Family had had a family conference to decide what to do with him, and Little Tommy Brady had never appeared in another episode.

Instead another boy appeared – Little Billy Brady. Little Billy Brady never called his mom a 'coot', a 'burnt boot', etc., etc.

Sven went up the stairs with heavy feet. They secretly put on their Dead Sister's clothes. They imagined themselves shopping.

A cream donut (12p), a King Kong key chain (36p), a packet of Wild West fuzzy felt (82p), a pair of sheer tights (£1.12).

It wasn't the same not being in the actual shop. It wasn't the same without their Dead Sister being with them.

They looked disconsolately out of the window. They had serious flippin' worries about their future.

It was at breakfast the following morning when the blow came. Their mother, at work in the shop downstairs, serving the fishermen their worms and copies of *Fishermen's Wives* and *Boating Beauties*, shouted up the stairwell, 'Have you told him yet, Harry?', in the shrill voice she used for shoplifters and school sports days when Sven was always bringing up the pack.

Then their father had slid the brochure towards them. Across the top in large letters was 'The Swiss Card Sharp Summer School', and below this, in smaller letters, 'Making Boys into Men' and 'Card Sharps™ since 1975', and an embossed glossy picture of a pack of cards.

'We're sending you there,' said their father. 'If you look at the small print it's not all about being a card sharp. They do "rough physical games under close supervision", and you can "learn to play the recorder or another musical instrument" and "make lifelong friends in one of the tightly packed but well organised dorm rooms".'

Sven traced the outline of the cards on the front of the brochure. They imagined a sweaty dorm room in the early hours of the morning, a recorder shoved up their ass in an unsupervised physical game, many *other* boys, fearsome ambidextrous card sharps laughing and braying at their white slender butt, taking bets about who was going to blow into the *stuck-up* instrument.

They opened the first page of the brochure. 'It says it's in a prison,' they said.

'It's in a *former* prison,' said their father. 'Faithfully converted into a modern home away from home, giving your most-loved one or ones the best chance in life. What's more, the facility being in a former prison means parents can sleep safe in the knowledge that your little varmint isn't going get out any time soon and indulge in the many nightlife temptations on offer to teenagers around the world.'

Harry Tosier-Gumshoe rose up from the table and adjusted the picture of Dead Sister fixed to the wall there. Every family meal she peered down at them – a constant reminder.

'Who knows,' said Sven's father, 'you might like it there. Just embrace the experience.' He wiped away a tear that had formed under his eye. 'And don't forget, not everyone has the opportunity we're giving you. Look – it says it'll make a man of you. Teach you how to fight your corner in a non-combative, non-physical way. And if that means no more missing teeth then we're all winners, aren't we?'

'I don't want to be a boy,' said Sven. 'A combative one or not.'

Harry took a deep breath, peered closely at the set of com-memorative *Michael Bentine's Potty Time* eggcups still on the table.

'I suppose I'll get to see Switzerland, at least,' said Sven.

His father coughed. 'Swiss is a kind of card sharp – the school is actually in Saltburn. Me and your mother, we couldn't actually afford to send you to Switzerland. I mean, we would if we could. But we can't. So you'll be staying right here in Saltburn. But locked up. So to speak.'

'Wow-ee,' said Sven. And they meant it.

'And even better news,' said their father, pulling his lips above and below his teeth, 'is that you leave in the morning! Honestly, son, me and your mother just want the best for you. Our beautiful boy.'

That night Sven dreamt of a daring escape. They scaled a wall. They dug a tunnel. They evaded armed guards. Running along the mudflats to the seal colony, they were invincible. The seals would raise them as one of their own. They would evolve to have seal powers. Sealman! Their bark is as powerful as their bite! Over water, underwater, you name it, they can do it all! They felt spectacular. They would be spectacular.

Then they woke up. Somehow in the night their big toe had got stuck in the bed post. Again. They tried to get it out. They couldn't. They called for their dad to come and save them.

At last their dad appeared, bleary-eyed, in his Crockett and Tubbs pyjamas (one thousand lots of them bought just as the last season of *Miami Vice* got canned).

'Toe stuck again, son?' he said. 'Leave it to Harry Tosier-Gumshoe. No job too small.' He guffawed heartily. 'Last week I dealt with Kwame Botha's dick that got stuck in the postman's wife. Metaphorically speaking. Haha. But don't tell your mother!'

Then, while their father was pulling at the toe – quite roughly, Sven thought – the bedcovers had fallen off. Sven always slept in the nude.

Their father, catching sight of them, had appeared to think carefully for a while, rubbing at Crockett's head on his chest before saying, 'Have you been taking those black-market puberty blockers again? What did your mother and I tell you about that?'

Then he noticed Dead Sister's panties on the floor. He shook his head sadly. 'And you've been wearing your sister's clothes?'

Sven shrugged. What was the point in denying it? And how could they explain that they still remembered the days when Dead Sister used to dress them up and they had run on the spot in their room – this room! – pretending that the sun was shining, a hearty slap-up dinner was waiting for them, that they were running through a field of corn, etc., etc., etc.? How they had felt breathless and safe? Etc., etc., etc. How, since she had gone, they had felt a hole open up in their life. Etc., etc., etc.

'Smaller testicles will probably not set you in good stead with the other boys at the Swiss Card Sharp Summer School,' said Harry. 'And nor will wearing your dead sister's panties. That's the last I'm saying on the matter. Now get yourself up and dressed. Your mother and I have got a little surprise for you.'

Then he had hopped from foot to foot.

'Oh dang it, you might as well have it now.'

He went out and returned seconds later with the thing Sven had always most coveted from the shop but which had always been strictly out of bounds. It was a man's head, roughly the size of a golf ball. The man had a shocked expression on his face. Fixed to the back of his head was a plug. The plug went up your butt, fixing it in place, so it looked like the man was trying to escape from your ass. A metaphor for Sven, although their father wouldn't have got it – the masculine escaping from inside them.

'You'll be the belle of the ball with that,' said their father. 'But use it wisely. It's all too easy to overdo a joke.'

All Together Now

The following morning, the rare extravagance of a taxi booked for the occasion, they were taken to the Swiss Card Sharp Summer School, situated on a bluff out past the nuclear-power station.

'Arbeit macht frei,' said Sven, squinting up at the metal sign on the gate.

'Now, now, don't be like that,' their mother said, looking at them pointedly. 'I've knitted you a willy warmer. If the other boys want one, tell them they're £1.06 a pop. Call it a quid – mate's discount. Every little helps!'

'Give them everything you've got,' his father said. 'And remember we love you.'

Harold, the taxi driver, beeped his horn. 'If you wouldn't mind! I've got a race at twelve.'

Harold was also a jockey, although he had never won a race thanks to his addiction to custard creams, which he dipped into cans of Bird's custard.

'This is us, then,' said their father.

Sven watched the taxi until it was a dot on the other side of the nuclear-power station before making his way with a heavy heart through the gate to his new life.

At the door, after first ringing, then knocking, Sven was greeted by a tall boy with long, jutting-out teeth who said his name was Octopus or Oedipus. He was wearing a badge with *Monitor* handwritten on it.

'If you'd like to follow me!'

The long, gloomy corridors smelt of the former prisoners' feet, Brussels sprouts and anchovy paste. In an effort, apparently, to make the corridors more hospitable, someone had placed rubber plants on gold pedestals at even intervals along them, but the plants only looked fearsome, their leaves like long skeletal fingers.

At last they came to a door labelled 'The Bunkhouse', in which Sven was allocated a bed, some sheets, a pillow, a towel and an introductory handbook, the first fifteen pages of which, so Octopus, or Oedipus, said, outlined the rules and expectations of the school.

Octopus or Oedipus was very full of himself, guffawing heartily at his own asides, sometimes just guffawing, like he was a wind-up toy and he simply couldn't stop himself. Later in life Sven imagined Octopus, or Oedipus, would become a policeman – the kind of policeman who got dismissed for taking the law into his own hands and spent the rest of his days as a volunteer traffic warden on Saltburn FC's match days. What would happen in their own life they couldn't imagine.

Right now, it was the worst of times.

Each morning the card sharps were startled from their bunks by a klaxon and, after roll call was taken in the former prison yard and a desultory breakfast was eaten – usually a green egg-like substance, something that might pass for tea – there were six long hours of card-sharp techniques, sleights of hands, false shuffles, false cuts, mixing the deck, bottom dealing and so on.

These lessons were taught by a trio of instructors – tall, wide men with broken teeth in mouths full of stories from the times they had been professional boxers in South America or the Andes – how they wouldn't have been knocked down so much at a lower altitude or if they didn't have the shits from such spicy and unusual foods.

Sven was so bored, had so little interest in the lessons, that while the other sharps were mixing their decks, as they came to call it, they would sit at the back of the room, transcribing on to the face of their designated set of cards stories they had made up about the former prisoners of the facility, grainy black-and-white photos of whom lined the long corridor walls. They gave them exotic names like Bones Malloy, Rupert the Third, and imagined being taken by them as a female lover, fussed and pawed over sweatily in out-of-the-way sepulchral rooms.

After lessons each day was a period of Designated Free Time, which Sven would spend alone in their dorm. They liked to put on their X-ray specs, fingerless gloves and the lime green socks given out at Chippy Chips with every tenth fish supper.

The glasses were huge on their face, the fingerless gloves pink, the socks, defects, going right up their thighs to their crotch.

Then they would sit quivering on their bottom bunk, imagining they were Jackie O on that day in Dallas, sitting in the back seat of her Lincoln Continental, her philandering husband's brains just blown across her pink Chanel suit.

'I'm a beautiful, powerful woman,' they would say. 'It is only circumstance of birth, the ability to sport a willy warmer in the anatomically correct place, being trapped in this unwanted body that have screwed me.'

Religiously, before they went to sleep, they would swallow their puberty blocker, purchased in the alley behind Ginny's Palace from Gustav the chemist, who had no morals and a serious gambling habit.

But, despite trying to keep themselves to themselves, Sven was bullied mercilessly.

Bert the boxer from Boosbeck was their biggest abuser. On seeing Bert shirtless on their first morning Sven had pointed out

— why did they do this? — that the tattoo across Bert's chest that stated 'IT'S A DOGGIE DOGGIE WORLD' should actually read, 'It's a dog-eat-dog world'. It was downhill from there.

At every opportunity Bert the boxer would think of new ways to torment Sven. There were Chinese burns, frogs in their bed, prawns stitched into the seam of their underpants, the head of their toothbrush put up Bert's bum then in their mouth, being made to sleep on their bed naked with no covers, being made to shower in their clothes, being made to stand on their head in the corner of the room while the other card sharps pinged elastic bands at them, being made to eat cat food on their hands and feet at Bert's feet while Bert called them a snivelling little weasel, being made to hold Bert's poo on their outstretched hand for sixty full minutes — and other much worse things that cut to the quick, like having to suck Bert's big toe while humming the National Anthem.

Sometimes at night to escape Sven would go up on to the roof of the prison and stare up at the stars, *Antares*, *Pleiades*, *Betelgeuse*, or out across the mudflats, where the fishermen would gather for their bacchanalian parties, dancing naked, ingesting magic mushrooms, indulging in the worshipping of lobster pots and plankton nets, those deities of the sea, and they would imagine their future.

It was a bleak one. For even in their wildest dreams they could not imagine a rescue — someone coming through the door and rescuing them from their misery.

Then Stanley appeared.

Holding Out for a Hero

Stanley, arriving four days late thanks to having to work with his welder father on the repair of Evans' Sausage and Pie van fleet, stepping into the Bunkhouse, had found Sven on their knees, the other sharps around them in a circle, jeering, while Sven was forced to lick some disgusting paste (it was Spam) off Bert's naked chest.

'It's a doggie doggie world,' Stanley said, reading out the tattoo on Bert's chest, grabbing the boxer from Boosbeck around the neck and launching him through the open window and down, via a pitch roof – *ka-dunk, ka-dunk, ka-dunk* – on to the parade ground below.

Bert landed on his arse, and lay there, stunned.

'And when you get back up here,' Stanley bellowed through the window, 'you can apologise to this wee person – and I mean properly apologise – and if you ever behave like that again I'll fucking kill you, so I will. I hate bullies, and you, my son, are one big fucking one. Or you were.'

From that point on Stanley and Sven were inseparable.

Stanley's father had a run-down workshop on the edge of Saltburn that dealt with 'All You're Welding Needs' and his mother was a dinner lady at Saltburn-by-the-Sea's Ecclesiastical Lower School, but she spent six months each year in the lunatic asylum up on the hill with the devout nuns because of her nerves, which drove Stanley's dad *bloody barmy*.

'But she's all right, me mam,' said Stanley. 'She's always there for me swimming.'

Stanley was a prodigious swimmer, and he dreamt that when he was older he would go diving for pearls in the Gulf of Mannar, of being the world champion free diver for five years in a row (at least) and of appearing in *The Guinness Book of World Records* for recording the fastest unaided swim between Saltburn-by-the-Sea and Stavanger, which was in Norway; but before all that, when he was sixteen later that year, he was going to join the army because his dad had already signed him up – there not being many jobs about here in Saltburn – and it was better to have a profession behind him.

'But what kind of profession I'll have in the army I don't know,' Stanley said, 'because the likes of me and you, Sven, are flippin' cannon fodder.'

Stanley wore a blue cable-knit jumper, had shoulders wider than a pit pony's thighs and, although he was only fifteen and three quarters, had to shave twice a day to maintain a bristle-free mien – although he didn't often shave because, he would say, tugging comically with both hands at full thick hairs on a square adult-looking chin, with a beard *like this* he could get served pints of ale at the Jolly Fisherman and admittance to Andy's Peep Show, where he could see real titties and ass through a wipe-down Perspex viewing screen.

Stanley's biggest secret was that when he was twelve years old he had welded his toes together with one of his father's blowtorches.

'I was thinking webbed feet like a duck or a grey goose or a swan would help me swim better, but the blowtorch flippin' bloody hurt, being hot, like, and me dad went bat-shit fuckin' crazy, hit the moon and back, but it did the trick, because look at these pair of bananas.'

Stanley kicked off his shoes. He peeled off his socks.

Jesusmothermaryofgod'sgapingarsehole, thought Sven.

Where other boys might have toes on each foot Stanley had a red ridged flipper.

After Stanley shared with them the secret of his feet Sven decided they should finally act upon the momentous decision they had taken not long after they had met up with Gustav the chemist in the alley behind Ginny's Palace. A secret shared is a secret halved.

So that night, while the other boys were engaging in some rough physical games under close supervision, Sven took Stanley into the broom and cleaning-apparatus storage cupboard, turned out the light and, standing on an upturned disinfectant bucket, whispered the words they had only ever said to themselves before into Stanley's left ear:

'I dress up sometimes in my dead sister's clothes.'

They looked down at their hands, kneaded their fingers together, felt a tightening in their butthole. In for a penny, in for a pounding.

'But it's not because they're my sister's clothes. It's because they're girls' clothes. I don't know why. I just prefer them. I feel safe. The truth is I want to be a girl.'

Sven closed their eyes. They could feel Stanley's breath on their cheek. It smelt of the herring mops, mulligatawny soup and fizzy cherry pop they'd had for dinner. They prayed. Please let me get what I want this time.

'You want to be a girl,' said Stanley, flicking on the light, grabbing Sven by the shoulders, pulling them in for a hug. 'Why should anyone give a flippin' flip about that sort of thing when there's so much other bad shit flying about? Stick with me and you'll be all right. Although don't stick with me in the army. I wouldn't wish that on my enemies. Two years I'm signed up. Then I'll be back. Or so I hope.'

Dress You Up

On the last day of the Swiss Card Sharp Summer School Stanley and Sven threw caution to the wind and skived off.

They went first to the mudflats, where seals gambolled and mudskippers skipped and where, in the shadow of the Saltburn-by-the-Sea nuclear-power plant, Stanley stripped down to a pair of flashy yellow Speedos. They were given to him, he said, eyes cast down, by Artur Rimbaud, owner of Saltburn-by-the-Sea Boys' Outfitters ('Clothes for *ALL* Occasions'), in return for sexual favours performed by Stanley's mother. This was part of her psychosis. On nights which harboured a full moon she would go out in a short yellow cagoule and no knickers to speak of and give herself arse over tit to the first willing man she came across.

Stanley sniffed and, looking surprised to see his fingers on his nipples, rotating clockwise, strode purposefully out to sea. And out to sea. And out to sea.

Having gone some distance, the land performing a sustained and graceful descent at this part of the coast, Stanley turned and, placing his hands on his hips, spreading apart his legs, so that he formed a kind of star, *Antares, Pleiades, Betelgeuse*, like one of the celestial bodies Sven had longed for on those sweltering summer nights when they had lain wide awake and alone on the fire escape outside their room staring up at the sky, he shouted, 'TODAY SALTBURN! TOMORROW STAVANGER!'

And then he was gone, swallowed by the water. *Everything that is good is taken away from me, and will be taken away, and will be taken away*, lamented Sven, before Stanley's arms came back up like pistons. It was a resurrection, a miracle.

Eventually Stanley returned, hair slicked back like a gangster, drips dripping from him, sporting goosebumps from his toes upwards.

Marching on the spot to keep warm, his mouth moved to the beat of his pumping arms and legs. 'When he, *I*, did, *do*, the swim *proper*, he, *I*, would have to have goose fat spread all over his body, *like a Christmas goose*, and somebody to follow behind him in an assistance boat because *I don't want to make a flippin' wrong turn and end up in flippin' Iceland, the flippin' Faro Islands or even flippin' Cuba*,' he said. And, laughing merrily, he pulled Sven up from the sand. 'Let's bounce and shimmy!' he said, and he taught Sven, then and there, there and then, a dance he'd learnt from a Cuban sailor, Jorge Felix Hernandez – hailing originally from Havana but now captaining tugs on the Humber estuary – 'One of me ma's conquests.'

And the two of them danced, laughing, because as Stanley pointed out, this dance was basically 'Just moving your feet real quick, but it feels good.'

And they felt good.

Because their dad would be working and because today was the day their mum volunteered at the lunatic asylum up on the hill, pushing the drugs trolley, Sven said they could sneak up to their narrow room on the third floor of Delicious Gifts and no one would be any the wiser or the worse off for it.

They thought they could watch one of their dad's Magnum, P.I. episodes recorded from the TV on VHS cassette – 'The Ugliest Dog in Hawaii' or 'The Curse of the King Kamehameha Club' or 'From Moscow to Maui', etc., or if you're not partial to a bit of Tom Selleck, they could search down the back and sides of the old sofa in the downstairs living room which their dad had purchased at an auction selling furniture from the set of the *The Liver Birds*. It had been an investment. He'd wanted to sell it, and for two years it had sat in the shop with a card on it – 'Nerys Hughes and Polly James Sat Here, *Liver Birds* Through and Through', but despite the fishermen coming in to recline on the sofa and have lewd thoughts about the two actresses it had not sold, and eventually it had been moved upstairs to the lounge.

But Stanley had other ideas. He had been carrying a cardboard suitcase around with him all day, which Sven had naturally assumed contained some specialised swimming equipment – flippers, deep-sea mask, octopus and stingray deterrent, plastic screw-in knob thing to stop salt water going up your bum – but now Stanley lifted the case up on to Sven's narrow bed and opened it up.

'What do you think?' he said, taking out a long yellow dress with flowers on it, a black bra and matching black panties, a pair of plastic high-heeled shoes, a large straw sun hat with real daisies and a stuffed green canary sticking out from the rim.

'They're for you,' said Stanley. 'Not your dead sister's. Yours. The start of your wardrobe. Now, come on mate. Try them on.'

Sven, their body shaking a little, told Stanley to turn his back and, feeling both self-conscious and free, they got changed.

When he was allowed to turn around again Stanley did that thing with his nipples again, wolf whistled and, grabbing Sven by the hand, pulled them down the stairs and out on to the street – 'Eyes forward, shoulders back, chest out, and act like the flip you mean it!' – where they paraded up and down the front, past Ginny's Palace, past Chippy Chips, past the Foetus Museum, past the shop which sold the huge sausage rolls which no one knew the name of but which everyone called Arkady's – Arkady being the owner, a Russian from Crimea, who had lost both his sons in the Chechen war, one to a bullet in the heart, one to a cut finger gone septic: first he'd lost his hand, then his arm, then his shoulder; the doctor only stopped the cutting when there was almost none of him left, *poor bugger.*

'I've never been happier,' said Sven, turning to Stanley. 'Out here in public, all this.'

But when Art Fiegelman, the fisherman, doffed his cap to Stanley and asked him who the young lady he was stepping out with was, and did she have a sister, Stanley, quick as a flash, said that she didn't, that this lady was one of a kind, one in a million, his love, Sven felt even happier. Ready to burst.

And then they did burst.

At the pier Stanley stopped them, pulled Sven in close, placed a gentle kiss on their lips. 'I wanted you ask you,' he said. 'Will you be my...' – he stopped, watched a seagull dive for a chip from a young boy's cone and fly off with it, gleeful – '...girlfriend? I didn't tell you. Tomorrow I'll be gone. The army. It's flippin' tomorrow. "Early call-up! Country in need!" I'll write, of course. But will you wait for me? Like I said, be my girlfriend? You don't have to say yes.'

The gull, parading in front of them now, dropped its chip, scuttled it across the pavement with its sharp beak, flew off with it again.

'Of course it's a yes,' said Sven. 'It's a yes, yes, yes!'

Sign Your Name

Dearest Sven our Captain being staunch & strident Welshman from Caerphilly whose grandfather piccolo player in 47th grenadiers & so tells us killed by stampeding elephant in time of Raj has military in blood

  & also complete obnoxious arsehole

  we hate him

  we being me + other poor signed-up sods ragtag bunch of sons of railway workers cabinet makers ship hands & all off cuff tattoo artists

  it is wonder what can be done with deconstructed Bic biro and hatpin

  eg your name tattooed on left buttock.

  for which Captain punished 2 mornings pre-reveille cleaning battalion bogs with single toothbrush and Birds baking soda

  ha

  Captain punish us all 1 by 1 for 1 minor infractions Yeats for excessive wind Butler for arse being too high during crawl training

  so we plan revenge

  and this is story

  last night broke into local zoo stole elephant named Kalamazoo after town in which rich American industrialist/ philanthropist who donated elephant lived Kalamazoo County State of Michigan

  with trail of peanuts & kind words led Kalamazoo to Captain's bunkhouse & affixed Kalamazoo to Captain's bunk & told Kalamazoo to run like wind back to zoo which did pulling bunk behind her

  Captain's screams more high-pitched than any piccolo I ever heard

today will be punished but worth it
Yours ever,
Stanley.

On the front of Stanley's postcard was the picture of a squat East German PT-76 tank, some tiny italicised writing, *Panzermuseum Munster*, and on the back Stanley's words cramped right up to the address and around a picture he had drawn of himself, head cocked, left eye winking.

Dearest Sven have learnt to shoot gun build dam from driftwood/biscuit boxes crawl across desert terrain while being fired upon by enemy insurgents enemy insurgents for now played by neighbouring unit also under training but 2 weeks ahead

Very full of selves they are Poulton-le-Fylde regiment rich father sons of bankers car salesmen sweatshop owners destined for officer rank

yesterday during unarmed combat they broke Smithy's jaw & shoved bugle up Butler's ass which unfair because who brings bugle to unarmed combat

now Butler has v sore ass and Smithy is in infirmary 7 days at least and has to eat scran through straw & can't sing Smithy is great singer voice like Sacha Distel

so last night for revenge our crew broke into Poulton regiment barracks & very quietly while they asleep we put super glue on the ends of their todgers but not being evil left instructions of how to remove = Brillo pads + Arkwright's Patent Cleaning Powder

ha

have you used Arkwright's Patent Cleaning Powder even on fingers stings like billy-o and stains bright purple so mebbe evil after all

Yours ever,
Stanley.

Like clockwork the postcards arrived each week. Always on the front was the image of a piece of army machinery and on the back Stanley's words, circling around a picture he had drawn of himself. 'Not much of artist but this is me. Always, Stanley.'

Fifty-two postcards.

One year passed. And in that year Sven finished school, enrolled in the local sixth-form college. Delicious Gifts continued to open twenty-four hours, meaning Dead Sister had to come up with new ways they could dress up and shop together, although thanks to Stanley, Sven had their own clothes now.

Regularly on *Look North with Arthur Seagull and Molly Splat* there appeared grainy images from the distant war – bivouacs, helicopters charging low over sand dunes, raids on windowless houses, skirmishes in marketplaces, snipers on rooftops, soldiers sitting shirtless at fold-away tables, field radios as big as suitcases, poor skinny sods with hats pulled low, eyes and mouths covered with camo scarves, and then, more and more often, body bags, rows of them, draped in flags.

Sven treasured Stanley's postcards, waited for the next one, stored them carefully in a shoebox under their bed.

Late at night they would take out the shoebox and read the postcards under the covers of their bed with a torch, dressed in the yellow dress Stanley had given them, imagining they were Jean Arthur in *Mr Smith Goes to Washington* or Myrna Loy in *The Thin Man Goes Home.*

Then one week the postcards stopped.

Every night Sven thought, *Tomorrow there might be a new postcard.*

The next day there was no new postcard.

Nor the next.

When there had been no postcards for twenty-eight days Sven skived off college and went directly to the station, took the express to Poulton-le-Fylde, where they presented themselves at the National War Office. This was housed in a former ice-cream factory, the old faded letters of which could still be seen above the door: Evans' Ice Cream: For When You Just Can't Stop Licking.

'I have a request,' they said, bold, the plan formed in their head, 'about a person I believe may be MIA.'

Then, unable to say Stanley's name out loud for fear of tearing up, Sven had written it on a slip of paper and slid it across the desk.

The man behind the counter was wearing a lime-green hat, goatskin gloves and a tie with three-dimensional snails crawling up it. He told Sven that operational information about combatants in action couldn't be divulged, but if Sven wished to purchase a commemorative Evans' die-cast model in the shape of a Matilda Tank to raise funds for 'our boys on the ground' then it would help the war effort.

The tank was £8.99. It came with 'genuine firing missiles' (safe for indoor use) and a pack of twenty enemy insurgents that could be set fire to, to bring about a realistic death. (Extra insurgents available in all good bookshops and convenience stores; 1p from each sale going to the war effort.)

Sven didn't have the necessary funds for the tank, having spent all the money they had on a cheap day return.

'Give me the info and I'll make it worth your while,' they said, pushing the return portion of their ticket across the desk in the manner of David Niven in *A Man Called Intrepid* when he was bribing a German foot soldier for secrets of the Nazi High Command.

'Stanley,' they whispered. 'Capital "S", one "L", ends in "E, Y". Between you and me. Nobody has to know.'

'I have a season ticket,' said the man, pushing the return back towards Sven. 'And a Frequent Breakfaster reward card. Once a week I get a free pain au chocolat and a cappuccino. So scram.'

It was as they were leaving the building that Sven saw the interactive recruitment diorama.

As they pressed the large green button to watch the 'short inspirational video' a small inset black-and-white screen flickered to life.

Two young men are sitting on swings in a car park. They pass a joint between them. One of the young men asks the other what he is up to tomorrow. The other young man shrugs, points around him to the desolate park where: two old bums dance to a slow waltz playing on a portable phonograph; a mangy dog pulls at the head of dead rat; a heavily pregnant woman, with another child in a pushchair, drinks from a can of beer and puffs on a cigarette, while another young mother, clearly drunk, drops a grey-skinned baby on its head; a third young man jumps to his death.

'Just another day in paradise,' the young man says.

Then, loud raucous music blaring out of the diorama's tiny speaker, a green car packed with joyriders zooms past, and as the joyriders spot the scene in the park one of them shouts, 'Hey, losers, joyride this!'

The car swerves, screeches, then, speeding up, takes out the bums, takes out the young mothers, takes out the dog and rat and crashes into a wall, exploding in ball of flames.

'Did you see that?' says the first young man, just as the second young man is decapitated by a flying hubcap from the exploding car.

As the first young man, caught in a shower of blood gushing from his friend's headless neck turns to face the camera and says, 'I need to get out of this place,' the screen segues to:

DON'T DELAY – YOUR COUNTRY NEEDS YOU*

JOIN THE ARMY TODAY

---

* Terms and conditions apply. No responsibility accepted for injury, serious injury, or death.

There follows a montage of shots of the first young man.

- Naked and buff and in shower with many other naked and buff young men. One young man turns to our young man says, 'What a great, toned body you've got! You must get loads of gorgeous girls.' Thought bubble appears above head of our young man. Bedpost with army cap on it. Below army cap many notches indicating female conquests.
- Young man leaps out of helicopter on to roof of burning building. He gathers two crying children up in his arms. He leaps from burning building on to roof of adjacent building. He leaps back into hovering helicopter.
- Young man in sand-coloured combat uniform. Speeded-up footage of him crawling across miles of deserts. He comes to castle wall. He climbs castle wall. He surreptitiously kills many bearded armed guards. He picks lock of heavily locked door. He breaches room containing Prime Minister tied to chair. He unties Prime Minister who says, 'What a hero. You have not only saved me, you have saved the country. You may even have saved the world.'
- Young man stands on podium. General steps up to podium and pins large medal on young man's chest. Young women in audience swoon. Thought bubble appears above young man's head. 'Joining the army was the best decision I ever made. While I still masturbate because masturbation is a healthy and natural thing to do, now I can always get girls and no longer have to take turns jerking off my stoned mates into a paper bag on a cold windswept car park. Happy days.'

The video ended and a short questionnaire appeared on the interactive touch screen.

JOIN UP HERE.

Without pause Sven selected 'No Death Wish' and 'No Major Psychological Problems', agreed that he came from a 'Disadvantaged Social Group with Little (or no) Future Prospects' and finally pressed the button to sign on the dotted line.

Stop the Cavalry

Sven left for basic training with his rucksack stuffed with items from Delicious Gifts: a stick of Ginny's Palace rock (12p), a cerise willy warmer with Sven's name stitched on it in lime-green thread (99p), an out-of-date tin of corned beef hash (65p), a set of commemorative beer mats, each one displaying a significant site from Saltburn-by-the-Sea – the towers of the nuclear-power plant emerging from the mist, the windows of the Jolly Fisherman lit up and casting light out on to the street, an aerial view of the lunatic asylum up on the hill, the art-deco public toilets on the front where the dirty old men hung out under the guise of holding seances (88p for the set), a porcelain seal, its beady black eyes seeming always to follow the viewer (£2), a triangular flag on a pink plastic stick that flapped gaily in the wind (8p), a polished winkle shell with the name of the town stencilled on it in gold lettering (5p), a novelty pencil rubber in the shape of Count Dracula (15p), Michael Jackson's *Thriller* on cassette (£1.05), a key ring in the shape of a magnet (25p), a fridge magnet displaying a view of the nuclear-power station from across the mudflats (80p), a lucky 1p piece sold for use in Ginny's Palace (8p) and (a replacement for the precious gift their dad had given them but had been *misplaced* at the Swiss Card Sharp Summer School – in fact Sven had shoved it so far up Bert the boxer from Boosbeck's bum no one had been over-keen to go in and look for it) the Talk o' the Town Co's golf-ball-sized man's head fixed to the small plug which you could insert to make it look as if a person was crawling out of your anus (£2.50).

Although Mary and Harry believed Sven was throwing away their life by joining the army, they had demurred when Sven had said over and over that their will was resolute and that if they were a soldier they would probably stop wearing women's clothes.

This last was a lie. If Stanley had taught them anything it was to be yourself.

The basic-training barracks were in the south, and from their train window Sven looked in awe as the misshapen northern fields containing donkeys with bits of straw sticking from their mouths, small crumbling disused windmills with lewd graffiti on their sails, stinking cow-silage enclosures surrounded by the cows themselves, gave way to wide multi-lane motorways, tall, gleaming skyscrapers, huge shopping malls whose car parks were filled with row upon row of shining cars, bars affixed to their bonnets for marauding bulls to bounce off during a stampede, racks on the backs for attaching cycles, motorbikes, go-karts, boxes on the top to store canoes, kayaks, tents, inflatable dinghies. They were, Sven mused, the Swiss army knife of cars – perfectly equipped to deal with every situation you were unlikely to find yourself in.

Having disembarked, finally, at the specified station, and having followed the pre-supplied directions on the laminated map, they found the barracks at the end of a long, dusty path with Roman ruins on one side and a closed-down gift shop and sauna on the other. According to the sign, the old lighthouse and adjacent sprat-packing factory had been 'requisitioned for army use'.

The training sergeant was a tall man with a beige wig and ill-fitting dentures with a green tint. On the first humid, drizzly morning after their arrival, a sleepless night in a stinking barracks with rows of metal-framed bunkbeds and a picture of the President Blu-Tacked to the wall, he gathered all the recruits outside the factory on a sand-packed parade ground and announced the first part of the training was to take place in the hills and woods behind the lighthouse, the area having been cordoned off to stop day-trippers, holidaymakers and other general busybodies straying on to a place where there would be live munitions.

After being given a brief induction to marching and half a bar of mouldy chocolate and some tepid tea in a green paper cup, off they went, sergeant ahead, recruits snaking behind.

There were five other young men, each one an identical height and each sporting the ripped abs and buzz-cut hairstyle of the Anatomically Correct Commando Dolls (£9.99)* Harry and Mary used to sell from a top shelf in Delicious Gifts.

Sven had had many erotic fantasies with and about their Anatomically Correct Commando Doll, given to them by their father in a brown paper bag in the bin alley behind Ginny's Palace, the rendezvous organised via a Post-it note secreted at the bottom of a crisp packet slipped under their bedroom door and with the mysterious words, along with the time and place of the rendezvous, 'Come in disguise.'

They had gone as the Shah of Iran, bastardising an old lobster pot and two of their mother's best sheets, and before they had even got halfway to Ginny's Palace they had caused quite a furore among the local fishermen; Cadan Bowes was still dining out on the story to this day, claiming, he said, he 'thought we were being invaded by aliens'.

In the weeks after first receiving the doll Sven had sometimes got through a week's supply of jizz in a single afternoon bunked

---

* Anatomically Correct Commando Dolls: For all those awkward questions your growing YOUNG MAN might have about penises, erections and masturbation, the Anatomically Correct Commando Doll will provide the answers with its unique Self-Explore-and-Play™ functionality. Each Anatomically Correct Commando Doll comes with a week's supply of erections and Jizz™. Extra erections and Jizz™ are available from all good retailers or by ringing 0800-222-JISSUM. (78p).

off school, and because of their desire to get the money to buy more jizz they had committed their only ever crime, rolling PC Ivan Gorenski and fiddling in his pockets for cash as he stumbled quite drunk and incapable one night out of the Jolly Fisherman.

In the Army Now

Being from the north Sven was not popular with the other recruits, and in the evenings when they would take out their bowling balls, head to the local Bowl-a-Rama and come back hours later, their eyes red with laughter, mouths redolent of cheap beer, winkles and crème de menthe shots, the tips of their fingers raw from throwing so many balls, Sven would still be on their bunk, their face turned to the wall, so their tears would not be seen.

Eventually falling asleep, they would dream of walking down Saltburn's promenade arm in arm with Stanley, their yellow dress gently lifting in the breeze, but then on waking they would find a small stack of bogies piled on their forehead in a replica of the Eiffel Tower, or their boots would have been filled to the brim with cold porridge or, one time, they even found a log of poo balanced perfectly on their upper lip so it looked like they had a shit moustache – which then became their nickname: Shit Moustache, or just SM for short.

The second week of the training programme was to take place down on the beach where, according to the training brochure, *From Waster to War Machine: It Could Be You!*, the young men would be split into single units of one and sent off to fend for themselves before coming back with 'a new sense of vigour and hardiness'.

Sven looked forward to this part more than the first week of drills and armament training, because it involved 'surviving in the wild' and 'living on your wits'. Having grown up on a bleak northern coastline, they knew how to scavenge for oysters, mussels, winkles, and how to ward off attacking seals and other aquatic animals with the flotsam and jetsam purloined from the seashore.

Having been taken down to the beach in a lime-green Sherman tank by the sergeant, they were each assigned a zone, given a ball of string and three potatoes in a paper bag and told under no circumstances were they allowed to communicate with him or each other.

On the first day Sven built themself a castle from driftwood and branches; on the second they constructed a boat from six tyres they found washed up and vines cut from the tops of trees. They made a fire from dried seaweed and caught fish with a harpoon they had fashioned themselves from a requisitioned abandoned shopping trolley.

On the third day one of the other young men turned up and asked if he could sleep in Sven's castle because the previous night he had frozen his fucking bollocks off.

Sven was not the kind of person who had been brought up to hold a grudge – Mary and Harry were forever providing dinners and made-to-measure willy warmers to cold, hungry shoplifters – and later that night, their stomachs full from the fish Sven had caught, Sven and the young man fell asleep side by side under the soft bedding Sven had fashioned from seaweed.

On the next night one of the other young men arrived, and the night after that another two.

Teddy Brewer, who had done the enormous poo on Sven's top lip, was the last to turn up. He did so on his hands and knees, naked apart from the seam of his underpants, his army cap and a number of sucking leeches attached to his buttocks. A chunk had been taken out of his side by a flippin' humungous seal, and a seagull had torn off one of his eyelids.

As Sven set about tending his wounds Teddy apologised for taking a poo on Sven's face. Sven, who had never been apologised to before by anyone, the Bones brothers especially, said there was no need to be sorry. If there was one thing they had learnt about humanity it was the necessity to be humane.

Two Tribes

Because Sven had excelled beyond anyone's reasonable expectations, a medal in the shape of a Matilda tank firing upon a defenceless line of enemy insurgents – babies with their heads blown off, mothers' arms raised in horror at the headless babies, a short man with his dick shot to pieces, a speech bubble coming from mouth saying, 'There goes my dick. You have to admire the sharpness of their shooting' – was pinned to their chest, and they were deemed to be battle fit and ordered to report to the parade ground at 0600 the following day, where they would be picked up for transportation to the war zone.

That night the other recruits took Sven bowling. Although all Sven's balls seemed to bounce out of their lane and miss all of the pins, they were announced the winner, and stood many small fiery drinks that were both sweet and milky.

'You'll be fine,' Teddy Brewer said the following morning as the jeep pulled up. He was still sporting the eyepatch Sven had fashioned him from an oyster shell. 'Look how you saved me. You'll show them what for.'

The jeep was driven by long thin lieutenant who wore odd socks and whose underpants were pulled up out of his trousers and over the top of his shirt. The back of the jeep was full of Michael Jackson cassette tapes, and one of these was played over and over on the journey to the airbase. The lieutenant had a large gap between his top and bottom lips, and all his words seemed to come from the end of a wind tunnel.

Upon arrival at the airbase they were waved through, and as they said goodbye the lieutenant gave Sven an extra-strong mint wrapped in a piece of tissue – 'To suck if your ears pop during the flight' – and two copies of Michael Jackson's *Dangerous* album on cassette.

The plane stood all alone on the runway. Standing next to it with his arms folded was the pilot. He was a handsome man who, thanks to the many glittery baubles attached to his arms and a fairy affixed to the top of his head, somewhat resembled a Christmas tree.

Having got Sven settled in the rear of the plane the pilot turned to Sven and smiled. 'I noticed you looking. If you're wondering, seven weeks' special ops in a Scandinavian forest over the winter period. It was a case of blending in and the look kinda stuck. The kids love it. Every Christmas Eve they put presents under me and sing 'Kumbaya' – not strictly a carol, but it's their favourite song, and who am I to piss on their chips? Season of goodwill and all that.'

He cast his arms about, causing the baubles to clash dramatically together and one to start up, via some internal musical device, Sven supposed, with a rendition of 'O Little Town of Bethlehem'.

'That's why we do it, isn't it? Go to war, I mean. Make the world a safe place for our progeny.' *The hopes and fears of all the years…* 'And blast a few folk. Perk of the job.' *…Are met in thee tonight.*

This being a flight to repatriate bodies, Sven was the only passenger, and so, taking the opportunity of being alone, they stripped off their clothes and, pulling out the yellow dress Stanley had given them from its hiding place in their pack, they put it on.

On their last night at the bowling alley Teddy Brewer had broken down and confessed how he had played Blanche DuBois in a school production of Tennessee Williams' *A Streetcar Named Desire.*

'It runs in my blood,' said Teddy. 'My father was a female impersonator.'

In the late 1970s he had been a stalwart of *How Much of a Woman Am I?*, a game show in which grown men had to compete in ever more womanly tasks while dressed as their favourite Hollywood film star. His dad had been Marlene Dietrich.

'He was gutted when the show was pulled – it was because of the New Wave of Comedy – political correctness that deemed his show sexist, out of fashion. He never really got over it – turned to drink and booze, and then drove his Mini Metro off the edge of Salthill Quarry, *'Where Have All the Flowers Gone'* blasting out from the cassette deck. He'd left a note taped to the dashboard. "Never forget who you are. I haven't forgot. I'm just not allowed to be." We buried him in his favourite dress, and the worst thing was I never even told him I loved him. That's why I gave Blanche DuBois my all. The standing ovation I got was for Dad. Proudest night of my life. But in the army I thought I'd have to quash all that, be the hard man, which led to my ill treatment of you. Sorry. It's what machismo does. Makes you think you're it. You're not. You're just shit.'

During the flight Sven played their *Dangerous* cassette over and over on their Walkman and thought of Stanley. They had once slow danced to 'Heal the World' under the pier. It had been blasting from the speakers on the Michael Jackson penny-drop in the arcade above. Slowly they had spun while Michael sang and coins crashed and jingled above.

Getting off the plane, Sven was met by an extremely sun-tanned man in fatigues, of which the knees and elbows were completely worn out. Another man was slumped, face-down, naked, on the back of an old truck, his ass in the air.

'I'm Mike One,' said the man. 'Over there, on the truck, that's Mike Two. Last night he had a hard time down at Billy Barnacles' Surf and Turf. We all did. Yesterday Mike Three had a letter home. His son Mike Jnr's got cerebral palsy or MS or something like that. And his wife's leaving him. With the kid's doctor. Well, you know, have a sick kid and you and the doctor spend a lot of time together. But what can you do? Fill in a self-assessment form and send it off. *Do you have suicidal thoughts? Yes, I do. Do you feel like hurting yourself and others? Yes, I do.* What I want to know is, who's reading them?' Then he said, squinting his eyes at Sven, 'Like the dress. Yellow. Nice colour. You'll blend in with all this fucking sand. But if you think the dress is a good idea to show off your non-combat suitability it's been done before. Mike Six, two weeks on the trot wore the same miniskirt-boob-tube combo, filled in the self-assessment, *Are you fit for active service? No, I am not. In a combat situation do you feel you have the potential to be the last man standing? No, I do not.* Last we'd heard he was down on the front in AG or S or somewhere like that. Still in his outfit, apparently. Shoots the shit out of shit during the day. Does bar dancing at night. Since the syphilis outbreak last year we've all been warned off the local girls, and one thing we all know about Mike Six is that he's very clean. Very clean. If you want a poop-shoot then Mike Six's would be it. I put that in my self-assessment. *Do you have sexual feelings towards other men? Yes, I do. Do you feel this might hinder your objectivity in a total-war situation? Yes, I do.* Did I hear anything? No, I did not. Now, where's your stuff?'

The airbase had one donkey on it, a small shop set up on a lopsided trestle table and a baggage-reclaim belt powered by a single skinny boy on a bike, the bike's rear wheel connected to the belt by a series of pulleys and levers.

Sven watched as the boy slowly fetched their rucksack from the plane, placed it on the far end of the baggage-reclaim belt, hopped on his bike and then peddled furiously until the bag was right next to Sven.

'Before you leave,' called out the boy, 'don't forget to stop by the shop.'

Then he got off the bike, put on a 'Today you have been severed by Mohammed' badge, and went over and stood behind the trestle table.

On the table were a range of small plastic aeroplanes, their wings melted and drooping, bottles of cloudy water and a book written by someone called Mike Eight entitled, *What to Do in a Case of Emergency! Life in a War Zone, Memoirs of a Near Survivor!*

On the back of the book was a photograph of a man with no legs and only one arm, sat upright in a wheelchair, being tended to by a group of elderly nuns. The nuns appeared to be in a kind of barn. The back half of the barn appeared to be on fire. The nuns had that look on their face which said, *Shall I save self or crippled man in wheelchair who is unable to help himself due to having many parts blown from body? If only goddam photographer wasn't here choice would be easy one. Myself. Because man shits through tube! I did not become nun, praise the Lord, to help man shit through tube. Became nun to help cute orphans, live in attractive nunnery, get away from bastard father who came to room at night and told me I was good girl, etc., etc., etc.*

The photograph was of Mike Eight, Sven supposed, and they were going to buy the book, if only to find out if Mike Eight was saved or if the book had been written posthumously by one of the nuns to raise money to rebuild the barn, do God's work, help other men like Mike Eight, when in the distance there was a huge explosion, followed by a dull rumbling under their feet.

Mike One sucked in his cheeks and looked pointedly at his watch. 'It must be a Tuesday,' he said. 'I fucking hate Tuesdays.'

Smalltown Boy

The base was housed in a huge rambling former pickle factory on the outskirts of S. Climb up a series of squat rusty ladders on to the flat roof of the factory and there all of S was: distant adobe tenement blocks, the ancient spiralling minarets of many mosques, sombre squares where lithe children would play war games punctuated by the sharp crack of faraway shooting rifles. Just outside the base, abutting the perimeter fence, was a white, square-windowed cottage owned by a tall hermit who claimed to be a direct descendant of the mighty king, Xerxes I, murdered at the height of his powers by Artabanus, the commander of his own royal bodyguard.

Each morning the hermit would emerge naked on to the same patch of crumbling concrete, swarming with the large red ants common to the region and said to be able to strip a goat of flesh in twenty minutes flat, and, by a contraption of his own devising, broomsticks bound end to end and then together at the top with hempen rope, tip a bucket of water over himself.

It was by this cascade they marked their reveille.

He's at it again. Hermit showering. Time to arise boys.

There were stories the west side of the pickle factory was haunted. The former owner, Babak Tehrani, said to have always carried a sharpened scythe in his belt and be not afraid to use it to cut fingers from misbehaving employees. It was these fingers, it was said, that did the haunting, stealthily entering all viable holes while you were sleeping – bum, ear, mouth, nose – before making their way to your heart, which they would grip with a deathly chill, causing nightmares the lingering memory of which would last throughout the day.

So the soldiers always kept to the east side, except when, in groups of at least four, they climbed the mighty west stanchions that swept up to the distant roof and dove headfirst into the still half-full pickling vats. Then, laughing, they would cavort and dive, tossing the remains of the floating onions at each other, before emerging stinking and slick. It was a vainglorious vinegary time.

Like the simple man of the cottage, that hoary descendent of Xerxes I, for the most part, thanks to the extreme heat, the soldiers existed in a state of nudity.

Strange times breed strange bedfellows, but this was not without precedent.

It was Mike Four, born Mihajlo in the town of Szentes, who told them of his Great Uncle Pataki, a member of that infamous

Cold War Hungarian basketball team that had travelled the length and breadth of the country by train and in the nude: 'They only donned their clobber on match days, because if they didn't' – and here he drew a finger across his throat – 'Khrushchev would have got wind of it and had their arses on spikes outside the Országház.'

'Országház?' asked Mike One.

'Hungarian Parliament. On the banks of Danube. Very beautiful building.'

'Set off nicely by arses on spikes,' said Mike Three, who was the funny one and who one day dreamt of appearing at the Royal Variety Performance – 'If I don't get my balls blown off in this blasted war, or other parts of me even less conducive to quick one-liners and startling repartee.'

'Like your mouth,' said Mike Two.

'Or your arsehole,' said Mike Five.

'I'm always talking out of it,' said Mike Three. Boom boom. (He *was* the funny one.)

Tuesdays and Thursdays were the only days when they routinely donned their uniforms, and on the nights before these days a kind of unstated ceremony would take place: floors would be swept, bedding shaken out, clothes neatly folded at bunk ends for the following day.

It was on a Monday night especially that some of the men would even go so far as to kneel and pray, *Dear God, protect me on the morrow, and protect my family and protect my loved ones, and protect the fishes in the sea, and protect the mighty whales, hammerheads, kraken* (thanks to Mike Five for these last watery benedictions, due to his former life as a fisherman on the *Saint Helena*, who plied her trade between the Barents Sea and Peterhead in Aberdeenshire), because it was on a Tuesday, by common agreement, decrees signed secretly in dusty tents, that the war itself would take place.

The fighting of the war. Actual killing.

Wednesday nights were an altogether more raucous affair. On Wednesday nights the men would shave together, standing in a line before iron buckets filled with tepid water, and then stick ginormous fake moustaches on each other's faces, a glorious find from the bazaar at A, where they had also purchased sweetly smelling incense sticks, tiny earrings in the shape of hissing snakes, elaborately decorated shawls that doubled as disguises if they wanted to go out in the early hours of the morning and chant with the other men to welcome the arrival of daily train from P, its carriages packed with produce and smelling sweetly of saffron, cardamom, ginseng and other herbs unknown to them.

After the shaving and the sticking-on of the Dalis, Fu Manchus, Lampshades, now fully moustachioed up, the men would preen before the base's single mirror boasting, as if they might have been in a fairy tale, about who was the fairest of them all.

This might go on for hours before the men fell exhausted on to their bunks, back first, to avoid the disturbance of their precious moustaches.

They had to look their best.

On Thursday Esta Esfahani would visit.

With whom they were all in love.

Love Cats

In a similar fashion to those incendiary leaflets dropped from aerostat machines on to Napoleonic battlefields – *Your general is descended from a baboon and eats his own shit, while you are prime boeuf being led needlessly to slaughter* – modern warfare vis-à-vis the general population was concerned not only with winning over bodies, but also hearts and minds. And to this purpose, Esta Esfahani, long-limbed and with lips a bee would sting you for, would come to the factory to teach the soldiers local customs, manners and the strange soaring language they heard drifting over five times a day from the mouths of the muezzins.

It being clear to all the Mikes right off the bat – turning up in a yellow dress might have been a clue – that Sven was not of the kind to fall for a person of the female sex, this newest recruit became a kind of conduit for all the Mikes, down which they would pour all their reasons why they should be the most appropriate and assiduous lover for Esta.

Mike One, a butcher by trade, dreamt of opening a sausage-roll shop in the East End of the Capital City. And Esta would be his wife, collecting prestigious awards in a glamorous and succulent pastry-case dress of Mike One's own making. She would want for nothing. Sausages would provide.

Mike Two, a self-styled sex machine – *The Pumper from Kuala Lumpur*, as he liked to call himself, his mother being half Malay, the other half being proud Scot, growing up in Govan under the shadow of the shipyards – claimed both men and women had always wanted him. While still at school he had been given nickname of *The Bike* – even Priest Gonçalo coming to him for womanly advice. Esta, though, had tamed him – for her he would become a one-woman man; would devote himself to her happiness, etc., etc.

Mike Three, the funny one, would write his own sitcom, *Me and Esta*. They would win a BAFTA each for *Outstanding Comedy Actor* and *Actress* and make the move seamlessly to Hollywood and jointly host the Oscars three years in a row.

Mike Four, the Hungarian, simply wanted to make love to a woman, having only previously been with Mike Six, he of the boob-tube and extremely pucker poop-shoot, during a drunken night in F that was never to be talked about – but always was, on and on, long into the night, until Mike Four, absurdly angry, would climb up on to the roof and sleep there under the stars, *Antares, Pleiades, Betelgeuse*.

Mike Five, the fisherman, desired to return with Esta to Peterhead and, while he sailed the seas in search of the mighty kraken she would work in the corner shop on the… corner, stacking cans of beans, spam, herring, smiling sweetly, waiting for her loved one to return from his travels.

Even Sven loved Esta, would wait breathlessly for her weekly visits. For, having exhausted enquiries with the Mikes regarding Stanley – 'No, we've never had a Stanley here, we've always been just Mikes, except for you – are you sure you're not a Mike? – she was their conduit to the outside world.

Each Thursday morning, after their lessons, she would take them into S, and it was here, in the multitudes, that Sven believed they might find Stanley, his webbed feet caressing the pavement, his mouth wide open, ready to tell anyone who enquired about his dream of swimming from Saltburn to Stavanger. Of setting the World Record. Never to be beaten.

Except he wasn't. Stanley was never there. Nowhere to be seen.

Searchin' (I Gotta Find a Man)

But still, on subsequent Thursdays, in the town of S, Sven searched for Stanley under the gilt vaulted ceilings of tearooms where old ladies with angry Pomeranian dogs were served cup after cup of sweet Moroccan tea by thin moustachioed waiters with neat rows of Bic pens in their chest pockets. They searched for Stanley in the pool halls, the men from which, tired of all those spinning, crashing colourful balls regularly spooled out into the sunshine to puff hungrily on their small portable hookahs, holding aloft their cues, looking like the rag-end of a defeated medieval army. They searched for Stanley in the many identical laundromats managed by doppelgänger petit hussars doling out detergent with all the reluctance of Draco's Council of Four Hundred in the city-state of Athens. They searched for Stanley in the fruit shops with their colourful shining produce displayed in even more colourful buckets on racks outside their dim interiors, the fruits protected from the sun by faded branded umbrellas, *Coca-Cola*, *Lunn Poly*, *Camel Cigarettes*, *Kodak*, *Prozac*, *Pan Am*. They searched for Stanley in the nail bars staffed by teams of fearsome Vietnamese ladies, identical with their tiny waists and pink, fume-cancelling face masks and with the pots of their polish flush across their bodies in belts like seventies Soviet secret agents; and they searched for Stanley in the tiny non-gambling casinos, with a single roulette wheel each, the real action taking place out back in drab covered shacks, or in concealed cellars where, under smoke-clogged ceilings, heavily bearded men gazed pitifully at the cards life had dealt them, each swearing, *Just one more hand and then I'm done*. They searched for Stanley in the many barbers' shops, interrupting the singing to pose their questions for all the barbers that sang in the town, taking up and passing along a single aria at closing time, 'O mio babbino caro', 'Largo al factotum', 'Quando me'n vo'. They searched for Stanley in the largely silent hairdressers as dusty copies of old English language magazines were passed to clients, *National Geographic*, *Caravan Club Monthly*, *Anglers Weekly*, the hairdressers secretly seething about the popularity of the singing barbers but also secretly a little in love with them and their closing-time concerts – 'Leave the door open – it's always nice at this time to have a little breeze. The noise? No, it doesn't bother me at all – I can hardly hear it.' They searched for Stanley amongst the fortune tellers garbed in colourful robes, their seeing eyes hidden behind mysterious dark glasses, with prophesies that always ended in *Flash Gordon* cliffhangers and, 'Behind the door, no… she's gone; the spirits are tired today…' – all the better to get their desperate clients to return. They searched for Stanley in the shoe shops, with fearsome foot-measuring machines that all the children were afraid of – 'No, mother, it'll eat my foot off, like a crocodile!'; in underwear shops, the windows of which were filled with scantily clad mannequins, the source of many a teenage boy's fantasy – which did not include the angry owner, who regularly came out to chase off any lingerers with a sharpened broomstick. They even searched for Stanley in the abandoned train yards, where the itinerant workers from G would congregate, skinny men with rope-like miraculous muscles who, lured to the town of S by fabulous felicitous stories of limitless work and untold riches, but finding neither, not even enough for the train fare home, were willing to do anything for an easy, fast buck.

And it was during his searches, no sign or word of Stanley, that Sven learnt that everybody, or as near to everybody as that word could encompass, in the tiny metropolis of S lived in one of eight very tall, sprawling, gargantuan buildings and – it was a fact much lamented in all of the above-mentioned commercial establishments – in none of these buildings, each divided into many hundreds of flats, garrets, penthouses, apartments, was there a single lift. Vertical movement, both up and down, was accomplished only by a series of wooden external staircases.

'And there is no other means?' asked Sven.

They were sitting on the terrace of Soufi's Al-Arabian Cakes, Sweets and Coffees with Esta and all the Mikes. On tables either side of their party groups of teenage boys were either engaged in riotous games of speed chess, hands flying through the air as battles were won and fought, or comparing illicit images of penises and boobs on their mobile devices. It was a Thursday afternoon: their day for cultural engagement.

'Not unless you jump,' said Esta seriously. Turning her gaze towards the staircases of the building opposite she pointed at the nets positioned all around its base. 'In England you have Beachy Head. In Japan they have seppuku. In S we have jumping from tall building.'

'Kind of like Spider-Man, but without the spider part,' said Mike Three. The funny one.

'And what's going on there?' asked Sven, also now pointing.

A third of the way up the staircase a bent old lady, bulging bin bag clasped in her arms, was shouting at two tall men, who each had a hard plastic suitcase balanced on their heads, while a family manhandled large tea chests up, or down, the staircase blocked in all directions.

'This is what we call the domino effect,' said Esta, and she explained that as people got married, had children, children moved out, family members died, divorces happened, people *disappeared*, an enforced move would be necessary to fit into an apartment that matched the size of your new family unit. And as one moved, so had to others.

'I heard Soufi talking when I ordered our drinks,' said Esta. 'That family you see at the top of the stairs had twins today. It is a blessing for them, but a disaster for many others – as many as two dozen families will have to move.'

'I wonder,' said Sven, an idea forming in their head.

On that fateful day when they had been captured under the pier by the Bones brothers and hefted by the armpits to the torture chair in the Martello tower, Sven had been reading their favourite superhero comic, *Removalman!* – mask made from a hessian sack, cape the colour of a tea chest, a large recondite R in its centre.

In each weekly episode bad guys planning a raid would turn up at their secret den to find their getaway van had been replaced by a chintz sofa, their cache of weapons usurped by a family of smiling Gonks; or a bank robbery would be stymied by the bank itself having been moved to a new location, a shop selling tights lower than twenty deniers in its place.

'I don't get it,' said Mike One.

They were back at the pickle factory.

Sven instructed the Mikes to turn their backs, then told them to turn around again when they were ready.

'Removalman!' they shouted, and performed, in situ, a perfect replica of the pose of their hero – arms straight out, hands folded forward, as if gripping the edges of a packing case, knees slightly bent to avoid injury to the lower back. The cape and the hessian headdress had been easy to fashion.

'Who wouldn't love Removalman?' Sven asked. 'And for us it will be the next level of our community engagement. They need to move apartments; we do the move for them, packing, lifting, unboxing – the whole lot! Get these people to love us and the war will be over. Trust me on this.'

Mike Three was good with words – not just funny ones – so it was he who created the advert. It was then passed to Esta, who translated it and organised its placement in the tea-shop window.

عمال الإزالة !
كل احتياجاتك المتحركة .
لا وظيفة كبيرة جدا أو صغيرة .
معدلات ممتازة .
لا تخجل ! جربنا!

The Removalmen!
All your moving needs.
No job too big or small.
Excellent rates.
Don't be shy! Give us a try!

A week later they received their first commission. One week after that their second. Within two months the removals were taking up all their free time.

The plan was working, except for the part Sven had not revealed to the others: spending so much time going in and out of apartments, mixing with the locals, they hoped they might hear word of Stanley.

Late at night, while the Mikes were asleep, or pretending to be asleep and secretly fiddling with themselves, Sven would compose imaginary postcards to Stanley with extraordinary military machinery on their front, echoing those glorious postcards they had themselves been sent all those aeons ago.

Dear Stanley,
Today the Mikes and I moved Frida Daghestani, age eighty-two, eyes bright like buttons. As I was lugging her record collection down from the twenty-fifth floor, to which she could no longer make the stairs, she told me how she had worked diligently on the Soviet Space Mission in 1963, going to space kitted out in a woollen space suit she had knitted herself. Before making her final descent down the stairs to her new home she insisted we help her up to the roof. There, climbing up on to the air-conditioning unit she stretched her crooked hands up into the air.

'Once I was even higher than this,' she said, and for a second, squinting, I could see her sprinting gaily across the surface of the moon.

A young girl again. Free.

Miss you, ever yours,

Sven.

Dear Stanley,
How is life with you, wherever you are? Today we moved Roxana Madani and her three children, Sara, Simin and Soraya. Their father Kamran – 'part-time tram driver, part-time waster – never should have married the bloody fool' – had died.

Roxana, who had, long ago, in order to account for their father's numerous long absences, told her children that their father was a spy, now told them that he had been killed on a dangerous mission – 'Foreign embassy, skylight; treacherous slippery roof tiles in stormy weather.' But it had been Roxana who had found him, pushed under his own tram for non-payment of debts by the Koshogi Brothers, conjoined twins and grand scions of a gambling syndicate that they ran with ruthless intensity.

In her flat Roxana had three hundred and six plastic bath toys, ducks, alligators, frogs, little steamships, mills with working waterwheels, submarines, water lilies, and a lacquered box in which she kept all her hairdressing equipment. In lieu of payment she cut each of our hair and, remembering how you said I had something of the Jean Seberg about me, I asked her to do it in that style – you know, like in the poster of *À bout de souffle* you had up in your room in the Swiss Card Sharp Summer School.

Stanley, you always leave me breathless.

Yours ever,

Sven.

Dear Stanley,

Let me tell you about Benyamin Turan.

By all accounts Turan had always been a bum, a womaniser, a scoundrel, a gambler. At fifteen years old he'd had 'Kiss My Crack' tattooed across his bum cheeks and 'Don't Mess With Me, I'm One Dangerous Motherfucker' across the knuckles of his left (punching) hand – apparently the phrase is shorter in Arabic: لا تعبث معي ، أنا موظر خطير.

By the time he was eighteen he had held up a post train, turned over a laundromat, robbed a pet shop.

People said there was no hope for him. It was going to end badly, with him ending up in prison or accidentally shooting himself in the foot or penis.

Then he met Yasamin and everything changed.

'If you want to stay with me,' she said, 'you have to go straight.'

'Like an arrow,' he said, and two weeks later he was looking around for a premises to open up a shop.

'We'll sell ants,' he said, having had an obsession with ants since he was a little boy. 'Ant paperweights, ant deodorant, ant cuddly toys, ant books, ant pencil ends, elaborate ant hats, ant jigsaw puzzles.'

The shop was a roaring success, and now they are moving to a bigger apartment. It has a bidet in every room and views over the distant olive plantations! At night they will be able to watch the trees grow – open the windows wide and smell the oil.

Dear Stanley, I dream of one day when we will be together. That I will find you somewhere out here. That I haven't made this journey for nothing.

Yours in perpetuity,

Sven.

Love Vigilantes

It was Captain Newheart who put an end to their growing removal business.

Captain Newheart, squat, wide-eyed, with a belly that hung grotesquely over his khaki shorts, carried about his person a book on war written by a Chinese philosopher, and his speech was peppered with its pithy phrases: wars are won not in the hearts and the minds, but in the legs and the arms; to surprise your enemy you must surprise yourself.

His first act, that first day of his inauspicious arrival, was a speech.

Revolution had broken out in P. Colonel D. had been assassinated in C. The enemy were gathering their forces around V. Martial law had been imposed in G. F was to be retaken at midnight.

'I don't know about you,' said Mike Five, the fisherman, 'but I'm just hearing letters.'

'J,' said Mike Three, the funny one. 'G, X, Y, Y, Y.'

Over the next weeks Captain Newheart increased the days in the Designated Fighting Area from one to three, stopped all community engagement and instigated mandatory PT (Physical Training) on the PG (Parade Ground) each morning. For this, the wearing of clothes – 'i.e. the designated uniform' – was mandatory.

On top of all this, he made roll call mandatory three times a day – roll call to be announced by the sound of a bugle (on day three Mike One said he would like to shove the bugle up Captain Newheart's ass, but Mike Two said that would be a waste of a good bugle), and so on.

It was the worst of times. It was the worst of times.

'Like being in the fucking army,' said Mike Three, the funny one.

Dear Stanley,

Last night Captain Newheart said that in the morning he has a big announcement for us. We are not expecting good news.

Mike Three's great-great-uncle, he tells us, was one of those men who died at the Somme – 'We set up here. You set up there. We fling ourselves towards each other in deadly abandon. For the King. For the Country.' Were ever two more ludicrous concepts created?

Here is where your heart beats (I am pointing at my heart). Here is where love resides (I am pointing at my head). So ask yourself. Would your king die for you? Would your country?

They would not. They would only order you to kill yourself.

Yours, you know it,

Sven.

Dear Stanley,

Did I ever tell you about my Dead Sister? Not the existence of her, for you knew that well enough. You remember, I suppose, the tiddlywinks competitions the three of us had? How you did not know a ghost could be so competitive. Or how she so loved Elmer, her pink cuddly elephant, with its squishy feet and nose that made an actual trumpeting sound when pulled?

But no, I mean, did I tell you how she died?

At first we had no idea what the frequent infections, the anaemia, gradual weight loss might mean.

We put it down to our intemperate weather, teenage hormones, a broken heart. I can still not forgive Ada Abara for standing her up outside Ginny's Palace and then later, that very same evening, being seen in Chippy Chips with Precious Biko, ordering a fish supper for two with extra mushy peas.

She was inconsolable and, day by day, breath by breath, her health deteriorated. Even a restorative trip to Poulton-le-Fylde did not restore her spirits, and that was when we knew something seriously was wrong, and we made that fateful trip to the hospital.

I was with Mum and Dad when they told us.

The doctor was a fine-looking Indian man that several of the girls at school had had a crush on since he had appeared on the front page of *The Courier* for having built Digger Johnson a new leg from scratch after Digger had fallen into the crocodile enclosure at The Boosbeck Wildlife Park and had his right peg chewed right off. Due to some childhood illness, the doctor, and I have forgotten his name, was only able to speak by fixing a tiny megaphone to his larynx, which gave his voice something of a loud computer sound.

'I'M VERY SORRY. IT'S LEUKAEMIA.'

Leukaemia.

'YES. LEUKAEMIA. A CANCER OF THE BODY'S BLOOD-FORMING TISSUES.'

Its path turned out to be a harrowing one.

I was with her when she died. The nurse had just visited, arranged the sheets. In the sky outside a plane had sliced the sky in two. I was holding her hand when she opened her eyes and said the last thing she would ever say – 'Be brave, Sven.'

And have I been brave? I have not.

Why did I let you go when I should have not? It was a lack in me. I should have lain down on that train track and said you were not to go. Over my dead body.

I am not a brave man. Person. Woman. Whatever I am.

Forgive me.

Sven.

It was barely dawn, the sun a creeping eyelid across the horizon, when Captain Newheart asked for their attention.

For once there was no bugle.

In silence he marched them on to the beaten sand of the parade ground. A lone donkey nuzzled the far side of the chain-link fence. Two yards from it stood a sign: 'WATCH OUT – MINES!'

'Watch out – mines!' said Mike Three, the funny one, each morning as he put his dick through a hole in the chain-link fence and pissed copiously.

'Now listen up,' bellowed Captain Newheart.

The men were gathered around him in parade formation. Adjacent to Captain Newheart was a flipchart. He was holding a pointer.

'News has come in that we have a deserter. And local intelligence suggests he's been hiding out somewhere near here.'

Captain Newheart pointed with his pointer to a crudely drawn map on the flipchart.

'How can we win this war when we can't win the hearts of our own men? One bad apple can destroy the batch. We must show this lot that we stand united.'

'The only united I care about is Manchester United,' whispered Mike One.

'Come on, you reds!' whispered Mike Three, the funny one.

'Our mission,' bellowed Captain Newheart, 'or your mission – and for this I require a volunteer, one brave volunteer – is to go out and find this deserter. Bring him home. Show these filthy ████████ what it means to be a soldier. To fight for your country, etc., etc.'

Sven closed their eyes, was back on that beach again, the Bones Brothers coming at them with a condom filled with sand, with the snapping claws of a live crab, with the rusty speculum 'for looking up buttholes' that Aart Jansen had stolen from his dad, the doctor, aeons ago.

'I'm Private Tosier-Gumshoe. Fifteenth Seal Regiment. Identification Number 35654. I won't tell you anything.'

They were not a brave person. Never had been.

Or was that true? Sven remembered that day – Stanley taking the dress out of the suitcase. Telling them to put it on. Walking along the promenade together.

Stanley had made them brave. Given them that power.

'I'll go,' said Sven, putting up their hand. 'Me. I'll do it. I'll go find your deserter.' Because they knew who it might be, and it was time to be brave again.

Smooth Operator

It was only when they were out of sight of the base camp that Sven stopped the motorbike they had been issued for their mission – an Armstrong MT500, made in Bolton so the little brass plate bolted to its side said.

'If not now, when facing certain death,' said Sven, 'then when?'

And right there by the side of the road they stripped down to their underpants and, extracting the dress from its hiding place in their rucksack – the very same yellow dress Stanley had given them all those years before – they slipped it over their head.

It was almost sunset when Sven pulled into S. The coffee shops, tables spilling out on to the streets, were full, the clientele sitting with one ear turned as the neighbourhood's barbers launched into their nightly aria.

It was outside Horatio's Pool Hall that Sven bumped into Benyamin Turan.

'I need your help,' said Sven. 'I'm trying to find someone.'

From a rooftop a muezzin called the faithful to prayer.

Doors opened. Shutters came down. Teacups were hastily collected.

It was on their motorbike in the desert that it had come to them. If Stanley had deserted they knew where he would go – well, not the where *exactly*, but the *kind of* where.

'They have feet like flippers,' said Sven. 'They like the water.'

'The water, you say?' said Turan. 'Do you know you're in the middle of the fucking desert?'

And then his eyes did something. Went rounder. Brighter.

'Oh, hang on. There might be something. I'll draw you a map. But I warn you. It's a long way.'

Ferry Cross the Mersey

For forty days and for forty nights Sven crossed the desert.

Christ! Did their feet burn with pain?

Yes, they did.

Was their skin red and raw and blistered from the sun?

Yes, it was.

It was on the twenty-fifth day that they began to have visions. It was their sister who came first. Not on her hospital bed now, but on the beach with them, laughing. At their winky. They were changing into their bathers and she had seen it, pointed, laughed.

'But I want to be like you,' they said. 'I don't want this thing. To be a boy. Masculinity. War. Empty posturing. Machismo. Pints with the boys. Football terraces on a Saturday. Lads' holidays in Magaluf. Catching crabs and laughing about it.' And they had wanted to talk seriously with her, the ghost, but she, the ghost, had done a kind of dance, ran into the sea, screaming.

Next to appear were their mother and father, standing behind the counter of Delicious Gifts, their faces sad. And as they watched a single tear ran down their mother's cheek and their father extended an arm, placed it around her shoulders.

'Don't worry. They'll be back soon. Our love. Only this time let us do better.'

And then more and more they saw Stanley, his arms coming up out of the water like pistons.

'Today Saltburn-by-the-Sea. Tomorrow Stavanger!'

At night when Sven closed their eyes, rested their head on a pillow of sand they had made, they could hear the Mikes on their beds next to them, testing each other from their battered much-treasured copy of *The Guinness Book of World Records*.

'What was the loudest sneeze ever recorded in history?'

'What is the name of the largest diamond in the world?'

'What is the record for putting Mars bars up your bum?'

'What is the fastest land mammal?'

'In which war did the most people die?'

'What is the biggest ever bomb made and how many people did it kill?'

'Who is the tallest man in the world?'

They were hallucinating. Or not hallucinating. For what is real, and what is not?

On their fortieth day in the desert Sven saw in the distance a line rising up out of the sand. As they came closer the line became a wall and, closer still, within that wall a gate appeared. Squinting upwards, shielding their eyes with a hand, they viewed the magnificent sign, standing on two poles to the side of the gate, the words spelt out in colourful neon, first in Arabic and then, underneath, in English.

ل وانظر البحر .

معدلات خاصة للعاطلين والأطفال وكبار السن والمعاقين .

وأولئك الذين يحتاجون إلى ابتهاج .

ممنوع الكلاب .

Ocean World.

Come and See the Sea.

Special Rates for the Unemployed, children, elderly, the disabled.

And those in need of cheering up.

No dogs.

When the Going Gets Tough

The ticket booth, a door on its side bent and swinging open, the glass of its hatch broken, was in the shape of a pirate ship. The row of concession stands behind it stood in an equally dilapidated state. Trays lay empty, wooden slats had rotted away in places, price lists had faded to illegibility, burnt by the sun. Only a few baseball caps remained on display. They were blue, 'Ocean World' stencilled into their brims in gold lettering.

Sven took one, placed it snugly on their head and called out, 'Hello! Hello!'

Past the concession stands was a wooden post with arrows pointing in different directions down pathways bordered by plastic fencing. The arrows were inscribed with beautiful Arabic writing, English underneath.

Nemo's Submarine. Whacky Wave-Maker. Poseidon's Grotto. The Pacific Slide – Risk it at Your Peril!

'Hello!' called out Sven again, louder this time.

Every ten metres or so down each pathway were bins in the shape of clams affixed to posts. Small informational signs indicated how long the waiting time would be if you stood there.

'You are twenty minutes away from your next fun time!' 'Keep your eyes peeled for Nemo! Why not ask him for a photograph!'

Sven came to the sign that read 'The Pacific Slide – Risk it at Your Peril!' And here was a staircase leading up to a hundred feet or more into the air, the top of the staircase connected to five or six slides, formed from brightly coloured tubes, but cracked now in places and, like everything else, faded and coated in a film of sand.

Sven was in a water park, but there was no water anywhere.

The Whacky Wave-Maker had no waves. Nemo's Submarine hung in mid-air, more of a rocket than a submersible. Even the mermaids, fibreglass monstrosities scattered here and there around the park, could not summon up a drop between them, their fishy tails, which once must have trailed in water, standing high and dry.

'It's sad, isn't it?'

Startled by the voice, Sven spun around.

The man was small, lizard-like, had a cigarette clamped in one side of his mouth, a broom in his hand.

'This whole place used to be fed from the ocean. The Americans built it – part of their reconstruction plan after some war or another. Then when they put the puppet government in place and left us to manage on our own they insisted we pay them a special tax on the water. But there was not just one tax – there was one to ship the water, one to move the water; one even to keep it clean. The ocean was in their region, you see? Their sphere of influence. And so we had to pay them for the pleasure. The cynical amongst you might say they did it to make money. But I think they were just showing off. Let's build a water park in the desert! Look what American imperialism can achieve! But of course once they'd gone we couldn't afford what in essence was simply a vanity project. We had other stuff to pay for. So this happened.' The man cast his arms about. 'We can barely keep the one pool going. But we do. There's failure and there's total failure. We won't have that. We have our pride.'

'You have a pool?' said Sven.

'Follow the signs,' said the man. 'The Lido. You can't miss it.'

Once in a Lifetime

Deckchairs had been set out. Towels folded neatly next to them. There was a small concession stand, its hatch open, cans of drink and packets of crisps on display.

But it was the pool Sven was interested in.

A perfect blue. Reflections of the sun. Chlorine tang.

And there at the far end: arms. First one and then another. Like pistons.

Sven watched as they came closer and closer. Watched the head emerge from the water. Water slide from the head.

Were they dreaming? Hallucinating?

Stanley.

'Lap two hundred and forty,' said Stanley. 'Once I get to two thousand and twenty-six that will equal the distance from Saltburn to Stavanger. The thing is to do it without stopping. Oh!' He lifted himself up on to the side. 'That's you, is it? Wearing the yellow dress? Hello, love!'

Sven plunged a single finger into the water. It felt real enough. Like it might be true. Lifting the finger back out, they placed a whole hand on Stanley's still-wet thigh and closed their eyes.

They could see then a beautiful future. The end of the war. Returning to Saltburn with Stanley. Being reunited with their parents, and although Stanley's parents would initially disown him thanks to his desertion and choice of girlfriend they would come around after a few months when they saw how happy the couple were.

Sven's parents, old and worn out after years of toil, would be more than happy for Sven and Stanley to take over the running of Delicious Gifts, although the couple would reduce the opening hours to eighteen so they could spend some time together and so Stanley could train for his swim to Stavanger. He would do this either in the Saltburn municipal pool or the sea itself.

On weekends they would take trips to Filey, paper bags crammed with stale bread and out-of-date sweets to feed the seals. One day, after Stanley had proposed down on one knee at the pier under gaudy flashing lights, they would get married. Sven's dress would be yellow, and Stanley would look handsome in a tight green suit. After marriage would be children, adopted from the Orphans of War Children's Home in Boosbeck. They would be lively but bookish children, who would love bunkbeds and Rubik's cubes, would compose music on Rolf Harris Stylophones, wear lime-green jelly shoes. On weekends the family would eat chips on the beach and ice creams in cones with hundreds and thousands and flakes in them. They would go together to the penny arcade, and when they lost everything they would take sound advice from the mermaid. There would be half days spent in the Foetus Museum or the Saltburn Aquarium, staring in wonder as the stingrays and the clown fish dived and flipped. There would be sunset walks to the nuclear-power station where they would feed the pit ponies peanuts through gaps in the chain-link fence.

On Stanley's thirtieth birthday, a beautiful calm spring day, he would finally make the swim to Stavanger. Sven would accompany him in a boat piloted by one of the fishermen, feeding Stanley morsels of food and water from a bottle with a special tube.

Waiting for them in Stavanger would be an authenticator from *The Guinness Book of World Records*. Stanley would appear in the book the next year, standing proud in his lime-green Speedos with his arm around his lovely wife, Sven, with a Jean Seberg haircut and a figure-hugging pink dress with a flamingo pattern.

Sven could see it all. It was all so clear. So much happiness. On and on. A bright, happy future. It was just a question of… It was just a question of… It was just a question of…?

They took their hand from Stanley's thigh, opened their eyes, and…

You have been reading Saltburn. We very much hope you enjoyed your stay as much as we enjoyed having you.

Peace.

ACKNOWLEDGEMENTS

Different versions of these stories first appeared on ABCtales in 2020. Thank you to all the readers there who encouraged me to keep going.

Thank you too to my publisher, Haywood Books, for taking a chance and putting these stories out there.

Life has been difficult recently. It's only writing that has kept me going. So, thank you, writing, for being there when I needed you.

This book draws much inspiration from a wide array of music – you can find a Spotify playlist by scanning the QR code below or by visiting: spoti.fi/43lc4Ds.

ABOUT THE AUTHOR

DREW GUMMERSON is a novelist and award-winning short-story writer of books including *The Lodger*, *Me and Mickie James* and, more recently, *Seven Nights at the Flamingo Hotel*. He is a Lambda Award finalist, and won the Leicestershire Short Story Prize. His stories have been featured on BBC Radio 4 and in various anthologies. Drew lives in Leicestershire.

LINKTR.EE/DREWGUM ⊕ 🐦 @DREWGUM